]

'If you are looking for a ⸻ ⸻ and lots of laughter, *The Mists of Simla* will serve you well. Balraj Khanna's novel takes one on a hilarious, gripping and exciting ride through the life of Rahul Kapoor, a handsome boy of eighteen. Mr. Khanna takes a simple plot- a boy aged eighteen goes to Simla to study and learns about life-and makes it an entertainer by humour supplemented with the caricature-ish characters, and by placing the story successfully in a time-frame which gives him the agency to incorporate interesting events in his story. *The Mists of Simla* is a mad but *masaledar* blend of events that often transpire in the lives of young men. It's got emotion, passion, loss, humour, heartaches, goons, war, friendship, enmity, sex, homosexual bullies, stern teachers, family, cricket, politics, fights and list continues. The narration is direct and it got me glued to the novel instantly.'

(Mihir Vatsa)

'Indian youth are going to scream. Enthralling! I loved it! Superbly executed! Perfect psyche of a growing young man on the right side of things, bold, brave yet innocently dipped in moral servitudes. The fragrance of family life especially when they meet in SIMLA is deftly handled, the way India is known all over, with every dish the devil raises its head skywards.'

(Balbir Singh Sambyal)

By the same author

Fiction
Nation of Fools
Sweet Chillies

Children
Rajah King of the Jungle

Non-fiction
Kalighat Paintings 1820–1920
The Art of Modern India
Krishna the Divine Lover
Human and Divine

Balraj Khanna was born in the Punjab, India, and came to London in the Swinging Sixties to study English. Instead, he took to art – eventually becoming 'one of the most distinguished painters working in England' (Bryan Robertson). His enduring love of literature culminated in three works of fiction, of which *Nation of Fools* was adjudged 'one of the 200 best novels in English since 1950'. He has also written extensively about Indian art.

Balraj Khanna still lives in London, next door to Lords Cricket Ground – which he describes as 'his spiritual home'. *The Mists of Simla* is his fourth work of fiction.

THE MISTS OF SIMLA

Balraj Khanna

Balraj Khanna

London W9 2PY

ISBN 978-0-9573981-0-8

For Francine

PROLOGUE

The summer of 1962 in India was like any other scorching, parched, punishing. Monsoon floods followed, adding injury to misery. This was normal. Normal and expected. The country was prepared for it all in its usual God's-will-be-done sort of way.

What was neither normal nor expected was the sudden appearance on its borders in North East Frontier Agency - NEFA - of a large Chinese army for which India was not prepared in any sort of way. China was supposed to be a friend. Delhi and Peking had been waxing lyrical about each other for years. Much-loved Nehru, apostle of peace, had gone well out of his way to raise the profile of the little-known Chou En Lai on the world stage. Against the wishes of the mighty US, he had championed pariah China at the UN. Nobody believed China would invade India. Least of all, the apostle of peace.

So Indians went about their business as usual, making do with what they had and trying desperately to get what they did not have. They sweated through the day but slept in peace at night.

Nowhere was it more apparent than in the sleepy little hill station of Solan, a place of pine-covered peaks and verdant valleys, where young Rahul Kapoor faced the important FA exam to get to graduate college. This college was twenty-five miles up the tortuous mountain road in glamorous Simla, the summer capital of the old British Raj. Indians loved Simla. In the Raj time, the common folk were not allowed to walk on its glittering Mall Road. But Indians still loved Simla. Simla was dazzling. Simla was bewitching. And although the British had been gone for fifteen long years, Simla remained dazzling and bewitching. Indians loved it all the more now that they could wear their shoes out walking on the once-forbidden Mall and gape at its Aladdin shops.

Almost eighteen, Rahul loved home. The very thought of going away pushed a needle through his heart. But Solan was Solan, a half-hearted scatter of corrugated-iron rooftops clinging to slippery hillsides where nothing ever happened. All Solan had was the scenery and a shoebox cinema which had never heard of Hollywood. Rahul was sick of Solan's boring scenery and its leaky shoebox.

Rahul knew that one behaved the way people treated one. And people treated him as if he was different from them. It was not his fault, therefore, if he came to believe that he was - different. He got noticed even without trying. The problem was, there simply weren't enough people around of the right kind to notice Rahul. The local girls couldn't even leave home, unless they were escorted by aunts with tandoors strapped to their bellies and brothers armed to the teeth and gums.

Rahul longed to be in Simla where girls wore bottom-hugging jeans and see-through nylon tops on its famous Mall Road, smoked and danced in dishy English restaurants, skated in swirling skirts and went to Hollywood movies - unchaperoned.

But there was this condition - Rahul had to pass the looming FA exam. It was an order nearly as tall as the mammoth Mount Solan for anybody. But Rahul was not just anybody. He was a Kapoor. He continued to hit, spin and chase the red five-and-a-half-ounce cricket ball even as the exams approached. He also prayed. Prayer moved mountains. Prayer filled the future with goodies.

Rahul prayed to the beautiful blue-bodied Krishna, with whom he had a special relationship. The God and the man had much in common - especially love for sport and girls. The whole world knew how the Divine Lover was ever surrounded by countless beauties, his many nubile *gopis* to whom he made love. Rahul was sure his day would come. He had full faith in Krishna, the God of Understanding. Rahul could talk to Him as a friend. He did so every day.

ONE

A dark cloud suddenly shot up from behind the sullen hump of Mount Solan, making the early-morning gold more radiant by contrast. Then the cloud just hung there, waiting for a push to spill it over and fill the panoramic valley.

The push did not come immediately and yet the July morning, dew-laden and clear, acquired a grim shade of grey. Rahul, watching with his sixteen–year-old sister Shobana from their long veranda, knew what was coming. He did not want it to come. He did not want the black cloud to topple the mountain. For sure as hell, that would be it, *khattam-shudh* - total destruction of whatever was left of the rotting Kapoor cash crops. The monsoon that year had come a month too early. This would be the fourth jharri non-stop rainfall on the trot.

Rahul was thinking. No, a hammer was at work inside his head.

Money.

The Kapoors were broke. They often were. But this time . . .

Rahul yawned loudly to chase money away.

There was anger in the cloud. Within minutes the immense valley became ink-black. Serpents of lightning stung it. Soon, the distant cannonade became an overhead affair. It frightened the life out of Shobana and their dog Terry at her feet.

'Mummy!' she yelled and ran as rain pelted down deafeningly on the corrugated-iron roof of their rambling Sun House. In its master bedroom, she jumped into Mummy's queen-size palang.

'Mummy, save me,' she said in English, hugging her. The family spoke English in the Sun House, the language of anybody who was somebody. They switched to Punjabi only when angry.

In their room, her little brothers Shoki and Bimbi, aged fourteen and twelve, were jubilant. They leaped off their beds and came running, chattering their teeth even though it was not cold at all.

'Mummy!' They jumped in after her.

Bed-tea arrived for Mummy and for Daddy. Bald old Santram with only a bodi topknot brought it on a silver tray - a heavily pregnant teapot, its tea-cosy shimmering with sequins, Royal Worcester cups and saucers. Daddy was served first in his king-size bed. There were bags under his eyes. He had spent last evening gazing at maps of NEFA. Then he had had a bad night breathlessness and coughing. This time of the year brought it on, the monsoon rain releasing some strange vapour trapped in the mountain earth. He had tried everything, from whatever Dr Gupta prescribed to homeopathy bullshit and the Ayurvedic bakwas. But . . . It was just this time of the calendar. Come September the first or second, and Prakash Kapoor, a handsome man of fifty, was fit as a fiddle.

Rahul turned up, followed by Terry. He too slipped under Mummy's quilt.

'What about the dog?' Prakash said.

'Acres of room here, sir,' Rahul replied.

'Kamla madam, you bore me idiots, not sons. Is that what I was married to you for?' Prakash said to his wife. But he loved the sight of her with their children. For a moment he did not have a worry in the world. The idiots laughed, the happiest idiots in the world.

'As much your sons as mine, ji,' Kamla said, taking a sip.

'What Ji-ji? Was told when marrying I was marrying not only a beauty queen but also one with a BA. So I was guaranteed classy offsprings. Intelligent. But just look at them!'

In fact, looking at his boys and Shobana did to Prakash what a gust of cool breeze does to a man when the mercury goes mad. 'You must admit you present a picture with your litter clinging to you,' he added.

'I probably do. Present a picture of a sort.'

'Changing the subject - this bitch rain.'

'Daddy, where do the birds go in a bad monsoon rain like this?' Bimbi asked.

'Silly boy, where do you think they go? And monsoon is a wind, not rain. Get that in your wet brain,' Shoki said. 'I read somewhere that in rain, if you run from the car to the house, you get the same amount of water as when you walk.'

'You can walk next time. I'll run.' Bimbi laughed. 'And did you know pears sink while apples float?'

'We are talking about rain, you fool. Personally, I love it when the rain belts down like this.' Shoki had said the wrong thing. 'I mean . . .' He bit his tongue.

'Do you now?' said Shobana, looking at him sideways as she always did at anyone or anything - without moving her head, only her flashing big almond eyes. 'I wonder why?' In a storm like this one, Shoki and Bimbi could legally play truant from St Luke's, their English school a mile away.

'Of course you are going!' Rahul snapped loudly. 'What are umbrellas for?'

'Brer Rahul, what I like about you is your tender heart,' yelped Bimbi, the baby of the family.

'And you too. GO. Both of you. Go bath and dress.'

'Mummy, he can't throw us out of the house in this storm?' Shoki appealed to the High Court. The High Court turned to the Supreme Court.

'Why are you looking at me? If the rain is too much for your sons, then keep them at home. Under your quilt.'

'Sir, they won't dissolve in the rain. I promise,' said Rahul. 'Or maybe they will, these dumb lumps of gur sugar. OUT, YOU FOOLS,' he barked.

'Owl Rahul. Owl Rahul,' sang the boys.

Rahul didn't like being called an owl, the ugly bird of the night that Indians loathe. Mention of it to him was like a red rag to a Spanish bull. He was ready to charge.

'An umbrella in the hand and a kick in your back garden . . .' Rahul gave two sharp kicks to Shoki's backside. Shoki caught his foot. The foot stank. It was not just Rahul and his cricket ball-danda all day yesterday, Rahul's feet always stank.

'Do you ever wash, big bruvver-ji?'

'Ask a silly question.' Bimbi caught Rahul's other foot and the three brothers wrestled, grunting and groaning deafeningly.

'SHUT UP,' Prakash shouted.

Silence. Still, the question remained – school versus storm? With his wife's and his daughter's eyes on him, Prakash half gave in.

'All right, you bastards. Go after lunch.'

The bastards hugged Mummy in glee.

'This torment,' Mummy said to the ceiling, and gloom rushed into the happy room.

The Kapoor 'cash crop' – vegetables that couldn't grow in the scorching plains - was as good as dead. Their fruits too, especially the new craze - strawberries. The Kapoors had been expecting a visitor for some time, a VVIP. This infernal rain meant he wouldn't be coming today either.

The Kapoors of Solan were high-caste Punjabi Khatris - the Kshatriya warriors and kings of ancient India while most hill folk were the lower vaishya traders by caste with a handful of top caste Brahmins thrown in between. In olden times, the King was always a Kshatriya while his Prime Minister and guru was always a Brahmin.

The Kapoors had their Sun House and the equally grand Moon House nearby. And they owned a whole hill sliced in terraces. Its yield fetched handsome money. But the monsoon could play dirty tricks – bad if too late, worse if too early. Prakash played the stock market usually successfully. The Moon House fetched sweet 300 per month when let out. Then there was the salary of his eldest son, Captain Prithviraj, or Pithi, serving in NEFA – 500 plus that the MOD sent to Prakash's account on the first of every month. All this painted a golden halo around the Kapoors.

But the Moon House had lain vacant ever since its last occupant, the Commanding Officer of Solan, had left the small garrison town two months ago. And Pithi's money had not arrived for three months due to some bungle at the Army HQ in troubled NEFA 1,600 miles away. Lastly, the shares had taken a nosedive, thanks to Mr Chou En Lai. The Family's golden halo did bring free credit, but things had begun to split at the seam. It was writ large on Prakash's face.

Kamla didn't look at her husband. Instead, she dispatched another skymail to the family God.

'O Krishna-ji, put some sense in the army's head in NEFA. And send to this house today the CO and make him want the other one.' The new CO had been in town for two weeks and was supposed to be coming to see the Moon House any day, every day.

Kamla prayed silently to the tin roof singing loudly. She felt the big raindrops bite her bare shoulders as she stole a glance at her husband.

Prakash too was thinking. 'Whatever happens, happens for the best,' he reminded himself of the old Indian saying. 'And this dhanda business of life goes on.' Anyway, he had seen it all before. Nothing could have been worse than it had been fifteen years ago in burning Lahore, his hometown now in Pakistan. Then it was not just money that was at stake, but his very life and the lives of his young family. Yet he had come through it all, albeit with a little help from a friend - a godsend.

Yes, Prakash had seen it all before.

Now his gaze was fixed on the open door. But he was not looking at anything. It was his way of sorting things out in his head.

The fireworks died down, but not the rain, although it now merely murmured on the tin roof. The Kapoors sat down to breakfast on the veranda, the long balcony overlooking Mount Solan across the wide stretch of the Cinemascope valley. The breakfast was hot milk, ice-cold lassi and tea. Along came toast and English jam, fried eggs on piping hot parathas, spicy lamb kidneys, spherical puris and channa masala.

Prakash only had tea. Then he walked off to the library to stare at the large-scale maps of NEFA which he had spread on a table. These were Ordnance maps of the world's highest mountains, gushing rivers and impenetrable jungles. They were incomprehensible. Yet Prakash could remain glued to them for hours. Kamla knew what he was looking for in them - an escape route for Pithi when . . . she dared not say it: *when the Chinese invasion came*. So she went away.

The doorbell.

'Our visitor.' Shobana sprang like a gazelle and ran to tell Daddy. It had to be Daddy to receive the new CO.

It was the wrong visitor – not the CO but old Gokul, headman of the Kapoor Hill. With him was his fifteenyear-old son Bhola. Each had a basket on his head. They laid them down on the veranda floor. The Kapoors did not want to see what they contained: the corpse of their Hill: rotting fruit and veg. One look and Santram dismissed them with a forefinger.

'Go and sit in the shed and wait for a tea-cup.'

Gokul and his son were barely out of sight when Lalaji appeared, the main grain merchant and grocer of Solan. The bespectacled Mahatma Gandhi's double was wrinkled, wore a khadi waistcoat and a white mullmull dhoti.

'Ram, Ram, Santram.'

'Ram, Ram, Lala-ji. Why have you come in this cat-dog rain? Is it urgent or important?'

Santram knew exactly why the old man had come, being in the same boat himself. Not only was he owed the past two months' salary, he had also lent Prakash several hundred from his own trunk to pay his workers and to lay out this breakfast for the family daily. The old servant had been with the Kapoors since well before Partition and had seen all. Regarded almost as a family member, Santram had everything he needed. He never complained. Like a god-fearing Hindu, he knew his karma in this life. It was to serve.

'It is one and it is the other. Both, you can say,' Lalaji said.

'A bit early, no? But I'll tell Kapoor Sahib you are here.' Santram knew the effect the mention of the big boss's name would have on the man.

17

Lala-ji's face shrank.

'Don't bother the Sahib. I've come for Bibi-ji.'

Santram led Lala-ji to the family room where Bibi-ji was. He looked unhappy. Ten minutes later when he emerged from the family room, he looked even more unhappy. He was muttering to himself.

'What, Lala-ji?' Rahul on the veranda beamed a Binaca toothpaste smile. He also knew everything.

'I am a fool number one, Rahul-baba.'

'You are the cleverest man Number One of the Solan Bazaar, Lala-ji. And the wisest.'

'No, I'm not. I came in soaking rain to demand money. I'm going out in soaking rain having agreed to postpone the demand. Indefinitely. And to keep supplying. Who can argue with Bibi-ji?'

Some time later, the doorbell rang again. The rain had now dwindled to a fine drizzle. Rahul, coating his already well-oiled bat with linseed oil in his room, heard Shoki shout: *'It's him.'*

Shoki was wrong. In fact, there were two visitors lanky cloth merchant Chadha and tubby tailor Kalidas. They had also come to see Bibi-ji. They carried two brown paper bags full of folded clothes. A look about them said they meant business.

The lady of the house was now at her toilette. Santram went and spoke to the bathroom door.

'Bibi-ji, it's the Cloth Palace man and . . .'

'Keep them on the veranda,' Kamla spoke back.

But Shoki shouted from his door, 'No, show them to the drawing room and give them tea, Santram.'

The servant gave his master's son a look of shock tradesmen in the drawing room of the Sun House?

'And tea for these men?' Santram repeated, hearing himself say in his throat, 'For these bazaar men?' Ram, Ram, Ram. Santram's bodi stirred.

In the drawing room, the men dared not sit down. They remained standing, holding the clothes' bags as if they held two infants in their arms. Five minutes passed. Then ten. Patient by nature being Indian, they knew it was their lot to wait. Five minutes on, Rahul, still in pyjamas and slippers, turned up.

'Welcome to the humble Kapoor hut, shriman gentlemen. Welcome and sit down. Why are you standing? Tea, Santram, tea.'

The men simply could not bring themselves to sit on a Kapoor sofa. They felt dumb in the presence of a mere boy they had seen grow from a toddler to a near sixfooter. They sat down cross-legged on the colourful Persian carpet.

'So how is life treating the Cloth Palace King, may I ask? Or should I say, vice versa?' The Cloth Palace King didn't know what to say. 'And you of the Savile Row of Solan, sir? Looks like you've been busy. Luck favours the busy. It brings rain, the rain of silver rupees.' Rahul laughed loudly. The tailor didn't know how to respond. He felt uncomfortable.

'What is this Savile-shavil, Rahul-baba?' he managed to say.

'A street in London where they tailor the world's best suits for the world's best gentlemen. From cloth sold by London's Cloth Palace King.'

'We've just come to give these to Bibi-ji, and take the payment.'

'Ah, my beautiful new blue suit. Beats any from Savile Row hands down. Can I try it on?' Rahul took the trousers of the blue suit and pulled them over his red and yellow striped pyjama legs. Then he put the jacket on. 'How do I look?' he said to the ill-at-ease tailor.

Shobana appeared at the door. 'Do you really want to know?' she asked.

'You said something, Shobi?'

'Tailor master-ji, do tell him how he looks.' Then Shobana ran away.

Tea arrived. As Santram began to pour it into the English cups, the men raised their hands – they couldn't possibly drink tea here, in this house. Ram, Ram, Ram!

'By the way, have you heard of a country called China, Lala-ji?'

'Who hasn't, Rahul-baba.'

'Do you know what it's famous for?'

'That I don't. Chopsticks?'

'No. Knives. Long knives. For back-stabbing.'

'Isn't that Chou man a friend of our Pandit-ji?'

'The Chini Chou is nobody's friend. He is stabbing us personally. He's eaten our shares and caused this rain with atom bomb tests to rot our crops.'

The lady of the house turned up. She wore a pale blue silk sari. Kamla had hurried. Without any makeup, she looked lovelier than when she took longer. And ten years younger than her forty-five.

'Many many thank-yous to you, shriman gentlemen, for coming here in this weather. I was thinking of dropping by one of these days with the payment. How much is it?'

The men murmured the sum. It removed the floor from beneath Rahul's feet. But not, it appeared, from his mother's.

'I know. You have to wait as I said the other day and as I am saying now.'

'But Bibi-ji . . .'

'But what, Chadha-ji? I know all the buts and shuts.'

'We too have families, Bibi-ji madam.'

'I know. I know. Do you think I don't? What do you want? The Kapoor boys to go to school naked? Rahul to walk on Simla Mall in kuchcha under-wear?' Kamla Kapoor got angry. 'Is that what you want?'

No, they didn't want that.

'So go, shriman-ji. I'll come one day when the new CO moves in the other house. When Captain Pithi's money is released. When. . .'

'When will that be, Bibi-ji madam?' said the Cloth Palace King.

'How long have we bought cloth from you?' Bibi-ji Madam sounded angry.

The Cloth Palace King didn't answer.

'How long have you been tailoring our clothes, Kalidas?' Bibi-ji madam now sounded very angry.

Kalidas too kept mum.

'How long? Speak.' Kamla raised her voice. 'Or have you lost your tongues?'

'Since forty-seven,' the two men said.

'Have you ever not been paid in the full?'

'Never.'

'Subject closed then.'

While this was going on in the Sun House's drawing room with its Persian rug, velvet-covered sofas, silverframed photos of the dashing twenty-three-year old Captain Pithi playing polo, Captain Pithi on horseback jumping a hurdle, Captain Pithi receiving a silver cup from Mrs General So and So . . . and the Royal Worcester tea service on a glass-topped table, there occurred the third visit, Visitor number four in a car. The rain had stopped.

'*It's him. Most definitely*.' It had to be, third time lucky. Alas, that was not the case again. For this was no ordinary car, being a long, black and beautiful Rolls Royce with the number-plate SOLAN I under a royal flag. Yet this was a welcome visitor, being none other than the Rana Saheb of Solan, another Gandhi look-alike - but with a difference. A twinkle in his eye.

Royalty!

Nobody loves royalty more than the Indians – they worship it. The mercantile coalition crumbled. It left, tea in English cups un-drunk.

'I will come as soon as I can,' Kamla said to the dukandars.

'Come when you like, Bibi-ji. Your own shop,' the tailor said, bowing to the Rana Saheb.

'Only your humble servants,' mumbled the cloth merchant.

'Rana Saheb, what a delight! Thought you were in Delhi?'

'Just coming up from the plains. Hot hot hot down there. Melting. Look at me. Half melted. Couldn't pass by without stopping for a cup and seeing my rose, my lotus flower. Where is she? And that wicked boy?'

The septuagenarian King of Solan loved the Kapoor children, especially Rahul and Shobana. The King had had four ranis, but not one 'issue'. He had poured buckets of cash in the pockets of 'UK-returned quacks'. But they never found out what the matter was with 'them', the ranis.

By now all the Kapoors had gathered in the drawing room.

'Highness, how lovely to see you,' Prakash said.

'How are you, Prakash? You should go down to the plains for this month, you know. Dry heat will do you good.' Highness noticed the maps Prakash had brought with him. 'What news from Pithi?'

'The same. "The Chinese put up one post, we put up one post. But the Chinese won't attack". Which is also what our PM says.'

'I disagree. Totally.'

'What, even with our Prime Minister?'

'Even with our dear PM. He thinks Chou En Lai is a friend. The Chini is a snake in the grass.'

'Don't trust him myself. Something about his face. Like Jinnah's. Dry and cunning.'

'Nehru may have a fine face, but it is the face of false hope that his newfound friend won't attack.'

'This is what the army says. The government too.'

'Our government is spitting out meaningless fancy words. It is doing bugger all while the Chinis are building up, lining up mountain guns.'

'Why aren't we doing the same with our guns?'

'Guns? What guns? Fools and ostriches never had any. I'd get the boy out of NEFA if I were you, Prakash. Want me to try? It will take just one phone call. But you also know people in Delhi.'

'Pithi wouldn't like that, Highness. He's a soldier. His job is to fight if it comes to that.'

'And it will – I'm telling you. That Chou will come from both the north and the north-east. From NEFA first - where we are the weakest, standing on less than half a leg. Listen to me, why don't you let me get him a cantonment posting? Are you listening?'

'Highness, Pithi is a soldier. . .'

'Kamla beti, you tell your stubby hubby. There's still time. It is going to be hell - the Chinis mean business, bloody business. By the way, have you heard that Nehru is passing through here soon?'

'We've been hearing that for some time now.'

'Wish I could stop him and talk to him. The man needs a good lecture. I have known him since the Jallianwala Bagh massacre. Travelled with him and Dyer on the same train that night to Delhi . . .'

Having Solan's King amongst them made the Kapoors feel good. Listening to him made them feel better. He looked at Rahul.

'Why are you dressed like . . . what should I say?'

'Like an idiot number one,' Shoki burped.

'When are you off to Simla then?'

'Soon soon, Highness.'

'Been to inspect the Front?'

'Yes, Highness.'

'What's the opposition like?'

'Mouthwatering, Highness,' Rahul said and in his mind's eye saw girls swarming up and down the Simla Mall in tight-fitting jeans and see-through nylon tops, their pink nipples showing.

Highness laughed.

'Prakash, this boy of yours will take Simla by storm. Mark my word. I give you my guarantee.'

'How do you know, Pops?' Shobana said. She called His Highness 'Pops', the only one in the world to do so, and he loved it. She had called him that since the age of two.

'How do I know? It's written all over his face. Bollywood looks, speaks English like Little Lord Fauntleroy, plays cricket like Pataudi. Plus the rest. You see, I know human psychology inside out. My job is to be able to read people like open books.'

'Read me, Pops.' Shobana took his hands in hers.

'Biscuit, you are a beautiful poem. One doesn't read a poem. One recites it,' the old King said, happy as a child.

'Then recite me, Pops. No one has ever recited me before.'

The King sipped tea from a saucer and recited a furlong of the great Ghalib before leaving.

The rain stopped, the sky cleared up and the sun began to sparkle fiercely. In the afternoon, another car was heard on the gravel outside. Rahul looked, and saw a fancy white American car driven by a very tall jet-black chauffeur in uniform and hat. Pops's Rolls was more than a car. It was an order – 'get out of my way, I am King'. This car was sexy. It said 'come ride me'.

Out of it stepped Uncle and Aunty Sarin of Delhi. Bishamber Sarin was Prakash's friend from their schooldays. Now a 'high high' in the government, he was a tank of a man. He looked menacing, but Uncle Sarin had only to open his mouth to reveal a high-pitched voice that made it seem as if he needed protection - a bird resided in his throat.

Aunty Sarin was half his size, but she had a boom to her voice that sent birds flying from electricity poles. It was well-known from whom Uncle Sarin needed protection. The 'come ride me' car also disgorged another couple, one Rahul had never seen before.

'The Malhotra of Simla. Ramakant and Devi-ji.' Uncle Sarin introduced his companions as everybody sat down. 'They are taking us back and we thought we'd stop by for a quick hello.'

Mr Malhotra was a quiet man who smiled when anyone said anything. Mrs Malhotra smiled only when she addressed someone. She looked like the centrespread of *Filmfare*. The film star dripped with gold - from her ears, neck and wrists.

From the moment they settled down, the walking gold-mine stole glances at the various photos of Pithi. Rahul guessed. A Malhotra woman. Must have a marriageable daughter. According to unwritten caste laws, Malhotras married only the Kapoors or Khannas, top Khatris all. Other Khatris like the Seths and Sehgals were all way below them. The conversation turned to Pithi almost immediately. It was natural with all those maps.

'You are a Delhi wallah, Bishamber. You walk the corridors of power or what-have-you. Tell us then: will there be war?' Prakash said after Santram had served them with a glass of sweet-lime nimbu pani.

'The whole world is with Nehru. Including JFK. Including Krushchev. Who can wage war against him? Not even that Peking Duck whatsisname, that Chou chap. Not that stupid.'

'But he has put so many divisions in NEFA.'

'This is called sabre-rattling. That rattle-snake in the grass is sabre-rattling.'

The talk now turned to other things - the rain that had killed the Kapoor 'cash crop'. The visitors were not unhappy to leave it behind, nor did they look forward to the floods it had unleashed in the plains. Finally, Rahul was noticed.

'Oh, yes?' Mrs Malhotra said, perking up when she heard that Rahul would be going to college in Simla.

Then she acquired a permanent smile as she favoured him with a prolonged look, making the boy rather pleased with himself. It puzzled him too - he had yet to open his mouth.

'Come and visit us, won't you?' Mrs Malhotra stole another look at Pithi jumping a hurdle.

'I will, Aunty.'

'Spitting image of you, both boys, Kapoor sahib,' Mrs Malhotra said, looking from Pithi's photos to Rahul. Prakash wondered if he was being flattered. Even though he was used to this sort of thing, he still did not know what to say.

The Moon House and its twin, the Sun House, stood a hundred yards apart on the same drive from Simla Road. Solan's new Station Commander came and saw and fell in love. On transfer from Poona, Colonel Rikhey lived up to his reputation:

'Likeable. All-weather likeable. Five-footia pukka sahib.'

His moustache and Howitzer laugh added inches to those Napoleonic few feet. He spoke perfect Indian Army English - direct and well edited.

The Moon House seen, Prakash took him home for a drink. With bated breath, everybody awaited them on the long veranda. The fact that the soldier had come to the Sun House meant only one thing: that he'd liked the Moon House. It meant three months' rent in advance. A collective sigh of relief was swiftly chased away by ripples of joy. The evening began to bubble with the likeable five-footia at its centre. It came as no surprise to Rahul that his father and their visitor had known so many people on both sides of the fifteenyear old Indo-Pak border.

The Colonel loved his friends 'across' but hated Pakistan and said Partition was 'oneman-made'.

'Mismanagement at top level - Mountbatten, Congress and the Muslim League. A triangular bungle. But essentially one-man-made.' The Colonel left the man un-named, but he did add, 'To every Churchill, a Hitler. To every Gandhi, a Jinnah. That's history, dear sir.'

On hearing that Rahul would be going to boarding college in Simla, the soldier became the second man to make the same prediction about him within the same twelve hours.

'He will take Simla by storm, young Rahul will.'

'How, Uncle?' asked Shobana.

'Written on his face. Handsome and intelligent.'

'Intelligent?' Shobana laughed. 'How can you tell, Uncle?'

'A trained soldier is a good reader of the human character.'

'Another one,' Rahul said to himself.

'Ever considered the army as a career, young man?'

'One soldier in the family is enough, sir.'

'Oh, what?'

Prakash manoeuvred a move to the drawing room. He wanted to talk to the Colonel about Pithi.

'Ah,' the soldier said, noticing Pithi's photos.

'My elder son, Captain Prithviraj.'

'Also a handsome young man. But then . . .' the Colonel stopped. He looked from Prakash to his wife. 'Where's he posted?'

'NEFA.'

'Ah, NEFA? Hot spot. Thirty-third Corps?'

'Fourth Division. Seventh Infantry Brigade at a fifteen-thousand-foot-high place called Bomdilla.'

'Tricky place, that. Very. Eyeball to eyeball.'

Colonel Rikhey was unlike any Indian Rahul had ever known - he did not have to be asked ten times to stay for dinner. Mother and daughter went away to see to it, while the men sipped whisky.

'Will China attack us, Colonel Sahib?'

'Our prestige as a peace-loving nation is sky-high. You don't attack a peace-loving person.'

'Then what is really going on? Why this sabre-rattling?'

'It's Chou's En Lai's way of saying to the world that he is important.'

'What if he attacks?'

'That he can't do to a friend.'

'But what if he does?'

'Then we'll throw him out, bleeding.'

This was just what Prakash wanted to hear.

'So fortifying to have you here, Colonel.'

They were called to dinner. A long table was laid out on the veranda lit only by twilight and a rising full moon. It gave sufficient light, making the spotless white tablecloth shimmer and the china and silver sparkle. The panoramic expanse of the Solan Valley began from the veranda's wood railing. A few wooded hillocks and a dark massive mountain at the far end stood out in the moonlight. On the valley's right side there lay a spread of a thousand of pinpoints of light, the Solan town. A magical sight.

'If little Solan has all this, who needs Simla?' The Colonel ate with relish. He used his snow-white napkin like a prince.

'Rahul Kapoor, remember this,' Rahul said to himself in his throat, wiping the corners of his mouth like the Colonel.

'We will have a return match as soon as Mrs Rikhey arrives here from Poona with the little ones.'

'How many, ji?' Kamla asked.

'Two boys and a girl.'

'Years?'

'Vinod and Parmod are fourteen and fifteen. Our Leela is sixteen,' Colonel Rikhey said, turning to Shobana. 'Just like you, beta. A flower.'

Just by hearing her name - Leela - Rahul realised somehow it was going to be meaningful for him.

TWO

A lot happened on the day of Rahul's last exam that sent him into a spin. Firstly, Pithi's money came through. Then a letter arrived from the CO's office with *On Indian Government Service* printed on its top and a cheque inside it.

'We are kings again,' shouted Rahul at the valley.

Thirdly, when Rahul got home at lunch, he saw the Rikhey family arrive in an old black Packard.

Rahul simply had to see Leela Rikhey - but how? He needed a brainwave. He got one - welcome gifts should be sent to the Moon House. It was a master-stroke. The Sun House agreed to his suggestion and put him in charge of the mission.

The Moon House too was a half-timbered affair. Painted white, the two identical houses were built on two breast-shaped hilly humps and guarded by towering eucalyptus trees that sang in a strong breeze. Creeper-encased verandas lined their ground floors while fragile-looking balconies were attached to the rooms on the first floor. Some of these gaped at yards and yards of nothing but air scented by the verdant valley. The houses had been built in the last year of the Great War by a Lucknow Nawab as summer residences for his two principal begums. These ladies were of blinding beauty and the Nawab loved them to distraction. Unable to bear the thought of any other male gaze falling on them, he had chosen sleepy Solan instead of naughty Simla for their homes, and had their multi-roomed abodes shrouded in foliage that grew and kept growing, completely hiding the two houses from each other.

This arrangement suited the two women, who lived to hate each other in their splendid isolation. Behind their ´morning rooms', manicured lawns sloped gently down to a pair of tennis courts, the only likely place that could have brought them together. But sport was forbidden to Muslim ladies.

Legend had it that so fierce had been the mutual hatred of these beauties, one could not live without the other, and that both passed away within an hour of each other. When word reached one that the other had expired and of how she had expired - she had hanged herself by her long chiffon breast scarf for no known reason at all except, possibly, loneliness, poor thing the other died on the spot from sheer happiness.

The news of this double tragedy in Solan led to a third death, that of the weak-hearted Nawab in the far-off Lucknow. Telegram in one hand, he clutched his chest with the other and fell to the marble floor of his palace, a corpse.

For reasons unknown to any, his houses in Solan had remained empty till 1947, the year of the Indian holocaust. The Nawab's grandson and heir to his fortune, Jafar Ali, was a Jinnah man. He was also a bosom pal of Prakash Kapoor, with whom he had been to Chief's College in the Mughal princely Lahore. The young Nawab resided in the Lucknow family palace. He wanted to sell the Solan houses and land in India, and follow his leader to his new home, Pakistan. Prakash's ancestral haveli in Lahore was more valuable than his friend's combined Solan estate. A Gandhi man, Prakash wanted to live in India. As Lahore lay in flames and mountains of Hindu/Muslim corpses rose, the Nawab flew to the murder city in his private plane and arrived at his friend's door with a proposal, a godsend for the much-harassed Prakash. A deal was sealed with a burra peg of Dimple Scotch and some pillowcases filled with cash in the Lahore Gymkhana Club at midnight on 15 August when Nehru in

Delhi began his famous speech. A week later, the Kapoors were in the Sun House in Solan.

Quickly, Prakash had both houses restored to their bygone glory. The newly established army station rented the Moon House for its CO, to whose current incarnation Rahul had come to offer the Kapoor welcome gifts - five baskets of fruit from the plains, covered with colourful translucent patang kite paper carried by five servants on their heads.

Two smart-looking orderlies in olive green inspected the fruit laid out in a neat row on the veranda. Then they stiffened up.

'Mrs Rikhey at home?' enquired Rahul.

'One minute,' replied one orderly, disappearing behind the jali door of the double-fronted entrance. Then *she* emerged – on the spot edible. 35, 22, 32. I'mdreaming eyes, Kiss-me-quick lips, honey cheeks . . . Lightning had struck.

'Mummy's in the bathroom.'

The lightning having struck, Rahul knew nothing any more.

'We haven't ordered any fruit.'

Those eyes. Those lips. Those tits. All Rahul knew was that he didn't want to go to Simla any more.

'But I have a note here in the Colonel's own hand, Miss-ji,' Rahul lied, pointing to his empty breast pocket under which his heart rioted like a 1947 Lahore street mob.

The Colonel's daughter gave Rahul a martial look. She turned on her heels and dashed inside the house. 'Mummy, come and see. A man's brought fruit. Tons of it, believe it or not. The idiot says Daddy's sent for it,' the idiot heard her yell.

'What fruit? I haven't ordered any,' Mummy replied. 'Tell him to take his rubbish away.'

Daddy's girl came back.

'Take your rubbish away. All of it. Now.'

'Miss-ji, I was ordered to bring this fruit here and I have. I can't take it back. I'll get the sack.'

'We don't want what we haven't asked for. So go go. Jao jao.' Miss-ji looked at the orderlies.

'But Miss-ji. . .'

The orderlies advanced and rested a hand each on Rahul's shoulders - not a neighbourly gesture. Just then a jeep ground its way up the drive and out of it leaped Colonel Rikhey and his two sons.

'Rahul, my boy. What's all this? Jolly nice of you folks. Jolly nice. . .'

An invitation with sides dipped in gold came for the 'return match'. It stole Rahul's sleep. Boy, he was going to be with her in the same room all evening for a cosy, comfy family meal!

Boy, oh boy! But the Colonel liked to play it big. He invited the whole garrison as well. In starched khaki with shiny brass buttons and polished leather, there was the lanky Sikh Major Long Beard and his pot-bellied fellow Sikh Major Short Beard. There was Captain Mustachio So & So and Lieutenant Ogle Ogle . . . a bloody battalion of them. Most of them had come with their doll-like wives - Indian officers' ladies made the best-looking army wives. Yet some of them stole lustful looks at their Commander' daughter, noticed Rahul, taking her clothes off with their sideways glances. One in particular - Lieutenant Ogle Ogle. The bastard was only a couple of years older than Rahul and (and this hurt) devilishly good-looking.

The CO's daughter seemed to be used to this sort of thing. In fact, she appeared to be revelling in it. The constant smile on her lips and her glowing cheeks said so. She flitted through the throng with a twinkle in her eyes - it was as much her party as it was Daddy's. Rahul had seen her look towards him once. Maybe twice. And that was all. Rahul had no right to feel hurt that she hadn't looked a third time. So why was he? He sought his best friend's help.

'Use your brains, Rahul. If you can't hit the stumps in the first over, try something different in the second. Bowl round the wicket,' Krishna whispered in his ear.

Rahul decided he would make friends with her brothers, Vinod and Parmod. Cricket did it.

Rahul's Middle College had an annual fixture with the Garrison. The boys had heard about it. Had he played in this year's game?

'Out first ball, alas. Took five for thirty though,' said humble Rahul.

'Five for thirty?' Eyes widened. 'Can you bowl a googly? Can you play the late cut?'

From that moment on they were eating out of his hands. Being a spinner, Rahul showed them the googly grip and promised to teach them to play the late cut which he himself could not play. At the same time, he watched their sister from the corners of his eyes. He noticed she was taking a particular interest in his own sister, Shobana, equally beautiful and equally ogled by those bearded and un-bearded wolves in military clothing. In this he saw the hand of God. He heard the sweet sound of opportunity knocking, although not as yet very loudly. He looked up and saw Krishna wink at him.

Now when God Himself winks at you . . .

Rahul knew his day had come. Or was on its way.

It was a buffet affair. In attendance were bearers in snow-white tunics, red and gold cummerbunds and loud crisp turbans. The two girls allowed themselves to be served. Then, plates in hand, they turned their backs on the wolves and their dolls and moved away to stand on a small balcony. Right in front was a drop of a hundred feet, then half a mile of void and the Solan mountain ablaze with a riot of glowing pinheads. A magical evening, an evening to fall in love.

'Hungry?' Rahul said to his admirers.

'Starving,' they replied in unison. Plates in hand, they came and quietly stationed themselves behind their sisters. The girls were not eating. They were laughing and talking - about him!

'No, honestly. He's such a joker, Shobana. You know? Had Daddy not arrived just then . . . Didn't he tell you?'

'Not a thing.'

'He had me totally fooled, you know. But somehow I did not think he was quite a peddler.'

'Oh, but he is. My brother - he peddles lies. Laughable lies.'

'So he's going to the famous Simla College. Wow!'

'Is it famous?'

'Very. Top top. He'll become a pukka Simla Pink.'

'Who's a Simla Pink?'

'You know? Rosy cheeks. Nose in air. Head in the clouds, speaks English so well no one can understand a word, treats the world like dirt.'

'My brother is too daft for that.'

'We have friends there.'

'And we have an aunt in Simla. But we never see her. Mummy doesn't like her.'

'Simla girls are fast. So he's going to Simla. Wow.'

'Only if he passes his exam. My brother's dumb.'

'Doesn't look dumb to me.'

'But he is. Deceives everyone with his looks.'

'Yes?' Leela happened to look back. Her cheeks turned cherry pink when her eyes met Rahul's.

It was precisely at that moment that Rahul changed his mind about going to Simla. His mouth full, he addressed his first mega prayer to the sky.

'O Krishna-ji, my dearest and best and true friend. Please . . .' And Rahul made a request. It was a strange request. So strange, even the God had difficulty in believing it.

'You sure?' the God asked the mortal.

Folding his hands, the young man addressed himself to the blue-bodied Eternal and asked for the direct opposite of what he had begged of Him before.

'Please. Let my number go missing from *The Tribune* on the D Day.'

It was the strangest about-turn in history.

'Life. An inexhaustible storehouse of strangeness.'

The girls became friends. They began to visit each other. Whenever Leela came to the Sun House, Rahul found a reason to be around. But he was not included in the girls' scheme of things. Nor could he demand to be – this was India.

He received only glances - sometimes he caught her looking at him. Her eyes drowned Rahul in a homemade syrup as sweet as it was intoxicating. But it was not good enough. Rahul wanted to be alone with her. And her eyes said - *me too*.

'What to do, Sir?' Rahul addressed the blue yonder.

'Games. Play games,' came the reply with a wink of the Divine eye. But they had been doing this anyway, playing games with their eyes. Their games were like a silent movie with no sub-titles. Hardly enough. Rahul had to do something, provide the missing words. He was clever. He could do it.

Rahul drew Leela's brothers into his orbit.

Vinod was mad about stamps. Rahul gave him his precious album. Parmod was addicted to collecting comics. Rahul had stacks of old ones. He gave him the lot. The Rikhey brothers had a secret for which they would have been beaten black and blue had it ever become known - they liked a fag. Rahul, a true friend, sometimes bought a Gold Flake cigarette and shared it with them down in the valley. Now whenever their sister came to see Shobana, he made sure they were there too. Soon the girls let them into their self-contained world.

'Games. Let's play games,' the Rikhey boys cried.

Playing cards was no good. With Shoki and Bimbi who would cry their lungs out if not included in a game, a pack of cards was not big enough. Nobody liked the carrom, really. Nor any other board game. There was little enthusiasm for tennis or badminton. And cricket?

'Boring. Boring,' the girls sang.

What was left then?

'Let's go for walks, dammit. Magic mountains. People come from all over India just for that,' the Rikhey boys said, repeating word for word what Rahul had put in their mouths.

Going up and down the familiar tracks was tame. So was picnicking in the Happy Valley a mile away. They had to do something more daring. And they did. Taking perilous pagdandi footpaths, they went down deep khuds, steep precipices overgrown with tall mountain grass, shrubbery and flowers wild and beautiful. Sometimes they all had to hold hands to get through a dangerous patch. Rahul liked these spots. Somehow he was always holding the hand of she for whom who he now lived. Once, the two of them got separated from the others.

'What now?' Leela said. Then she slipped on the carpet of pine needles and fell straight into Rahul's arms ten feet below and clung to him for her life. Paradise. But far too briefly.

'Didi, you all right?' cried kill-fun Vinod, parting the curtain of six-foot-high golden grass.

Somehow, cricket took on - Rahul convinced the boys that they had to learn to bowl the off spin and play the late cut. He knew they never would - the clever Colonel's sons were clumsy beyond belief.

Cricket was played in the disused tennis courts. Held in by the mountain with the sighing, whispering and singing euca-lyptuses on one side and the open Solan Valley on the other, it made quite a sumptuous playground. The three Kapoors and the two Rikhey boys with the cook's son and Gogo, plus two or three of Rahul's friends - Bharat, Rohan or Brij - could make an easy five-a-side. One evening, none of Rahul's friends turned up. But Shobana and Leela did.

'We want to play,' Leela said with her martial tongue.

'You can't,' said Rahul firmly.

'Why not?'

'It's a man's game, however boring or whatever you call it. And we love it. All right?'

'Yes, all right, all right. Don't be so touchy. We too love it. And we want to play.'

'I'll have to consult my esteemed friends. Gentlemen . . .'

The esteemed friends had no objection. Instead of the usual ordinary game, a proper Test Match would be played - India versus England. The ladies were appointed captains with everybody fielding.

'It's a cricket bat, not gulli ka danda, dammit. Hold it as one. Straight,' Rahul shouted from long on at the England captain, also his.

'Show me how,' his captain ordered.

Feeling as tall as the tallest eucalyptus, Rahul rolled up his sleeves and breezed to the popping crease with his cheeks beginning to burn. In a clasp of approximately 35 inches, he showed her how to hold a cricket bat and how to play a forward defensive stroke. She fitted in him just right. Her maddening 35-inch twin peaks soared into his bare arms, crushing him with shame and delight and making him wish he wore a box, even though they were playing with a tennis ball. Leela was a slow learner and missed ball after ball. Then, just like that, she hit an exquisite six over the trees, scattering the fielders like chicken. Everybody ran after the ball down the wooded mountainside. Left by themselves, the England captain and her coach remained as they were, hypnotised. Then Leela dropped the willow from her grasp as if it was a gulli-danda bat and turned and faced him. Rahul tightened his embrace, his straight rock-hard lunn thrust against her silken soft belly. He took her lips in his. She shut her eyes and went limp. For how long? Neither of them knew.

'Do you think anyone can see us?' she said, waking up.

'Only the Colonel sahib.'

'Boy, then you had better start running. To Simla.' Leela herself ran after the fielders.

Stunned, Rahul stood on. He picked up the bat and waited. Minutes passed, hours passed. But she did not come back. Rahul found himself practising straight drives. Suddenly he felt foolish – his lunn was still soaring. While he waited, time dealt with it. Then they all came back with the ball. Leela marched purposefully to the wicket – Ted Dexter about to hit another hundred - took the bat from Rahul and waved at the demon under-arm bowler, Shobana, to recommence hostilities. For the rest of the Test she did not look at him once.

What now?

Nothing. Absolutely nothing. Shobana often went to the Moon House, but Leela didn't come to the Sun House any more. Rahul burned like an Australian bush fire. He couldn't understand it. But his friends could.

'She's made herself scarce because she's ashamed of herself.' Bharat knew about these things. 'Psychology,' he shrugged.

'No, you fool. She's thinking.' Brij also knew psychology.

'Of what?' Rahul asked.

'Women. More complicated than the inside of a clock. Even God doesn't really know what makes them tick,' Brij went on.

'How the fuck do you know then?'

More days passed, dragging forward with a cruel lurch the dreaded D Day - and Leela remained out of sight. But the day before D Day was another big day, the Independence Day, 15 August. It was going to be an important day for his country, his town and for him, India's fifteenth birthday. He was bound to meet her then.

August was known to be merciless. Early every second or third morning, jet-black clouds from Simla side rolled over Mount Solan. Soon after came the divine fireworks, followed by torrential rain. It was an awesome seasonal ritual that went on for a couple of hours. Then suddenly the great waterworks stopped, as if the Chief Engineer up in Simla or somewhere higher had turned the tap off. The clouds dissolved and lo and behold, there was a clear blue sky and biting sunshine. In the afternoon, an umbrella once more became a must.

Independence Day in Solan was celebrated in the morning, just as it was up and down the country. A parade was held on the Military Maidan, a long flat ridge that had pushed itself up a mountainside. The whole of Solan thronged there in colourful clothes. Hordes of hill folk from the depths of the valley also turned up. The Station Commander hoisted the tricolour. When rose petals from the flag rained down on him, he took the salute and the army band played *Jann Gann Mann*, the national anthem. Everybody - man, woman and child - stood to attention, muttering the Tagore song, some with goose pimples on their cheeks, others with tears in their eyes. Then the Station Commander proudly made a speech. India had clocked up another year of freedom. There was much hugging. And that was that. The Solan wallahs went back home, the hill folk to their hamlets and the proud Station Commander threw a party in the Moon House.

Knowing 'our wretched monsoon', Colonel Rikhey had had a large shamiana marquee erected the night before for the VIPs - just in case. He also had the time of the function put forward an hour from eleven to twelve noon – 'to be double sure'.

The Rikheys dropped in at the Sun House early that evening, all of them, including *her*. They sat in a large semi-circle on the veranda, facing the vast void of the valley, sipping tea and talking about the weather. But why wouldn't she look at Rahul?

'Worried about your exam results, Rahul?' the Colonel asked.

'Do I look worried, sir?'

'Yes, you do. Mighty worried. You needn't be. You are going to come up trumps, young man. You think it will rain tomorrow?'

'Yes. Cats and dogs.'

'WHAT? You want the whole show ruined?'

Yes. Rahul wanted the whole show ruined. Having made herself invisible for so long, here she was at last but without once looking at him. So how could he be sure of meeting her tomorrow? What was the point in it now, in this Independence tamasha masquerade? It was a bloody charade, anyway, this dumb patriotic harlotry. India was independent, it was independent. It had to be. They had fought for it. So what was the big deal?

'Prakash, your boy is an original. But sometimes I don't understand him.'

'I don't either.'

The Rikheys stayed there a whole hour but she didn't glance at him once – not until the family rose to leave. And even then it was more like seeing through him - as if he was a glass wall or something - than looking at him with a lover's eyes.

'Cheer up, young man. Say cheese and smile. Always look on the bright side of things. And always say that tomorrow will be better than today, that tomorrow will begin with a bang.'

Tomorrow did begin with a bang – there wasn't a single square inch of cloud in the sky. By nine it was very warm. By ten, hot like a tandoor.

'I told you, darling,' was said in the Moon House. 'Oh, no,' said the same voice an hour and a half later, when the sunny skies turned first grey, then black. Heavy rain and hail hit Solan with a vengeance. But flag-hoisting went ahead and the national anthem was duly sung. The people didn't mind the foul weather at all - braving it made them feel all the more patriotic. Colonel Rikhey's long speech was all about DRAGON CHOU. It couldn't be heard in spite of the loudspeakers, since a noisy wind lashed out. The Colonel cleverly cut his speech short.

As he uttered his last words – *'we will throw the Chini out if he dare come in. Jai Hind'* - all hell broke loose. The timing was unbelievable. The furious wind whipped out the pegs of the great shamiana from the rain-soaked earth, the bamboo poles collapsed, and away flew the colourful marquee into a ravine, like a cordless kite. Chaos erupted. People ran helter-skelter, mostly into each other. Leela Rikhey ran into Rahul Kapoor. They found themselves behind some bushes with a deep abyss only inches away on one side.

'Why have you been avoiding me all these days?'

'I haven't. I have been busy.'

'With what?'

'Oh, with this and that. You know.'

'No, I don't. You lie.'

'Honest.'

'You don't care for me. I mean nothing to you.'

'Don't say that.'

'Then what should I say?'

'Something nice.'

'I love you. We kissed at the Test Match. Did it mean nothing?'

'What? I can't hear.'

'You kissed me. Did it mean nothing to you?'

'Don't scream. Someone will hear you. Then?'

'No one can hear a cannon in this fucking racket.'
'Language. And don't shout. I'm not deaf.'
Silence.
'So you don't care for me. I mean nothing to you.'
Smouldering silence.
'If you don't answer, I'll jump off this cliff.'
'Pardon?'
'I swear I will. Want to see?'
'Yes.'

Rahul would show her what he was really made of. He really was going to do it. He really, really was.

'Mummee! Mummy's calling me. Must fly. Bye.'

With one foot raised over his grave as it were, Rahul asked himself the somewhat silly question - Should I? Or should I not? The purpose of the whole exercise had been to make her beg him not to. Now that she was no longer there, Rahul saw no merit in carrying the matter to a fatal conclusion.

He looked up and saw a greater monsoon storm than the one that beat on him. It was in the eyes of Mummy and Shobana - they were crying their lungs out at the untimely loss of a dearly beloved son and brother. Mummy had stayed at home to be with his father, who was unwell again. And Shobana was somewhere in that mad pele-mele. Rahul found her with the Rikheys.

Brother and sister got a lift in the Rikhey Packard. There wasn't any room for Rahul really - what with the five of them, Shobana and the driver. But Colonel Rikhey had a soft spot for the Kapoor boy. He waved the driver away and decided to drive the old car himself. Fortune began to smile at Rahul again and he congratulated himself on his wisdom that had inspired him to retreat from the edge of the abyss instead of offering himself to it as a sacrifice to his wounded pride and a broken heart. For he was asked to squeeze in at the very last minute. He did so, and as it happened, found himself next to none other than his very tormentor herself at the back by the door. As they set out on their mile-long journey home along that tortuous mountain road, Rahul slumped in the seat like his neighbour, arms crossed on his chest. Unseen, first his right hand found her left hand, then her right breast under her Burberry raincoat. It was firm and the size of the juicy langra mango.

Rahul had never held a young maiden's breasts before, but he had held an unshakable belief that they were the most beautiful things in all creation. Till that rainy, soggy moment he had no idea that by simply taking them in your hands you could release such a flood of joy. Why, the delight they ignited in him was devastating. He could have died of it. He wanted to die that joy would then become everlasting, eternal. But if God had located so much joy in our persons, life was for living. Forever.

Rahul shut his eyes to live 'forever', his hand where it was, doing what it was doing. But when he opened them, he shuddered. For in the driver's little mirror, he saw the Colonel's eyes on him. The man knew what Rahul was doing, fondling his daughter's breasts behind his back, looting his family honour. The Colonel was about to stop the car, drag the bastard out by the hair, break every bone in his body and relegate it to the very abyss which due to a bit of commonsense he had managed to avoid.

A mad, runaway lorry tearing its way up towards them made the Colonel avert his gaze. Rahul seized the opportunity and withdrew his hand. While the soldier negotiated with the loony lorry, Rahul's neighbour tugged at his hand and replaced it where it had been seconds ago.

'Bloody fool,' the CO swore at the lorry driver.

'It was your fault, darling, driving in the middle of the road. Then you always do,' said Mrs Rikhey.

'But did you see how fast he was going, sala haramzada bloody fool? He must be doing fifty. In this weather. On this road. Must have been a Sikh.'

'Maybe he's saying the same about you, darling.'

'What a day! It went all right - I mean in spite of the storm.'

'But we couldn't hear a word of your speech.'

'You can read it at home.'

Soon after they arrived, the Moon House became a mela, a fairground of 'army and civil', of soaked uniforms, saris and Congress white kurta pyjamas plus other forms of attire. The Rana Saheb also came. But he only stayed for a cup of tea. Then he asked to be driven to the Sun House to call on 'poor' Prakash. The rain suddenly stopped. Clouds vanished, the sky cleared up.

'Lovely, lovely,' croaked army and civil in unison.

There was one cloud, though. It was in Rahul's heart. How could she go about flitting through that throng, wide-eyed with glowing cheeks, without once looking at him? As if nothing had happened. As if he didn't exist. And how could she smile like that at everyone except him and especially at that cheap creep Ogle Ogle, so soon after what had happened?

'Don't be greedy, Owl Rahul. You've had your hands full for the day. Say thank you to your lovely Krishna. Say cheese and look at the bright side of things. Say tomorrow will be . . .'

Tomorrow was the day of reckoning. Rahul wished tomorrow would never come. Because he knew what it was going to bring.

Rahul had been playing a sickening game of self-deception. He knew some prayers cannot be answered. He also knew what the world's response would be if his prayers were.

'All that glitters isn't gold.'

'The glamour boy was only a fart, after all.'

'Nothing to him. Prince Charming, my arse.'

'Full of shit like the rest of us.'

These and other remarks from his friends and foes rang in his ears as Rahul made his way to the railway station with his brothers and Terry at dawn the next morning. But Rahul did not care as long as he did not have to go to Simla.

Carved in the belly of the mountain facing a yawning valley, Solan's little railway station had high Swiss gables overhung with flower bushes in bloom-primroses, begonias, petunias, marigolds ... a hanging Mughal Garden. Bharat, Brij, Rohan and other friends of his were already there, a dozen or so boys with sleep-filled, worried faces. At the deserted station they amounted to a crowd. Nobody spoke. Tensely, they awaited the arrival of the train from the plains that was bringing the newspapers. Even frisky Terry was restrained.

'Why are you so quiet, oi? You sat the exam, too?' Bimbi said, putting an arm around him.

It was grey and fresh and there was a touch of menace in the morning, an air of foreboding. The platform danced with deep breaths and cold sighs. All eyes were glued to the black hole of the tunnel in the wooded mountain out of which the tiny, toy-like train would suddenly emerge at six. It did so on the dot - Indian railways! Always late, but never when they are bringing sad tidings. Shattering the still of the morning with a deeply hoarse whistle, it oozed its way out of the hole slowly like a giant earthworm covered in steam and smoke.

The black metallic monster of an engine hissed to a halt just in front of the boys. The engines inside their ribcages also came to a stop. Then there was hustle and bustle. Copies of the dreaded newspaper, printed in Ambala Cantt sixty-five miles down in the burning Punjab plain, Feverishly, the lads scanned its pages, each one looking for his number and score. Grunts and shouts! Finding their numbers missing, brothers Ram and Sham tore up the newspaper.

'Third fucking rate,' they groaned.

'We knew it,' yelled Rahul's brothers. The whole world did - a Kapoor boy. It had to be a first.

For the first time in his life Rahul wished he was not so brilliant. Being so had sealed his fate. It was relegating him to a life he did not want just then, a life of glamour that Simla gave to those born with a silver spoon. He wished he was a mere Tom, Dick or Harry laloo-panjoo. A yokel. An idiot even.

All Solan came to congratulate the Kapoors.

'What did I say?' The Rana Saheb smiled proudly.

'I told you.' The Colonel embraced Rahul.

In the hustle-bustle of the house, Rahul managed a moment with Leela. She had the old kiss-me-quick look. But something was amiss.

'You all right, Leela-ji?'

'What?'

'Don't be sad. I'll come home every weekend.'

'What? Didn't hear you. Heartburn. Chickpeas.'

49

Surely she meant heartbreak, not heartburn.

'I really don't want to go.'

'Where?'

'This bloody Simla - where else? I wish an earthquake would flatten it.'

'Oh! You mean . . .'

Her brothers appeared! Rahul had to shut up

'Will you come tomorrow?' he asked her.

'I'll see.' Then Leela flew away.

But she did not come the next day. Nor the day after. She just disappeared.

'She must miss me. How can she not? How can she resist me?' Rahul could not understand. Casually, he asked Shobana how her friend was.

'Busy.'

'Busy doing what?'

'She goes riding a lot these days, you know.'

'So?'

'Guess who with? So, Bruvver-ji, I would forget stinking Solan-Volan's rains and enjoy the famous mists of Simla.'

Santram took Rahul's stuff by bus the day before, a Sunday, to lay out everything in his college hostel just as his young master liked.

The Nehru visit to these parts was beginning on Monday, so Simla Road became a madhouse on wheels, a tangle of road-blocks and police the next morning. But Prakash had a water-tight plan to beat it all. He'd drive off Solan at the first cry of the cock. That would give them time for breakfast at the Cecil, Simla's Savoy, and let Rahul make it to his first lecture, English with Professor Nath, at ten.

But Prakash had another of those nights.

'I am fine. I am fine,' he said next morning.

'You are going nowhere, ji. You haven't slept a wink. And I have sent for Dr Gupta.'

'Madam mine, I'm fine. Fit as a fiddle, fresh as a cucumber.'

'More like fresh as a fiddle. Madam yours says you are not setting one foot out of this house. Rahul, go and telephone stationmaster Gauri Shankar to ask if he can find you a seat on the early morning railcar.'

'Double over-packed,' Gauri Shankar said.

So it had to be the 7.30 Simla De Luxe bus.

Rahul wore his new blue suit and a polka dot tie.

'Humm!' Shoki, Bimbi and Shobana rolled their eyes. They beamed with pride at how their big brother looked. Their parents looked away - it encouraged the evil eye to gloat at your offsprings` good looks or good fortune. Kamla hurried to the kitchen and touched the coal-black back of the chappati tavva with the tip of her little finger. She came right back and put a little black spot on Rahul's left cheek - this would keep the evil eye away from her boy. A tear fell from her eye.

'Mummy mine!' Rahul clasped his mother in his arms.

'All right, you two,' his father said, looking away.

Heart in throat, Rahul bent down to touch his parents' feet in farewell. Shoki and Bimbi walked him to the bus station. On the tree-lined drive to the main road, they bumped into *her* of all people. She wore riding breeches, jacket and cap, and again looked on-the-spotedible. She noted his suit and all, and smiled and gave Rahul a long sidelong glance which said 'I love you'.

'Where are you off to so early dressed like a Lord?' she said, and shattered his heart in a thousand pieces. She didn't even know he was leaving, or worse, had forgotten!

'To peddle apples and pears at the bus stop. And your very good self in this gear?'

'Take a guess.'

'Let me see. Swimming. You are going swimming.'

There was no farewell.

The Solan bus stop was a rough patch on the Simla Road past the single-storey wooden Khalsa Hotel. Overlooking the narrow Lower Bazaar, it had rickety khokha wooden shops on one side and the Military Hill on the other. A seasonal puddle of mud water in its middle made it the breeding ground for flies and mosquitoes and also the meeting point of stray dogs and cows. It was always asleep. But it leaped to life when a bus or two arrived. Then hawkers from thin air flocked to it, holding aloft round brass trays with fuming glasses of tea or ice-cold nimbu pani and plates of chaat and biscuit-khatais. The Kapoor fruits and fruits from the plains - bananas, oranges and mangoes - also suddenly appeared. At this time of the morning, however, there was never anybody to be seen. Not even the dogs and their larger four-legged friends. But this morning, things looked different.

'Look, look!' Shoki cried in disbelief.

'What the hell?' Bimbi yelled.

'Looks like the fifteenth of August!' Shoki said.

In Gandhian white khadi, two thousand people sat on their haunches, filling the bus stop and covering the Military Hill.

'Looks like a mass shit-in,' Bimbi said. It did indeed look like one, the way people were squatting on their haunches.

'No. They've come to see Rahul off,' Shoki said.

It was obvious why they were there, to greet Nehru, as if he would be coming by bus. A few policemen stood idly by with lathis in their hands. Behind them stood Inspector Bansal.

'When is the PM expected?' Rahul asked.

'Sometime today,' Bansal replied.

'What if he turns up only at five p.m.?'

'What if he turns up at five p.m.?'

These people, like most Indians, had a love affair with Nehru. They had come for a darshan glimpse of their man. They didn't care how long it took. Anyway, they had come prepared. They brought with them parathas, pickles and umbrellas.

Rahul's bus arrived. It had failed to cross the collective Kapoor mind that there might not be room on it for him - there was always room for a Kapoor anywhere. But not on this bus. The conductor had never heard of the Kapoors and the more he heard that Rahul was one, the less he seemed to like the fact.

'The bus is full,' he said.

Rahul was not going to be late for college on his very first day even if it meant sitting on its roof rack with the luggage. First, he poured a bucket of the Kapoor charm on the man to make him see how urgent it was. Then he offered him an irresistible something - a glimpse of his wallet that contained 200 rupees, a month's allowance and twice the conductor's salary. But the fellow was deaf and blind. He was a toothpick of a man ten foot tall, an ace coconut picker.

'When the bus is full, the bus is full. Even the diggy.'

Rahul had no choice but to seek out Inspector Bansal. The inspector took the man behind a bush to talk him out of his 'gandoo arsehole rules'.

The conductor shook his head. 'Rules are rules.'

Inspector Bansal had his own rules. He gave the Man a loud kick in his diggy. Rahul got a seat, but made a life-long enemy.

The ride from Solan to Simla is a treat, one of the seven or eight wonders of the world. That is, if you have the stomach for motoring in those murder mountains. Rahul Kapoor did, being brought up in them. Not so his fellow passengers, all twenty-six of them packed in that mini Tata Mercedes bus - it stank of vomit. Rahul stuck his head out of the window for fresh air, thinking of *her* heartburn and his heartache.

Ten miles on, directly below an ancient temple ruin atop a minor peak, the unthinkable happened. Rahul should have known it would, it not being his day from the very start. The bus began to go phuph, phuph, phuph. . . Then it stopped.

'Ahhh!' people cried in relief - another stop! The jovial Sikh driver jerked his head from side to side and screwed up his handsome bearded face in a philosophical smile – this was not the first time. He leaped out and buried his turbaned head under the bonnet of the bus engine. The toothpick followed him and bent over him like a bagla crane. Then all the male passengers spilled out.

'It never rains, but. . .' shrugged the driver.

'What, what?' said ten voices.

'The gearbox.' The philosopher kicked his bus.

'So what happens now?'

'I haul my arse back to Solan and get the part.'

'Long time?'

'One hour. Maybe two. Depending.' Depending on how early or late he got a lift either way.

Rahul's hopes of making it to Professor Nath's lecture were dashed.

'Ma chod motherfuckers,' he called the bus company owners and threw his head up. Spotting the temple ruins at a height of a five-minute climb and knowing he had all the time in the world, Rahul began to trek uphill. He found the ruins as they should be - desolate and grand. He poked his nose in cells filled with luxuriant growths and thought of her and sighed. He passed through crumbling arches and ornate columns and sighed. Two hundred feet down below on the road, a De Luxe bus coming from Simla stopped by Rahul's bus. Wonderful. Now the driving ace would get a lift and go to Solan and, with some luck, get back in an hour. Rahul could still make it to college on time.

He saw the driver and the conductor of the Simla De Luxe also examine the damage. Minutes later, when Rahul looked down again, he heard the two buses blow their horns. He saw everybody clamber into the two buses and the next thing he knew, both vehicles had roared off in opposite directions. Obviously, the bus from Simla had the part Rahul's bus needed. The conductor of his bus had struck back and stranded Rahul in mid-jungle.

Rahul raced down, screaming blood-curdling Punjabi deliciousness: 'Go do kama sutra on your mother. On your sisters too . . .' His day in total tatters before it had begun, he wanted to cry as he started walking up the steep Simla Road.

Twelve miles on at Tara Devi, Rahul came in sight of Simla, a long crescent-shaped spread of an English town hoisted piece-meal to Himalayan heights. It was a picture postcard. Venom for the De Luxe conductor howled. But something about Simla that Rahul had read somewhere painted half a smile on his pained mug.

'What wonderful architecture! If the monkeys have done it, they should be shot, lest they do it over again.'

Anyone looking at the picture postcard would have under-stood why the English chose that dizzy mountain to plant a little England on it. It was all spotless azure skies, lush green slopes (if dangerous), and the breath of heaven itself.

The road passed by Tara Devi station where a mini-mini goods train was making its way up to Simla five miles away, a snail with a load on its back. Rahul ran and jumped into a tiny wagon full of coal. It proved to be the most luxurious rail journey of his life. The picture postcard became bigger and bigger as his toy train laboured its way up. Getting close to the main Simla station, Rahul got a good view of his college across the valley.

The Simla College was perched on a chittan in the Elysium Hill which thrust itself upwards awkwardly where the moun-tain city's lifeline, Cart Road, performed an acrobatic bend before moving on. Rahul knew it well, having been there once to register. It was a smiling spot with smiling views and vistas. In the Raj's heyday it used to be a glory of a hotel, the Elysium, one of so many, where, in the 'season' - from April-May to September - the sahib dallied with his mem and drank Pimms and danced the evening away. During this season when the endless plains of the subcontinent a light year away sizzled in the sun and then got drowned in the monsoon, Simla breathed that divine air. It became the sahib's Deauville, Nice and Monte Carlo all rolled in one and pushed up the Himalayas. Luxury hotels sparkled naughtily and ballroom floors creaked happily under the weight of nightly flirtings. Cuckolded husbands and forsaken wives took it all in their stride. They laid back and thought of England and sang 'God Save the King' whenever required to do so, usually nightly.

Rahul's college, the one-time palace of pleasure, had of late found a different function as the only coeducational college north of Delhi.

THREE

The sun was already dipping behind the hills when Rahul had the first sight of his new home - the Simla College Hostel. It sat nervously on an awkward ledge at the side of the wooded Mount Jakhoo, overlooking the Queen of Hill Stations. A whisker separated it from a precipice of creepy emptiness - architectural daredevilry. Had King Ludwig of Bavaria invested in real estate in Simla?

SCH was a two-storey, 30-room huddle of timber and masonry with a corrugated iron roof, the building materials of all Simla. A narrow balcony encircled its first floor. A very long veranda jutted out on the ground floor. Two men sat on the steps there, pulling at beedis. One of them was his very own Santram. The servant sprang to his feet when he saw Rahul coming up the rickshaw-track from Lakkar Bazaar, his face red like a chilli.

'Rahul-baba, what happened? Been waiting all day with heart in throat.'

'The fucking de Luxe conductor. Threw me out under the temple ruins.'

'Oho. Temple to Tara Devi is twelve mountain miles! Oho.' The devoted old family servant's heart melted for the boy he had looked after from the day he was born. 'What about the other buses?'

'All fucking full up. None stopped.'

'Not even a PWD truck?'

'Not even a PWD truck.'

'Oho. You must be knackered double plus. Come rest in your room. It's all made. Tip and top.'

'Hope the room came with a bed.'

'Soft as a maiden's bosom, sir,' put in the other man, a short, fair-complexioned hill man not much older than Rahul.

'Bahadar Singh,' Santram introduced him. 'Best Hostel mundu. Your servant.'

Like Rahul's college half a mile away, his hostel too used to be a glory of a hotel in the Raj days, Teak Hotel. Immediately from the long veranda unfolded the kingly Simla Valley and the endless undulation of pine-and-deodar-covered peaks stretching far into the horizon.

Rahul's room was on the first floor at the back. Handsomely proportioned, it had a large curtain-less window and a skylight. Santram had laid out everything neatly. Tired as he was, Rahul still wanted to go out on the balcony behind his room to see the other side of the valley. The way to it lay through Rahul's 'English bathroom' which included a mystery object - a bidet.

'Oi, what's this?' Santram pointed to the bidet.

'Never been used since '47,' said Bahadar Singh. 'Indian ladies don't like it.'

'But what is it?'

'Them memsahibs used to wash here after.'

'Why doesn't it have a lid, like the loo?'

'Been puzzling myself about that, to tell you the truth.' Bahadar Singh was sturdy-looking like all hill people. He had blue eyes, like some of them.

Bahadar Singh opened the balcony door. More pine-and-deodar-covered heights and depths far and near greeted them. But there was a difference, a breath-stopping one, since beyond the valley in the dying rain of the sun's gold rose snow-capped

Himalayan cones behind at least four different ranges of mountains. An awesome spectacle.

'That there is Shali Peak behind the Mashobra range,' Bahadar Singh said in English like a guide at the Taj Mahal. 'And that is Snowdon Hospital.' He jabbed a finger at a vast complex of white and green buildings down in the valley. 'Used to be the house of C-in-C. Wavell was there before he became Viceroy and moved on to Viceroy Lodge there behind. That on the left under is Chapslee, house of the Maharajah of Kapurthala, and that above it is Auckland House, lovely, lovely girls' school on Elysium Hill by your college, Rahul-baba.'

'All right, Bahadar Singh,' Rahul said. He had had enough of nature for the day, month and the year. Unable to remain upright any more, he wanted to go inside and lie down on the bed 'as soft as a maiden's bosom', though a slab of concrete would do in its absence. Santram understood.

'Achcha, Rahul-baba, then. If I don't go now, I'll miss the last bus and I too'll be walking.'

When left alone, Rahul lay down in his bed to review his entry into the realm of higher education.

Not exactly triumphal. Wait till the boys heard about it back home. They'd go epileptic.

His legs aching and his body throbbing, he shut his eyes. He heard someone walking on his tin roof, light footsteps, like a thief. Then a monkey with a face as pink as that of an Englishman took a peep at him from the skylight. The fellow smiled at him.

Rahul fell asleep. Sometime later he woke up with a start. He was cold, his clothes felt damp. A thick, translucent mist filled his room like cigarette smoke in a gamblers' den. He had left the bathroom doors ajar and the famous Simla vapour had just wafted in. Rahul hugged himself and felt the first pangs of loneliness. He shut the bathroom doors and came down to the common room. It was empty. He felt desperately hungry. He went to the dining room. That was also bare. But kitchen noises came from a door in its middle. A man of about forty with blue eyes emerged from it. He had a front tooth missing. A jet of air accompanied his words.

'Jhandoo, head cook. Been at the Teak twenty years.' Surprisingly, he too spoke English.

'Where did you learn to speak English?'

'From the English.'

'Where's everybody?'

'Where they are every evening. On the Mall Road.'

'Why is everybody on the Mall Road?'

'It's see-and-be-seen time. Simla is like women who look better after dark. Everybody comes out to see and be seen. Same as English did. Worst thing they did was to leave Simla. Wish they would come back - we are ruining it. They knew how to live. Best people. And they tipped. Indians don't. Mean lot. Even the rich. Richer and meaner.'

Rahul didn't like to hear that.

'I'm very hungry. Any food-shood?'

'Too early for dinner.'

'A cup of tea and a bun? Possible?'

'Too busy.'

The bastard! He could have made an exception, his first day. Rahul had seen a cheap wooden dhaba eatery right below the hostel hill. He went and had a cup, two long rusks and was back in his room within minutes. Five minutes later, he fell asleep again and only woke up at noon the next day. He shaved and bathed and dressed and had some lunch and realised he had missed another day's college - he had no lectures in the afternoon.

He turned up there anyway. The college buzzed. Glamour cascaded down the hillside bathed in honey. Everybody looked happy for being there. Everybody spoke in English only. And so many girls, all with the Simla rose in their cheeks! Each one dressed just for one transparent purpose - to kill. Silk, georgette, taffeta . . . even in plain DCM cotton they looked unearthly.

Was Rahul noticed? Just from the corners of those mascara, kohled Diwali sparklers. A note was taken of a lonesome new someone. There was no question of anyone speaking to him, a new nobody. Girls didn't speak to boys anyway. Only to each other. And they talked nonstop. Their chatter was a mountain stream bubbly and unstoppable. But it was posh chatter. And delicious.

The boys? Simla-smart, they too had rosy cheeks. They ogled, drank cup after cup of tea and they also talked. Simla College was tall on everything - looks, style and talk. Especially talk. Rahul met two of his teachers briefly, Professor Lall and Professor Dyal in black gowns. Then he was accosted by two tall fellows a year or two older than himself.

'Welcome to Simla, young sir. Kumar. Mahendru,' a suited-booted Simla-smart someone introduced himself and his equally well turned-out companion. There was a good long handshake.

'Rahul.'

'What a lovely name. Suits you.' The two men took a bow.

'Final year. Science and Maths. We are also at the hostel,' Kumar said. 'You must feel lost here,' he went on. 'We did too on our first day. Everyone does. Anything we can do?'

'No, thanks. I'm fine.'

'Lonely? You must be. But not to worry. You have two new friends now. Us,' Mahendru said.

'Once you get used to Simla, you won't want to live anywhere else. It's magical,' Kumar added

'Both to look at and to live on.'

'Anything we can do at all, just knock at room 25, the last below the hostel veranda.'

Just then, they were called away by a black-gowned professor passing by. As Rahul looked around, someone else approached him.

'Mull. Rishi Mull. A Simla wallah.' This fellow was his age. He took his hand and shook it hard.

'Kapoor. Rahul Kapoor. From Solan.'

'Delighted to meet you. Aren't you?' Muscular and short, five foot six as opposed to Rahul's five eleven, Rishi Mull was good-looking in a roguish sort of way with a short crop of wavy black hair.

They were both from the same year, and class. They talked and watched the endless fashion cavalcade on the college compound that gave them much to talk about. Rahul's new-found classmate had a certain manner about him. He spoke to Rahul as if he had known him all his life and their talk became a long chat, with him thumping Rahul on the shoulder like an old friend. Inevitably, their conversation turned to girls.

'I say, how all these beauty-bitches eye you.'

'What do you mean?' Rahul didn't understand.

'I mean they want to gobble you up, Mr K.'

'What on earth do you mean, Mr R?'

'Just that. By the way, what did the Sewage Rats have to say?'

'Sewage Rats who?'

'Those two. Kumar and Mahendru. Avoid them.'

'Why? They seemed quite nice.'

'Just do.'

A college peon came to say Rahul must report to the college admin office for some formality.

'OK then. See you later, crocodile,' Rishi laughed – he had cracked a joke - and waved him on.

After the office, Rahul had a cup of tea in the packed tuck-shop. But he felt lonely in that crowd. He walked back to his hostel. He felt lonely in his room too. He fell asleep again. It was quite cool when he woke up. Thick mist clung to his windowpanes. The blue rectangle of his skylight was woolly white. Rahul threw some water at his face to wake himself up fully. Then he made his way down to the common room. Half a dozen younger boys lounged there in deep Raj-time sofas. They looked lost. First years, thought Rahul. Just then, in walked his new friend, a cigarette dangling from his lips. He spoke to the younger boys.

'So you haven't met? This is my friend Rahul. Rahul Kapoor of Solan. Surely you've at least heard of him. Played for Himachal Under Eighteens last year. Rishi Mull at your service.' Rishi made a bow – d'Artagnan meeting Aramis, Athos and Porthos.

Of course the first years had heard of Rahul, their looks said as they introduced themselves.

'Do you also live here then?' Rahul said.

'I don't. Not even allowed here,' Rishi whispered.

'Why not?'

'Your warden doesn't like my beautiful face. Why? I can't understand. Fancy a walk on the Mall? Just the right time. Teeming with women, each one of them itching for it.'

'I'm starving. I'm itching for food.'

'We'll grab something at Davico's. Great place packed with Anglo bitches. Parsee ones too. All of them itching for it. Itching.'

'A lot of itching going on here.'

'Is true. Believe it or not. Simlaah! Our Monte Naughty Carlo. And the Mall is its Promenade des Anglais which is in Nice, in fact . . . '

There was a noise outside on the wooden veranda someone with a heavy walking stick.

'Oh, it's that prick One Legga.' Rishi ran to the window. 'Your one-legged Gregory Peck. Don't tell him I was here. See you in Davico's at seven.'

Rishi opened the window and melted in the mist. Enter the man with the walking stick, the hostel warden, Professor Nath, also Head of English.

'Shut the window, boys. So much mist. And it's chilly. Don't you feel it? No sense, no feeling.'

'Good evening, sir,' the room said in unison.

Professor Nath had an artificial leg. He was a handsome man of forty. He did look like the actor mentioned by Rahul's strange new friend.

'Where are the rest of you? Loafing on Mall Road, no doubt. Not the place for boys from decent families. You are welcome here. Live by these five simple rules if you want to have a happy life here.'

He pointed his stick to a notice which said: NO ALCOHOL. NO GAMBLING. NO FEMALE VISITORS. NO VISITORS AFTER 10 P.M. MESS BILL PAID STRICTLY WEEKLY.

'This is your home now. Forget where you come from. Forget your past. Think of it as a foreign country - like Pakistan we left behind in '47. Who's been smoking? You, Kapoor?' Nath first sniffed Rahul's hands, then his face.

'Good. Why weren't you at college yesterday?'

Rahul explained.

'Thank God for giving you two legs. And today?'

'I slept, sir.'

'I'll buy that today, but not tomorrow. Good luck to you all. You are going to need it.'

Who the hell was this 'delighted-to-meet-you-aren't you' specimen Rishi? Did Rahul want to go to see him?   No, he did not. Yet he opened his trunk and took out two-ten rupee notes. On second thoughts, he put them back and stuffed the rest of the cash in his wallet. His first day on the Queen of Hills. Rahul wanted to feel rich.

By seven the mist lifted to cast a magic spell over Simla, the sort that had bewitched five generations of the British, bringing to them their Cheltenham and Chelmsford. As it was downhill all the way, Rahul was on the Mall within minutes.

Simla's Promenade des Anglais was certainly 'teeming'. Swarms of dressed-to-kill people walked up and down with holiday gay-abandon, looking each other up and down. Thousands of them going to a mela.

There were more men than women. Men walked hand-in-hand or arm-in-arm with other men, like lovers, but men and women did not. Some women did wear jeans, but none, alas, wore see-through tops.

'Maybe tomorrow in the sun.' There were scores of young women in European clothes, Anglo-Indian and Parsee. But Rahul couldn't tell who was 'itching for it' in spite of the languid looks he received.

Dazzling shops and restaurants were strung along like a necklace of pearls for half a mile, the most glamorous and expensive half-mile in all the Himalayas. Its star was Davico's.

The star of Simla hit Rahul for six with its medley of sweet sounds, sweet smells and very sweet faces. A hundred kindred spirits in white sharkskin jackets and revealing blouses sat in the lap of naked luxury. Many were in each other's arms on the parquet dance floor. A bare-shouldered, shimmering-bosomed mermaid sang songs in English, and Tony D'Souza's band played English tunes. It was a dream. It throbbed like the human heart. Rahul was fascinated. More than that, he was terrified. He wanted to run. But as Rahul turned to go, a hand on his shoulder stopped him.

'I say.' Rishi led him to a table at the back.

'Is it still India we are looking at?' Rahul said.

'You are looking at what India wants to be.'

'What about . . . ?' What about the real India - all that poverty, hunger, disease and the rest?

'These people have worked their arses off to get where they are. Not their fault if the country starves. They are only having a bit of fun and listening to Dee Dee, for God's sake. What's the matter with you? A beer bottle?'

'But I don't drink.' Rahul had promised Mummy.

'Don't give me that crap. You are in Simla now, city of the stars. Not a leaky pisspot hill village. Beside, I've made a great new friend today and I want to celebrate. Bearer . . .' Rishi ordered a bottle of Golden Eagle lager brewed at Solan. 'Now let's hear all about you. The good and the bad. The good points first. Me, I'm a cocktail of both, the good and the witty side of me far out-weighing the other.' Rishi laughed like a very old friend.

'I can see that. Plus the style. Buckets of it.'

'That's what matters in Simla. Style. Who said style's the man?'

'Whoever did probably had you in mind.'

Rishi made Rahul talk, saying nothing about himself.

'Bucky lugger,' Rishi said after a while.

'What?'

'Forgive the old spoonerism. I meant to say Lucky Bugger.'

'I don't understand.'

'You have the chequebook of luck in your pocket today. So cash in a cheque. This is Simla. Anything is possible.'

'Speak in the Queen's English. Not your own.'

'Lady Luck is smiling. Look casually to your right.'

At a table fifteen feet away sat two dusky beauties in European clothes. They were both staring at him.

'Not Anglos - Anglos have mid-complexion. They are Christians with a touch of the tar brush - from Bangalore or Mangalore in South India. Equally friendly-givers of you know what,' Rishi hissed.

Rahul looked again and saw the ladies smile. He smiled back. Minutes later their eyes met again, and again there were suppressed smiles. This went on as they drank beer and the dancers danced and the bearers criss-crossed the floor and the mermaid sang 'Stupid Cupid' and other old English hits still popular in Simla. After one glass Rahul thought he understood what Rishi meant about the cheque-book. This was Simla. Anything was possible here. A dance with a stranger? Maybe something more? What more? Rahul daren't give expression to it. But his friend did.

'Ever had Christian pussy?' said bosom pal Rishi.

Rahul gave an honest answer.

'Thought not. What would you say to one tonight?'

'Frankly, I wouldn't know what to say.'

'But you'd be game.'

'What? Speak proper English, for God's sake.'

'I mean, you'd fuck her?'

Rahul laughed his head off. He had fleetingly hoped that something more than a mere dance with a stranger might happen. But the thought of the ultimate dream of his life . . .?

'Just because someone looks at you?'

'These are not idle looks, Rahul Kapoor Mister.'

'How the hell can you tell, Maharishi Mull?'

'How the hell can I tell? Rahul, you have a lot to learn about Simla.'

'Learn what? How to build sandcastles?'

'Yes.'

As the two new friends speculated, their half-built sand-castles collapsed. Two gentlemen in black bow ties and white jackets materialised from nowhere and approached their good Christian neighbours. They bowed with great charm and Rahul lip-read them asking, 'May I have the honour of a dance?' The ladies rose. The men held their chairs back and the four of them walked to the floor, ladies in front. Rahul made a note of it.

'Don't worry. The world's full of pussy.'

It was a quick-step, but it was not over quickly. A foxtrot followed, a tortoise trot, more like. For it lingered on. Finally, the dancing over, the ladies came back to their table, alone. They glanced at the boys and one of them smiled at Rahul. Minutes later, two other men turned up at the girls' sides and again, Rahul lip-read their request to dance. This time, the ladies declined. This was both good news and bad. Good in that the girls had darted a quick glance at the two boys while saying no to the men, and bad because maybe they had decided against dancing for the rest of the evening.

'Kapoor, the one in the green is giving you the come-on. Go and ask her for a dance,' Rishi mumbled.

Rahul started to go weak at the knees. He had never asked a lady unknown to him for a dance before. He wasn't going to now either. He said no.

'Don't be a fart.' Rishi stood up. 'I'm going for a pee. When I come back, I want to see you on the floor. Or at their table.'

'A favour, Mull - stay in the loo for the rest of the evening.'

'And another thing. Give us a build-up.'

'What's that?'

'What I gave you in the hostel about you playing for Himachal Under Eighteens.'

'Why did you lie?'

'But it worked - you should have seen their faces. So build me up with word surgery. Say I'm President of the college union, cricket Captain and what not. Say my old man is the

70

Rajah of Kulu, but that I'm too shy to talk about it. That sort of thing.'

'Why?'

'To make me irresistible, you follow? I'll do the same for you. Works wonders with women. They are all the same. Dumb. They like being dazzled.'

As the builder-merchant of words moved on, Rahul sipped Golden Eagle and pulled at a Gold Flake. Out of the corner of his eyes he saw the girls converse with the liveried bearer, also their waiter. As Rishi was taking his time, Rahul ordered another beer. When the man brought the second bottle, he also brought a suggestion - why didn`t the young baba ask the lady in green for a dance?

'Why do you say so, bearer?'

'Because the lady herself is asking for it, believe it or not, Baba sahib,' the bearer whispered in English, bending down to pour the beer and keeping his back towards the girls. 'But she ask me not to tell you she is asking for it.'

Anita wore green, Helen red. Older than Rahul, twenty-one or twenty-two, they were Goan Christians from Delhi where they worked as secretaries in the new American Chancery. Kenneth Galbraith was their ambassador, 'a sky-scraper of a man'. They had been in Simla a whole week, staying at the YWCA, and were going back early tomorrow morning. What had they been doing all week long? Fending off men for most of the time. Indian men were creeps. All of them 'without exception'. Of course Rahul was different. They could tell. He was brotherly, the sort a girl could feel safe with.

'Tell us the story of your life, Rahul.'

Instead of telling them the story of his life, Rahul gave his friend a build-up.

'You must meet Rishi.'

'He looks weird.'

'Rather popular around here, Raj Kumar Rishi of Kulu. President of the college union and a published poet. And as if that's not enough, the son of a so-andso dances like Fred Astaire. . .'

Rahul had overdone it. What if the son of a so-and-so couldn't dance at all? He called him over the moment he showed up. The four of them hit it off. What was utterly unbelievable was that the son of a so-and-so did dance like Fred Astaire.

Rahul danced with Anita. First she danced as if she was dancing with a brother. Half an hour later, she did not. The closer they danced, the better they danced. It caused havoc in Rahul. He was ashamed of himself and wished he wore a cricket box. But Anita seemed to notice nothing. Sometimes she smiled and rested her cheek against his. Rahul was mesmerised. All the signs were saying just what he wanted to hear - he was going to lose it tonight, his virginity. He had read somewhere that the average American male lost his by the age of seventeen. He might not be American, but he was certainly not an average male and was nearly a year past the age limit.

The band took a break and the girls excused themselves.

'How much have you got on you, Squire?'

'How much what?'

'What do you think?'

'Oh.' Rahul told him. Rishi raised his left eyebrow, meaning it was more than enough.

Anita and Helen had been drinking soft drinks. When they returned, Rishi suggested Pimms for them. After some no, no, no, they succumbed to his tender persuasion. Unseen by the ladies, he winked at the understanding bearer, giving him the licence to display his largesse with the measure. Then Lord Mull ordered a tableful of this and that.

'I thought you were students,' Anita said.

'But we are,' replied the Prince of Kulu.

The dinner was lit by those Christian smiles. It was difficult to tell which was more delicious. Every table was lit with similar smiles. The lights were dimmed after dinner. People danced again. This was Davico's at its mellowest. And sexiest. Anita pressed herself against Rahul, her breasts crushed into his chest and her Chancery against - what could he say? - his Chancellor.

'Bad boy,' she brushed his ear with her lips.

'But you said I was different.'

'How wrong I was.'

'I am sorry if I have offended you. I'll go away.'

'Silly boy.' Her clasp said 'don't budge an inch'.

'I can't believe it.'

'What do you mean?'

'I mean this.' Rahul had fallen in love.

'I can't either.' Had she also? Rahul dared not think any more about it.

'Do you mean it really? Do you swear?'

'Silly boy.'

More beer, more Pimms and more dancing. Then just like that, Helen said they must go.

'Must you? Why?' Rishi was heart-broken.

'We have to get up very early in the morning.'

The bill came to one hundred and one rupees with the tip and all. Rahul had spent half his month's allowance on a single meal. But he counted out the notes like a Rajah. It was midnight and Tony D'Souza announced the last dance. Helen said she wanted to dance this number with him.

'But aren't you hot in that suit? Take off your jacket and dance with me. You haven't danced with me once.' She helped Rahul remove his jacket and dump it on his chair. Rahul did not want to dance with her, only with Anita. But Anita was talking to Rishi. She showed no interest in the last dance.

Rahul lost not his virginity, just his wallet. It was not in his jacket when he got back to SCH at 1.

The loss of money hurt more than the ten hammers in his head. How was he going to survive? What was he going to write home?

At five according to his watch, the wretch poised his head over the English loo as if it were a French Revolution guillotine.

'Cheap sluts.'

Only if he had laid one at least.

'Taking Simla by storm. O Highness.'

Sometime later there were noises. Floorboards creaked. Doors opened and doors slammed. There was the sound of laughter, of tap water hitting a steel bucket. Someone somewhere sang a haunting Hindi film song. The room next to Rahul's was the hostel gym. Chest-expanders dangled from its walls. Dumb-bells and other weight-lifting paraphernalia littered its old hotel parquet floor. Suddenly, mountains began to be lifted and dropped - on Rahul's head.

'Fucking Indians!' Why did they have this gandoo habit of getting up so early?

Sleep at last. Luckily, Rahul didn't know anyone around. No one came looking for him. Hours later, his sleep was broken by rain and hail hitting his tin roof. It was only Mundu Bahadar Singh tapping at his balcony window. Rahul felt better now, much better. He let Bahadar Singh in through his bathroom door.

'Sir . . .' The Warden wanted to see Rahul. 'Don't know for what. But Warden sir never calls a boy to his house unless it is worse than bad.'

Rahul knew. His father.

Professor Nath lived in The Lodge, the ex-hotel managers' residence a hundred feet away. A wooden wall had been erected around it. Boys called it the Great Wall of China for reasons that became clear to Rahul instantly.

Rahul had that rising lump in his throat. He saw his father in the Solan General with wires attached to his body. Rahul was in a desperate hurry to get in The Lodge. Someone else was in an equal hurry to get out. They collided head on at the gate.

'Don't you look where you are going?' The English was very posh and the very angry speaker very attractive.

'Normally I do.'

'Why did you make an exception today?'

'And your good self? Do you leave your eyes behind when you go out, I mean?'

'Idiot,' said the angry person. 'Total idiot.'

Mr Nath also looked very angry. But it had nothing to do with Rahul's father. Relief.

'Kapoor, this is a respectable college hostel.'

'I know, sir. That's why my father sent me here.'

'Here you behave yourself. Here you live like a gentleman's son. Understand?'

'But I do, sir.'

'You don't - and I want to expel you.'

'What have I done, sir?'

'What have you done?' Mr Nath roared. 'You abscond from college on your very first, second and third day. You come back at one a.m. You drink four bottles with Anglo whores and that pimp, and dance and do whatnot, and you dare ask what have you done?'

'Professor Nath, sir - '

'It's his influence, that badmash Rishi's. He and his useless twin will infect your brain and soul. Penniless, they live off tourists. They will eat at your expense, wear your clothes and steal from your pocket. The Mulls are that sort - to be avoided at all cost. You follow?'

'I don't, sir. My private life is my private life.'

'You have no private life here. This is SCH. Simla College Hostel. I am its warden. I make the rules, you obey them. If you don't, you get the boot. Understand? Any questions?' The Warden waved Rahul away as if he was a bhangi untouchable.

Any questions?

Only one – what was he going to eat? And where? WHERE? His 20 rupees wouldn't pay even a week's mess bill.

Rahul looked up at the deep blue sky above – Simla sky was always blue. WHERE?

'Any idea, Sir?'

'Seek and you shall find. Simla is a rich city and rich cities have more cheap places than expensive ones,' came the reply.

Rahul went up and down the great mountain city. He walked and walked till Simla's heights and depths cramped his calves. When the dense evening curtain fell, he turned back, resigned to going to bed on an empty stomach. But just then, he came face to face with a sign - 10AM-10PM.

10AM-10PM was a wooden shack stuck to a rockface at the bottom of the slanting Lower Bazaar, Simla's runny-nose slum street. For 60P, this dhaba eatery gave dal and as many chapattis as you could eat. It wasn't quite Davico's, but choosy beggars were unheard of even in Simla.

Only the scum of the earth ate there - coolies, road-sweepers and odd-jobbing hill-hands who had never seen soap. The question arose: what if Rahul Kapoor, son of Prakash Kapoor of Solan, was seen dipping his fingers in the 10AM-10PM house dal? His name in dust, no girl would ever look at him again. Nor would anyone even want to be seen with him in this glittering city of nawabs and snobs.

But Rahul had to eat.

However, luck was on Rahul's side for once. For no one from his world, the glam-fab world of Simla College, ever set foot in this bazaar.

A light year from the Pearl Necklace of the Mall, the karma of the Lower Bazaar was to serve the Pearl Necklace. Rahul needed a foolproof strategy to sneak in there unseen by anyone from the college at least once a day, if not twice. As he thought about it, Rahul became nervous. Very nervous. But he knew he was also clever. Very clever. He knew he could do it. And how.

Yet, as he was about to leave the SCH the very next day for lunch at 10AM-10PM, Rahul's knees caved in. He couldn't go through with it. But his stomach howled. So he took the sheet off his bed, pulled his pyjama leggings from under his pillow and a muffler from his wardrobe. Reaching the slum bazaar, he looked to his right and left, full of shame to the point of extinction. Phew! All clear. Hurriedly, he pulled his Indian leggings over his smart 'English' pants and wrapped up his mug with the muffler like a coolie so that only his eyes showed. Looking to right and left again, Rahul cloaked himself in the bedsheet.

In the 10AM-10PM, Rahul became one of the ten scum of the earth dealing hungry dog-like with dal and chapattis. No one gave him a second look except the pot-bellied Mahatma Budh, proprietor Mangal Sen. But then he would, wouldn't he? Boss-owners of all eateries want to know who comes in and who goes out, eating how much.

The moong dal had never been Rahul's favourite. Today, it tasted like the queen of lentils. And the thick rubbery chapattis? Now Rahul realised the truth of the saying that human civilisation was built on bread.

Rahul ate till he could eat no more. He left the place bowled over by his own brilliance - he had done it, fooled the world and filled his tum! Rahul had twenty rupees. He could last out till his money order came from home. The beauty of it was that nobody would ever know.

Boys occupied the left side of the Lilac Room - college rooms were still called by their old hotel names. The girls were on its right with a passage between them, like in a church. Professor Nath sat at his desk, facing them all. Behind him was a long window. It offered his class of sixty a breathtaking view of the sweeping Sanjauli Valley and the magnificent Mahasu Mountain with those ice-cream cones towering behind them. There was poetry in the window. There was a poetry book in every hand, except Rahul's. He shared Rishi's. Whispering, they were oblivious of all else.

'Number One Eight, move to another chair at the back.'

The professors addressed the students by their rollcall number. But Rahul didn't hear. Professor Nath tapped the wooden floor with his walking stick. Rahul still didn't hear.

'Something gone wrong with your ears that you can't hear?'

This time Rahul heard.

'Sorry, sir. But something is the matter. Water.'

'Been swimming? As far as we know, there is no river, pond or a public swimming pool in all Simla.'

'Rainwater, sir. It rained this morning.'

The class found it funny. Not so Professor Nath.

'Make sure it doesn't get to the brain and move to a chair at the back of the room by the door.'

'But there is no chair there, sir.'

'Then take the chair you are sitting on with you.'

'But I am sharing Rishi's book, sir.'

'In that case sit without one. And do not bother to turn up without your poetry book next time.'

Rahul was on Rishi's left. Three more boys sat on their right. Rahul stood up. Rishi picked up his chair and passed it to the fellow next to him, the Sikh boy Mohan Singh. Mohan passed it on in turn. By the time Rahul got the chair in his hands, the boys made sure they had wasted enough time, causing an epidemic of loud sniggers. Professor Nath was not amused. He struck the floor again.

'Order, order,' shouted Mohan. 'Order in court.'

Professor Nath stood up and the class quietened down. Professor Nath had been going on about his pet 'poetic licence' - it came up daily, whether the lecture was on prose, poetry or drama. Rahul suddenly asked: 'How can poetic licence apply to prose and drama as well, sir?'

'It so happens we are discussing poetry only today. Would you like to tell us what the difference is between a ballad, a sonnet and an ode? Rahul Kapoor, stand and deliver.' Professor Nath spoke in an unusually soft, poetic tone. They were reading Keats's 'La Belle Dame Sans Merci'. Yesterday, they had read a Shakespeare sonnet.

Rahul stood up. But he could not deliver.

'Sir, I don't know the difference between them. But I do know what is in common between them.'

'You do? So you are not the dunderhead that you look. Tell us, then. What do a ballad, a sonnet and an ode have in common?'

'Sir, they are all poems of one sort or another.'

There was loud laughter. Open rebellion. Mutiny. 1857. The girls never laughed loudly. That would be unbecoming of them. The Nath nostrils widened in anger from wall to wall. He chose a victim.

'You find it amusing, do you, Miss Number Two? Why don't *you* tell us the difference? Please stand,' he said to the girl who sat right opposite him.

This was unfair. For Number Two was the shyest of the class. And she hadn't even laughed, only held a hand to her mouth. She stood up in dead silence, giving Rahul a long look - obviously she had no idea at all. It was a heart-rending look. He had made her the sacrificial goat. His heart sank. Rahul hoped to Krishna she had an answer.

She did. In a voice as sweet as her face she told the class the difference between a ballad, a sonnet and an ode. It took all of a minute.

'One Eight, can you jot that down in your brain? And if it is water-logged, in a notebook or something like that.'

'Sir, why are you always after me?'

'Maybe it's because I don't want you to waste your time and ours. Maybe it's because I want all of you rotters to learn something,' Professor Nath blared out at the half of the class on his right. This coincided with the bell. 'Dismiss. And remember to invest some time in your homework essay. Two thousand words and you have two weeks. Don't forget to use your poetic licence.'

Outside, Rahul's eyes met those of Miss Number Two again. This time her eyes were not accusing him. They were sorry for him for being what Professor had called him - a dunderhead.

And Rishi, who had an arm around his shoulder, said: 'Bucky Lugger. Bucky Lugger.'

'Meaning what now?'

'Meaning Miss Number Two has eyes.'

'We all do.'

'But she has EYES, Mr Kapoor.'

'Meaning what, Mr Mull?'

'Use your bloody poetic licence, son.'

'What the hell is this poetic licence, Dad?'

'Oh!' Rishi's eyes lit up. 'One of those things. A must. Good for your social standing.'

'Where do you get it from?'

'From the Main Post Office, you fool. Where else? Like the radio licence. Costs nothing. One, one ten maybe. Must get one myself one of these days. Good for social standing, as I said. Very good.'

They saw Miss Number Two coming their way with a few other girls. The girls went past the boys as if they didn't exist. As was expected of them, the boys pretended they didn't. This was life.

Rahul had no social standing that he knew of. If shelling out a rupee brought some extra, he would lash out, even as things were. College over, after picking up his disguise from the hostel, he went straight to Simla's Main Post Office on the Upper Mall by Scandal Point. The green-painted wooden building, supported by delicate columns and arches, was big, bustling and beautiful.

'A poetic licence?' The man at a sales window of the busy hall was taken aback. Rahul was surprised. Then, not really.

'Fucking Indian clerks!' Rahul knew the breed inside out. 'God's chosen few. The only difference between them and a snail is a bit of brain. And guess who has it?' But he was patient.

'Yes, a poetic licence. You know? To practise.' Rahul spoke clearly, one word at a time, so that the fool understood.

'Of course!' The fool understood. He sold poetic licences every day. Didn't he? 'In one minute I am back with it from the stock room. Wait, please.' The man then went away and did something he had never dared do in all his working life. He knocked at the door of the Postmaster General, the karta dharta boss of all the five thousand post offices in the state of Himachal Pradesh.

'Sir . . . ' He explained. 'Sir, you have to come.'

With the PMG came all his staff. He took the clerk's seat.

'Young man, to be frank, we have sold out.'

'Oh, no.' Rahul had come all this way.

'But I would like to be of service.' With a flourish, the PMG wrote out something on a sheet of paper, stamped it and passed it to Rahul through the window grille. 'Hand-written, but it will do provisionally.'

'How much?' Rahul was over the moon. But wait a minute - why were the men around the man suppressing smiles, and why did they look at him as if he was an idiot or something?

'It's free. We charge for everything, but hand-written poetic licences are sold free.'

As the PMG spoke, the big, beautiful green wooden building collapsed like a house of cards. Rahul, now crimson in the face, ran. He ran to where he knew Rishi would be at that time - ogling on the Mall - to give him what he knew he should be giving to himself as well - an all-time kick up the arse. But he stopped.

'Think, Owl Rahul. You've already made an ass of yourself.' Making a fool of oneself before strangers was less painful. It didn't matter after the event - but before a friend, it could lead one to suicide.

Rahul had to check out Simla for his homework. But his cheeks burned with anger, making him bark, 'Stuff your homework, Nath.' They throbbed with shame, killing his hunger. But within minutes, his empty stomach took command.

A little later, fully kitted out in his bedsheet and the rest, Rahul found himself staring at 10AM-10PM. His eyes met those of the dhoti-clad Buddha seated lotus position on his wooden gaddi throne, facing a low wooden writing desk-cum-cash box. The Buddha beamed a beatific smile at Rahul, slapped his half-naked right thigh and leaped up from his throne.

'Mr Rahul,' the man said from Uncle Sarin's throat, embracing Rahul. The gesture made the young man almost stumble over an invisible Simla rock.

'Mangal Sen-ji!'

'I know it all now, Mr Rahul. But my lips are sealed. So don't worry.'

'But what do you know?'

'I've been watching you since you first walked in. I knew from day one you were different. You sit different, you stand different. You eat different, you speak different. So I knew you had a secret. So yesterday I sent my son Billoo to follow you. Billoo saw you take off your pyjama and the sheet and go to college hostel where a mundu told him who you were. It's not my business to know how you became penniless. Not my business at all, but from now on you are eating in my house food cooked by my housewallih. You pay same price when you get your money order from home. Agree?'

'But?' Rahul was lost for words.

'No but-shut. What but-shut? You are eat-now and pay-later house-guest. Come.'

Hit for six, Rahul allowed himself to be dragged along. Well, well, well. Rahul looked up at the sky.

'Krishna-ji, Sir. You are amazing. And I love You.'

Mangal Sen's house was an extension of 10AM-10PM above the rockface. It consisted of two over-furnished rooms with walls plastered with prints of gods and goddesses, Krishna among them.

'Sit, sit, sit,' Mangal Sen said, kicking his shoes off as they entered the baithak front room. Then he sat down cross-legged guru-like on a durrie covering the wooden floor. Rahul kicked off his shoes and sat down facing him, disciple-like. Mangal Sen looked at a connecting door and shouted, 'We are here, Housewallih-ji.'

Soon, a young girl appeared carrying two round brass thalis heaped with food. She was certainly not the housewallih, being only fifteen or sixteen. She had the biggest eyes Rahul had ever seen and they looked nowhere other than at his face.

'Daughter Kaki, this is college student Mr Rahul-ji. He'll be our guest from now on. Daily. And you know how we Indians treat our guests? As royalty. Go tell your mother that we are having parathas today, not chapattis. Parathas with desi ghee. The best. So how do you feel, Rahul?' The Buddha slapped the disciple on the thigh.

Rahul felt good. Somersaultingly good, after the bloody post office.

The meal in a brass thali - Rahul's favourite cauliflower, bhindis, yogurt lassi and a phirni sweet was princely. Worth at least two fifty. At 60P to be paid later, it was daylight robbery. But where was the catch?

'Come in, Housewallih-ji,' shouted Mangal Sen at the inter-connecting door and in walked Mrs Mangal Sen, a walking-talking carbon copy of her daughter but with a very motherly half smile on her very motherly face. If the Sens didn't belong to a lower caste, Rahul would have happily called her Auntie. So he had to address her as Mrs Mangal Sen. She seemed to like that, being called by an English prefix. Smiling to herself, she hitched her sari and sat on a chair instead of the floor.

'So?' asked the Housewallah, raising his left eyebrow. In answer, the Housewallih made a bow to a print of Goddess Kali, puzzling the guest.

'Anything you like, I cook. Just anything. What you like for tomorrow?' she asked the guest.

'Oh, Mrs Mangal Sen. Anything you care to cook. You have magic hands.'

'O, ji. This boy has magic tongue.'

'Told you,' said Mangal Sen.

'He speaks magic words. So leave it to me. Kaki,' Mrs Mangal Sen shouted at the interconnecting door. 'Tea, girl.'

As if Kaki was standing behind the door with tea, she came in with two fuming glasses of it. All his friends back in Solan used to call him Lucky Dog. But this was something else. Rahul saw Krishna smile and whisper, 'Make hay while . . .'

Rahul did just that. He made hay night and day. But something nagged at him - where was the catch?

Near the end of Week Two of delights, as Kaki handed Rahul his lunch thali, her hand touched his while her parents looked away. It was not an accident. Rahul had found the catch. He put the brass thali on the floor and stood up.

'One minute,' Rahul said, and walked out. As he made his way down to the road, he left all he had on him - a fiver - on the Buddha throne. Outside, he donned his disguise. Then his heart stopped: Professor Nath sat in a two-coolie rickshaw that had stopped right in front of the dhaba door for a breather! But Rahul was confident he could not be recognised. He walked past Nath with a sure foot.

'Kapoor?' Professor Nath called.

But Rahul kept walking on.

'KAPOOR.'

Rahul still didn't look back. The next second, a hand held him by the shoulder and pulled off his muffler.

'Sir, what are you doing here?'

'I am going back home. But what in the devil's name are *you* doing here?' Professor Nath's eyebrows arched and his forehead creased with revulsion on seeing a boy from his hostel emerging from that dung-hole in this slum. 'And why are you dressed up like a road-sweeper?'

Rahul raked his brain to say something suitable. He found just the words.

'Doing your homework, sir,' he said and took off his disguise.

'I asked the class to write an essay on Simla ... '

'I am doing some research to find the soul of Simla. The Mall is not it. The real Simla is here where real India is. I wanted to experience the real thing.'

Professor Nath slapped his forehead in disgust and urged his men to move on.

'Chalo, chalo, bhai.'

Unknown to them, there stood behind them two other SCH inmates – the smart fellows who had befriended Rahul on his first day at college, Kumar and Mahendru. They had seen all, heard and understood all. They shook Rahul's hand heartily.

'How lovely to see you, Rahul. We've been looking out for you at the hostel ever since we first met. But you are never in the dining room,' Kumar said, shaking his hand a second time.

'You are right about the soul of India being in these hovels and not . . .' Mahendru said.

'But what are you two doing here?'

In their suit-boot, they presented an odd sight.

'Like you, we too have been in search of the real Mother India,' Kumar said.

'Fancy a bite somewhere nice like Baljee's?'

'No, Mahendru. It has to be Davico's for our first of many meals together. Lunch is on us, Rahul,' Kumar said and gave a strange look, making him feel uncomfortable.

'No, thank you very much.' Rahul had been told at home never to accept hospitality that he couldn't repay. 'I'm meeting a friend from Solan at the bus stop and I'm already late.'

Rahul went without eating all day. The evening was long a-coming. When he heard and saw the boys rush down to the mess for dinner, he felt 'mice running amok in his empty stomach', as they say in India. But all he could afford was a cup of tea and a bun. A bun at 8 p.m. when all the others were scoffing mutton? Word would get around that Mr Solan had 'paisa problems', that the fancy fellow was all gas with not a chavanni coin to rub on his belly button. Tongues would wag. Girls would not look at him and boys would die laughing.

Rahul inspected his face in the wardrobe mirror. It made him unhappy. Never before in all his life had he gone hungry. Now it was going to become a daily thing. They say man gets used to anything. Rahul was not getting used to going hungry. He went to bed on an empty stomach.

Next morning after a mug of tea and two buns, Rahul hurried off to see Simla's most famous building, the Vice-regal Lodge. It looked like some Scottish castles he had seen in pictures - solid and ugly. Unimpressed, he walked right back, hungrily looking for another 10AM-10PM. At Scandal Point, black-gowned Professor Lall passed by him.

'Vagabondising again, Number Eighteen?'

'Doing my homework, sir.'

Professor Lall slapped his forehead in the same unbearable disgust as Professor Nath had done outside 10AM-10PM. Fucking teachers. God was not thinking clearly when He made them.

Simla was a far-flung affair of timber, corrugated iron and white-painted walls at 7,000 feet. At its base was its lifeline, Cart Road, which linked Simla to the rest of the world. A few hundred feet above, at an angle of 45 degrees meandered the Mall, where the heavenly-born Indians displayed their plumage in the season. Much of Simla lived in between, on terraces packed with about-to-slip-away shacks and houses. Between the Lower Bazaar and the Mall there lay the Middle Bazaar - all three were linked to each other by flights of steps. Middle Bazaar was the crowded commercial heart of the Queen of Hill Stations. Here people had to shove and push to get on. They had to shout and yell to be heard. Here the air was raw in the nostrils. Small-boned hill cows past their milk-giving age poked their noses at garbage heaps. And stray dogs outside better-class dhabas hoped to be thrown a half-eaten chapatti or a mutton bone. Here, business was always brisk.

The great fruit, vegetable and meat market buzzed. Urgency rippled to the sound of jingling coins. The egg and chicken market was loud with argument. Its dozen 'shops' had no walls, only a tin roof. Men in olive-green homespun woollen jackets with buttons up to the neck sat cross legged on durries, presiding over baskets full of snow-white eggs and string-and-cane cages in which strutted noisily that day's lunches and dinners through the length, breadth and heights of Simla. Eggs were sold in units of one. Chickens came as small, medium or large. The human eye did the weighing with astounding precision.

Like Brussels, the capital of Belgium, the first city of Himachal Pradesh had a vegetable named after it. It was smooth-skinned. It was baby-bottomed. It was dimpled. It was the big, green Simla Pepper, eaten stuffed with spicy mashed potato or mincemeat. Not far from Simla in the hills was a small village called Jutogh, which was renowned for another vegetable - the Jutogh cucumber. With black salt, it was heaven on Simla.

'And, sahib, come back in early season for a taste of some English delights - wild strawberries and gooseberries. You'll leap with delight.'

Rahul would have leaped with delight if he could afford a single banana. He looked everywhere for another 10AM-10PM without any luck. But he had his essay under his belt. Rahul made his way back to the world he understood, the Mall. He had to take a flight of hundreds of vertical steps. It left him gasping for breath.

Back on the Mall, Rahul ambled down its graceful slope to the smart store Gaindamul Hemraj to buy a razor blade. He spotted a bookshop on the way - Maria Bros. Fond of reading, the Kapoors liked even looking at books. So in Rahul went. He had never seen anything like it - books crowding shelves, books scattered on tables, books stacked up in columns supporting the roof! It was a mad sight. It was a lovely sight.

'Ever seen anything like it?' said someone.

Rahul turned and came face to face with a young Chinese man of his age but six inches smaller with a six-inch smile.

'Frankly, no. It's amazing.'

'World-famous shop this. I'm not joking.'

'I believe you.'

'Your first time here?'

'Yes. Yours too?'

'I'm local. I come here every other time to look. And I look. Mr Maria doesn't mind, the proprietor. Always charges me half price. So nice he is.'

They looked, wide-eyed. Literature, art, history, philosophy, biography were in serious competition for attention. Staggered, they came out.

'Rahul. I am at Simla College.'

'Lin. I work with Father at our shoe shop by the Fire Station on the Mall. Many Chinese shoe shops on the Mall – Chinese shoe best shoe. Guess who Mr Maria got all them books from? From them Rajah and maharajas whose fore-fathers made libraries a hundred years ago for show. The books were never opened, never read. Only seen. Clever Mr Maria got them as raddi cheap rubbish after `47 when the maharajas tumbled. Now he sells them to America, Australia and Japan with "waiting lists". Was nice meeting you. See you next time.'

At Gaindamul Hemraj, Rahul found himself looking at someone familiar - the friend of Uncle Sarin of Delhi and the husband of that gold mine. But what was the name?

'Namaste, Uncle.' He managed a working smile.

'Oh, hello there. How is Simla treating you?'

'Very well, sir.'

'Doesn't look it. Studying well? Eating well?'

'Very well, sir. Extremely well as a matter of fact.'

'Then why have you lost so much weight?'

'Oh? Must be walking the steep slopes of Simla.'

'All Simla does that. It should become a town of walking beanstalks then. You are coming to lunch on Sunday and meeting Aunty. Understood?' The man tapped Rahul gently on his cheek. He wrote down his address on a chit, pushed the chit and something else down his top pocket and moved on.

Rahul pulled out what the man had put in his pocket a hundred-rupee note! Oh, Krishna-ji! And the chit? It had an address on it only, but no name.

Rahul's best memory of the man was his car, the sexiest car Rahul had ever seen. Then came his wife. Every bit of her to which gold could be attached, had gold attached to it. Her fingers were dipped in it, her wrists were encased by it. Gold choked her long neck and it dripped from her ears.

Rahul bathed and dressed carefully with a dash of Pithi's present to him - Yardley aftershave. First impressions! He sought out Bahadar Singh for directions. The mundu raised his left eyebrow.

'Instead of going to lunch, catch the choo-choo train to Kalka and then the big train to Bombay.'

'Why, Bahadar Singh?'

'To conquer Bollywood. You have contract in pocket, sir sahib.'

'Exactly what I'm going to do.' Rahul showed him the chit.

'Green Gables?' Bahadar Singh cried loudly in the large dining room. Even though the mess was shut, it being a Sunday, there were still quite a few men around, Kumar and Mahendru among them, staring at him oddly, making him feel uncomfortable once again. 'Take Upper Mall at Scandal Point. Go past the Main Post Office and come to the conical white little Krishna temple. Then dip down right. Your lunch is on the left before Cart Road.'

The Krishna temple was a dark and empty chamber with a pleasant smell of the holy dhoop incense. Kicking off his shoes, Rahul went in. He spent a quiet minute with a small statue of the God. THANK YOU, SIR.

Coming out, Rahul had the strange hunch that he was being watched. How stupid.

Green Gables sprawled above Cart Road with tall rhododendrons. A milestone nearby said Annandale *1M*. That sexy car lorded it over the driveway, reflecting the sweet Simla sun. The wrought-iron gate was shut. Rahul simply jumped over it.

'Rahul-baba,' the chauffeur Rahul had seen at home in Solan called out from the porch. 'Come in the Morning Room.' The man ushered him into a big square room. The colour green was everywhere - a light shade for the walls, a richer one for the chairs and sofas, and something in between for the furry carpet. The room opened to the back garden of the house where dahlias and flowers of a hundred kinds bloomed. At the far end rose a rocky retaining wall, lined with shapely poplar trees.

'Beautiful house,' Rahul said.

'Sahib bought it from Mrs Bull for a peanut in '47. Mr Bull went with a heart attack in '46 so she was lonely. She wanted to go back to Blighty. And she went. I came with the house. Now I am going and they are coming,' the man said and left.

But nobody came. Ten long minutes later, a boy of twelve appeared. He wore grey worsted shorts and a blue blazer with the Bishop Cotton School insignia. He spoke perfect English.

'Hello. I am Bobby. And you are of course Rahul?'

'That's right.'

'Rahul. I like the name. Can I get you something?'

'No, thank you.'

'How do you like our Simla? I hope a lot.'

'Quite a lot.'

'Good. I am at Bishop Cotton. Brilliant school – India's Eton. I love cricket. We have a great side. I hear you played for Himachal Boys last year.'

'Who did you hear that from?'

'You know - word gets around. Please excuse me? I'll go and tell Mummy and Daddy you are here. We have some important guests. Back in a sec.'

Rahul felt nervous. And also foolish for feeling nervous in the company of a mere kid. There were noises, but far away. They came no nearer. Rahul waited. He was also a guest - the master of the house had invited him personally. Very soon he would show up. His madam too, that walking goldmine. Naturally. Rahul sat on. As time ticked by, his cheeks began to throb with anger. More time passed. Now he began to feel insulted.

'Rahul Kapoor, give them another five minutes.'

In fact, he gave them ten. Then, his cheeks ablaze, Rahul came out of the Morning Room and nearly stumbled. For there on the veranda stood three young ladies of dazzling beauty, among them, Miss Number Two of his class. She aimed a quick quizzical look at him. But as young men and young

94

women weren't allowed to talk to each other, Rahul walked on, burning with insult and anger. And his empty stomach was howling.

The Mall pulsating with anonymous shirt-sleeves was just the place for someone mortally wounded. Rahul wanted to walk. He did the famous mile of the Mall and kept walking on. For some reason, he also kept looking over his shoulder. At Clarke's Hotel, he thought of turning back. But a furnace still raged inside him. Besides, it was a silk and satin afternoon dyed in gold, not one made for sulking in his room.

Past Oakwood House, the Maharajah of Patiala's Simla residence, Rahul took a deserted sidetrack carved in dense foliage. Tall pine and deodar trees shot perpendicularly from 45-degree slopes embroidered with shrubs of all kinds. It was lonesome, just how Rahul felt. The hillside seemed to want to cry, just what Rahul wanted to do. Then something distracted him - a noise. Two young men were coming his way from the opposite direction – Kumar and Mahendru.

It was strange, meeting them here in this jungle deep and dark. Very odd.

The men hurried up to Rahul and embraced him one by one, as close friends do when they meet. But he hardly knew them. There was something unsettling about their show of affection.

'What are you doing in this godforsaken place, Rahul?' Kumar asked.

'I am out for a walk and I love it here.'

'What a coincidence. Let's walk together.'

'But I must rush back. Someone is coming to see me,' Rahul lied to them again.

'You are always doing that. Let's walk and talk.'

'We were just talking about you, in fact,' Mahendru said.

'Why?'

'We have been doing that ever since we first met.'

'Why?' Rahul repeated, feeling ill at ease.

'Certain questions cannot be answered. We felt deeply hurt when you turned down our invitation to lunch the other day.' Kumar put an arm around Rahul touchingly.

'I told you I was meeting a friend from Solon.'

'Never mind. We are both Godfearing Hindus, Mahendru and I. As such, we believe in karma.'

'And we believe it was our karma to meet,' Mehendru chipped in. 'We believe it was in our stars for you to come from so far to be with us.'

'Oh, really? I don't see that in my stars at all. In fact, I do not have any stars.'

'If certain questions cannot be answered, certain others don't need answers.' Mehndru said sagely.

'Forget it. Let's talk of other things. Of you. You look . . . what shall I say?'

'Let me say it for you, Kumar. Beautiful. The most beautiful boy in all the college. The moment we saw you, it was a first sight sort of thing. We would love to get to know you, Rahul.'

They advanced, arm-in-arm. Rahul realised he was trapped.

'Yes, we would love to get to know you better,' Kumar murmured. 'To be of assistance.'

'We know you have a little problem,' Mahendru beamed. 'Who doesn't have problems? So let's help you out.'

'Hostel mates, yaar. Let's become really good mates, Rahul.'

'What do you mean, Kumar?'

'Then from good mates let us become intimates.'

Rahul shivered, with fear and anger.

'Bad place this, Simla,' whispered Mahendru. 'Full of bad people, my dear.'

'We will protect you,' Kumar said, hugging him.

'Protect me? Who from and how?'

They were passing a wild rose bush in bloom. Kumar stopped and plucked a flower.

'Marry us, beautiful boy,' Mahendru proposed.

'With this rose, we thee wed,' Kumar said, pushing the rose into Rahul's shirt buttonhole. 'No one need know we are married.'

'You mad dogs . . .' In a quick move Rahul freed himself, bent down and picked up a two-pound rock one of them was going to have a cracked skull if they laid a finger on him.

'Simla is a wicked place, pretty boy.'

`We'll look after you. Ensure no one harms you.'

'You will, will you?' Rahul was trembling - with rage.

'You don't know Simla. Bad men around. They could do bad things to you.'

'But we will protect you.'

'Please come quietly with us. We know just the place for a discreet and happy ceremony. It can be our own little secret.'

'I presume you've both got mothers. I suggest you go and plug them post-haste,' Rahul hissed.

'Kumar, you heard what the cunt said?'

'I don't believe my ears. I must be going deaf, Mahendru.'

'You fucking are, Kumar.'

Two pairs of nostrils flared, becoming flame-throwers.

'Little cunt.'

'And we were being so nice to you. We were about to give you money for food because we know you are nothing but a pauper.'

'Solan choot. One little push. No one would ever know what happened to the pretty boy.'

This wasn't the time or the place for heroics - there were two of them. But nor could Rahul back off.

'You can try.'

They stood nose to nose. Rahul throbbed with a fear he had never known. But before a blow was struck or a push given, there came a loud shout from another pagdandi above theirs:

'Oi, oi, oi!'

Kumar and Mahendru ran and dissolved in the dense foliage.

'Squire Rahul!'

Rishi and his brother. Or rather his double, his identical twin. Who was who?

What fearful symmetry! Despite the danger moment, Rahul recalled the line from somewhere.

'Meet my little twin Kishi. Came into this world eight minutes after me. He is the college wicket-keeper.'

It was a strange place and a bizarre moment for introductions. But boy, was Rahul was grateful!

'What are you doing *here*? And why is your face red like a chilli? Been in a fight or something? Who were they? Not those sewage rats?'

'Some mad Simla shits looking for a fight.'

'What happened? They beat you up?'

Rahul was about to tell them. But this was something he had to sort out himself. Arm-in-arm, the three of them walked back to the Mall. Passing by the inviting Kwality restaurant, Rishi tapped his belly. Kishi pulled out the corners of his pockets.

Hungry and with no money, they walked to SCH for Rahul to pick up a couple of rupees from his trunk.

It had been a day of shocks for Rahul. But the biggest was yet to come. It stood on his table in his room in the shape of a tall, shiny brass tiffin in a cloud of mouth-watering smells. His mundu stood next to it.

'What's this?' Rahul said to Bahadar Singh.

'Sir sahib, somebody's servant in best clothes brought it from the Malhotras where you went for lunch.'

'The Malhotras?' The Twins whistled.

'That is tall, Squire,' Rishi said. 'Timber, real estate, petrol stations . . . you name it. Moreover, Mr Malhotra is the Dad of guess who?'

Chicken, mutton, veg, pillao . . . pudding.

The starving 1947 refugees had a kingly feast. Only afterwards did Rahul realise he shouldn't have touched a morsel. If he had even a grain of self-respect, he should have sent the thing back unopened. Who the hell did these Malhotras think they were? What did they think *he* was?

Rahul noticed next morning that Miss Number Two had eyes. His chin up, he gave her a view of his back garden to admire. Rahul was making a point. But as the day wore on, he stole an occasional glance at her - just to see her face. Gradually, his thinking changed.

'She had nothing to do with it. So why are you taking it out on her, you gas-filled ass? Nath's right about you, dunder-head.'

Back in SCH, Bahadar Singh announced a visitor as Rahul began to get changed for the cricket net - Bobby and their beautiful servant. Rahul knew why they had come and wished he had had the tiffin carrier washed.

'My didi Indira says you are in the same class.'

'She's very clever, your didi. A genius. Knows everything. What else did she say about me?'

'Not a lot, really. She said the boys in her class are rather simple. Stupid, she said.'

Rahul felt a cricket boot up his bare backside.

'Wasn't the food good?' Bobby asked.

'Five star. But you shouldn't have.'

'We had treated you badly. That was the least we could do.'

'How thoughtful. I ate so much, I haven't eaten anything since.'

'I mustn't forget to tell that to Mummy.' The boy laughed.

'Bahadar Singh, can you wash the tiffin?' Rahul asked hurriedly.

'You must have been furious with us. Quite rightly, too. The thing was, we had some VVIP guests. They arrived unexpectedly and I'm afraid we got terribly involved with them.'

For a boy of twelve he was extremely smart, thought Rahul.

'However, I have come to apologise and to invite you to lunch again next Sunday. Ramlal, take the tiffin from the mundu and have it washed at home.'

'I don't know what I'm doing next Sunday.' Rahul knew exactly he was doing next Sunday - nothing.

'That means you are not doing anything.'

Rahul was going to say, 'I'll see.' But the boy shut him up.

'And don't say "I'll see" or something of that sort. It's pukka then. OK? See you on Sunday.'

Only after the boy, the servant and the tiffin had gone out of the room did Rahul realise that he had accepted the invitation by not refusing it. He felt happy – his injured pride had been mended. He felt unhappy too - a week was a long time in Simla. How would it pass?

It was all quite simple.

The VVIP guests were a man and woman from the le Corbusier-built Punjab capital Chandigarh in the plains. Their surprise arrival - half an hour before Rahul - had made the Malhotras run like strangers in their own house.

For months, some 'hush and hush' business had been going on with this VVIP couple. Conducted by two middlemen - two aunts - it concerned the eldest of the three Malhotra girls, Padma, and the VVIPs' son. This had gone on for sleep-wrackingly too long without there being a green flag from the Punjab.

Then out of the blue that Sunday the boy's parents themselves turned up at the girl's door! Now that meant only one thing. It threw the Malhotras into a pool of panic as sweet as it was deep. Fainting with joy, Mr and Mrs Ramaknat Malhotra were busy swooning over the couple from the plains when Rahul had come face to face with the girl herself and her sisters.

Padma was adorned like a princess by her two sisters for the Private View. The kitchen had become a red hot chilli as this, that and the other was tossed and turned over coal fires. Barefooted servants ran hither and thither noiselessly. In all this, the boy from Solan simply got forgotten. But Simla, not being entirely ungraceful, remembered Solan, although only after the green flag had been duly waved by Chandigarh. The Malhotras hastened to undo the wrong by dispatching a tiffin full enough for four once the VVIPs had been fed.

It really was as simple as that.

FOUR

Atma Lal had the snow of Himachal's famed Himalayan peaks in his skin and the blue of its fast-flowing rivers in his eyes. The BSc student had one love in life Einstein. Atma had pinned a notice on his door $E=MC^2$ - in bold letters. Underneath, it said *Knock Only If You Know the Meaning of It.* No one knew the meaning of the equation that had made the atom bomb. But it did not stop anyone from walking through his door. The other boys called him Atom Lal. He loved it. Atom Lal had one hate in life - Karl Marx. Nobody cared for poor Marx in SCH. In Atom's case, it was personal.

Atom's father was the Tikkoo of Roopgarh, a small hill kingdom nearby. It had only two things to its name beautiful women and apples. Its women the rest of the world never saw, though it did the pale yellow Tikkoo apples. They were not very sweet. But in India anything that can be eaten gets eaten. Tikkoo apples got sold and the kingdom got by. Then a few years ago, they found some tin ore. This brought sudden prosperity to the little kingdom and a big headache to its Tikkoo. The tin ore was his personal property, he being the King. Those who mined it thought differently; they formed a union and demanded a share. When the Tikkoo shook his head, the workers shook their fists. The Tikkoo dismissed the lot and imported cheap labour from Punjab. Not a good move. Strikes and riots followed. One summer night, the Tikkoo's wooden winter palace caught fire for no known reason. Whodunnit? That bastard Karl Marx dunnit, that's who.

Rajkumar Chuba Ao hailed from the far-off NEFA. He was the Rajkumar of another tiny mountain kingdom 1,600 miles away above the smiling tea gardens of Assam. Well-built, he was small with Mongol features and eyes. He wore a tiepin and went to the Mall with an ivory-handled walking stick. He spoke pidgin Hindi – 'like an Englishman' and, having been to a public school in Darjeeling, he spoke English – 'like an Englishman'. He took to Rahul because of his brother serving in NEFA.

Mohammed was different - dreamy eyes, red lips. He was so beautiful, it was said that girls were jealous of him. There were rumours and other unspoken things about him: 'With a boy so beautiful, who needs girls?' And he giggled a lot - he put a hand on his wide-open mouth and giggled. Nicknamed Mohmi, he was of the house of Bhopal in Central India. It was said he had saris in his trunk. And that he liked to suck lollipops.

The body-builder Balbir was not a prince, but he was more princely than the princes – the Fourth Year glamour boy never let anyone else take the bill in the college tuck shop. The only one in SCH to wear a diamond ring, he had a deep wardrobe and changed clothes at least twice a day. Balbir came from Heaven on Earth, as the Mughals called the Vale of Kashmir. He ate egg yolks for breakfast and spent an hour every morning in the hostel gym, lifting weights. On Sundays, he had his sinuous body massaged with mustard oil by a hostel mundu. Balbir was always asking everybody to feel his Atlas biceps. He was often called Mr Universe.

Balbir's best friend was classmate Ranbir, a Sikh boy from Kenya. Ranbir was jet-black. He only wore black black jeans, a black shirt, a black leather jacket and a black patka. He was 'the Negro Sikh' behind his back. Balbir and Ranbir laughed a lot and studied in each others room till late at night.

Besides these and those two 'sewage rats' Kumar and Mahendru, plus thirty more from all over the country, was the stardust-coated Ajit, last year's cricket captain. Cricket in mountainous Simla was something, though there weren't many on its giddy heights and dizzy depths to play the 'glory game'. Between the God up there and the mortals down here, there was only one other being - the cricket captain. Ajit hailed from the Mecca of Indian cricket - Bombay. He looked every inch a cricketer – 'a clean cut above the rest'. With his silken black hair pressed down with Brylcreem, he stood like a cricketer - straight. Rishi said he had what a cricket captain needed:

'The right amount of gas in his ass.'

The blackboard had two quotes in Professor Nath's hand:

1. *At a turn of the road, I catch sight of a conical hill, covered with a deluge of white bungalows, dominated by a church behind, and above which rises a steep sugar-loaf of fir-trees. 'That is Simla! There is Mount Jakko!' I replied with pleasure and thankfulness. To taste such pleasure, we must be sick, wounded, roasted and worn-out in the dreadful plain of India.*

William Howard Russell,
The Times, 14 June 1859

2. *A man seeking legal advice, addressed his letter 'To Any Honest Lawyer in Simla'. The post office clerk wrote across it in red ink: 'Not in Simla' and returned it.*
Simla Gazette, April 1929

'I have taken these from the best essay handed in and would like to congratulate its author for excellent research and presentation. Well done, Number Two,' Professor Nath said.

Number Two turned purple and Professor Nath fixed Rahul with a hard stare. Rahul knew he had had it. Nath was going to expose him, tell the class where the penniless upstart had been eating: in a hovel disguised as a coolie! His heart racing, Rahul saw his name going up in smoke, his reputation being blown apart. He picked up his books and was going to dash out of the classroom to find a cliff to jump from and finish it all. But Pofessor Nath smiled broadly instead, told him to sit down with a hand and got on with the lecture. Phew!

There was a heated discussion about generations in general - the pre-war generation, the post-war generation, the rock 'n' roll generation, the beat generation…Freed from the fear of crushing humiliation, Rahul found himself raising a hand.

'Sir, can I ask a question?' he asked, standing up.

'Only if it is intelligent.'

'It is. Very.'

'You surprise me. Ask.'

'Sir, to what generation do we belong?'

'What on earth do you mean, One Eight?'

'I mean to which generation do we young Indians belong?'

'Humm,' Professor Nath said, not knowing what to say. 'Personally, I don't think you belong to any generation. You are only a gap between generations.'

'Are you saying I am neither here nor there, sir?'

'Dead right. Now having reminded us of your generation gap, will you do us the favour of closing your vocal gap firmly for the rest of the lecture? AND SIT DOWN.'

'Yes, sir.' Rahul dropped himself in his chair. The old hotel concert-room chair first creaked then it just split up noisily. Rahul collapsed on the floor and Rishi fell on top of him out of sympathy. The class then collapsed and Rahul peeped to see if *she* was looking. Rahul's back was broken. As was Rishi's.

Professor Nath blew his top off.

'Idiots. Total idiots. Was it for you that we fought the Englishman and went to jail?'

'Sir, did you really go to jail?' Rahul asked from where he was. Artfully, he checked again to see if she was looking. She wasn't.

'Pretend,' Nath cried, slapping his forehead. 'At least pretend to be intelligent. God doesn't give everybody good looks. So people pretend to have them. They go to all sorts of lengths to make themselves look beautiful. Ladies blacken their eyes and redden their lips and cheeks. And men shave their beards off . . .'

'Sir, you are insulting us,' cried Sikh Mohan.

' . . . Or they keep them on to look even more beautiful.' Laughter broke out again. But it was happy laughter, not rebellion. 'So if God didn't make you intelligent, which evidently He didn't, try to pretend that you are. Jot it down in your pea brain that you are going to try. Any questions?'

'Yes, sir, and it is a personal question. What accident gave you a bad leg? We feel concerned. That's why I'm asking,' Rahul said.

Nath was taken aback again. And touched.

'Kapoor boy, stand up and sit down. When it's time for me to tell you the story of my life, I will. Today we are talking about Simla. Englishman's Simla. Simla in history. Simla in Literature. OK?'

'Not OK, sir. Friends, Simla wallahs and country-men all want to know, sir.'

'You want to know how I lost my leg?'

The silence of the class was his answer.

'It happened on your famous Mall . . .'

The Mall? The class gasped - motor traffic was prohibited on the Mall. How could an accident take place there?

'The Simla Mall is more than a road with smart shops and restaurants and what-have-you. It is a habit, an English habit. Everybody flocked to it. Before the war, they came mounted on handsome horses wearing the whitest linen of the most stylish cut and showy uniforms and white kid gloves. They came to enjoy the good Simla air, but more to see and be seen. Unmarried young Englishwomen thronged here looking for husbands. They wore broad hats on the Mall, and were fol-lowed by dashing officers and unmarried box wallahs. They came, they saw and they conquered each other later at dances and balls held every night every summer . . .'

But what did this have to do with his missing leg?

'The English, not the Indians,' Nath continued. 'We were not allowed on the Mall Road for a hundred years. You want to know what generation you belong to? You belong to the first generation of free Indians. My generation could not go for a stroll on the Mall. I gave my leg so that you can walk there.'

'Sir? How? What happened?'

'The year was '41. None of you was yet born. The Congress was fighting for freedom. All our leaders were in jail - Gandhi, Nehru, Patel . . . the lot. The war was in full swing. Hitler had eaten up all Europe and the Japs were at our doorstep. England was fighting for its life.

Indian soldiers were fighting for England in the Middle East, Burma and in Africa. Over two million of them. And Indians still weren't allowed to walk on the Simla Mall UNLESS PROPERLY ATTIRED, painted signs said, meaning suit-boot-tie and hat.

'The dhoti is proper attire for a bania. The pyjama is right for anyone. The salvar is a must for a Muslim. But not on the Mall. Only suit-boot-tie and hat. And our leaders said, "Don't wear them".

'There used to be a dentist in Simla, Dr Nand Lal Varma, a close friend of mine. He was the local Congress leader here. In a meeting one afternoon that autumn, Dr Varma spoke, an emotional man with a loud voice. "Shame!" he cried. "The English-man makes us fight his wars so that he can continue to rule us. But he won't let us walk on a piece of land which was ours, is ours and forever will remain ours. He has built a Parliament in London in which he boasts of English justice. What does he call this? I call it shame. His shame. Shame, shame, shame. Do you call this improper attire?" Dr Varma shouted, standing up and pointing to his spotless white Congress khadi kurta and cotton pyjama. "Let's go and see who stops us."

'And we all stood up, three hundred of us. We came down from the rented hall below the Grand Hotel armed with nothing but the courage we were drunk on, shouting our demands - Freedom. Free-dom of speech. Freedom of movement.

'We came to the Upper Mall. People poured out of their homes and joined us - Simla, a peaceful pleasure ground of the pleasure-seeking English-man - had never seen anything like it. Imagine to yourselves what it must have looked like that day - Simla Mall deluged with Congress white khadi. When we reached the General Post Office, we saw the English Superintendent of Police, Watkins, with a hundred men, white and desi, right where the statue of Lajpat Rai stands today at Scandal Point.

'We did not want a head-on collision. Thousands of people had joined us by now. Our jaloos became five hundred yards long. The police formed a wall in front of the Scandal Point, brandishing their lathis.

'"Move back! Move back! Disperse! Go home!" Watkins shouted, pulling out his revolver and raising it in the air. "What do you want?" he yelled when we were eyeball to eyeball.

'"We want the freedom of the Mall. This is our home, these are our streets," Dr Varma yelled back.

'"Get lost, you niggers, you blackies," Watkins screamed and fired a shot in the air. As we surged forward to set foot on the Mall proper, he ordered a lathi charge. I was at the head of the procession, walking hand-in-hand with Dr Varma. We were the first to be struck down. I fell, with one leg broken in two. Mounted police suddenly appeared, on tall horses. My broken leg was crushed under the hooves of one.

'It had to be amputated from the knee down. You can say I left one of my legs on the Mall that day so that you can stretch both of yours on it today. I was only a year older than you are.'

The class was dumbfounded. The bell had gone ages ago, but no one had heard it. When they looked back, they saw the next class standing outside the Lilac Room door, waiting to come in. But nobody from Professor Nath's group stood up to go. They wanted to hear the end of the story.

'Then what happened, sir?' asked Number Two.

'Two weeks later, Simla wallahs had the freedom of the Mall. They've been walking on it ever since, wearing it out. The only thing they are good at is walking on it. Dismiss.'

Sunday came along.

Again, Rahul jumped over the gate. Again the same morning room. Mr and Mrs Malhotra sat there. Young Bobby stood behind them.

'Rahul, my boy. How are you?'

'He looks in fine fettle, Daddy. So smart, I say. What aftershave are you wearing? Yardley, no?' Bobby said.

'Hope you didn't mind too much about the other day. It was one of those things. Marriage and so on. Nerve-wracking. Your parents are so lucky that they have only one daughter,' Mrs Malhotra said.

'I understand, Aunty.'

'Homesick? I bet you are.'

'Our home is your home. How often do you write home?' Mr Malhotra said.

'Twice a week, sir.'

'Good. Sit down. Treat this as your own home.'

'My didi says you are wicked,' young Bobby said.

'I said nothing of the sort,' Miss Number Two said, coming into the room with her two sisters, the bride-designate Padma, and the middle one, Sushma. It was unusual for girls of the house to appear before a young man. It was unheard of if he was a total stranger as Rahul really was.

'And you said water gets into his ears when it rains.'

'I never.'

'And you said every time he sits on a chair it breaks.'

'I'd better not sit on this one then.'

Rahul sprang up, and everybody laughed, Ramakant loudly. Rahul realised that even if he had not given him a penny, he would have revered the softly-spoken man with a simple heart.

111

Rahul remained puzzled by the how-come and why of this warm welcome by a family totally unknown to him. He was not formally introduced to the girls, but he already knew that Miss Number Two was called Indira. After a little more chit chat, Mr and Mrs Malhotra left the morning room with Padma and Sushma. This was very strange - leaving their younger daughter Indira with Rahul whom they had only just met. But Rahul wasn't complaining.

'Lunch will be soon soon,' Mrs Malhotra said from the door.

'How do you like our house? Everybody falls in love with it at first sight,' Bobby said.

'I, too, have,' Rahul replied, looking at Indira.

'Is it true chairs break when you sit on them?'

'Number Two-ji, what other lies have you spread about me?'

'But you did break a chair in Professor Nath's lecture.'

'Oh, he gave me the poetic licence to do so.'

Indira laughed and Rahul's heart broke like that concert chair.

'What is poetic licence really?' she asked.

'Just a licence - as for the radio. Useful to have. You get it from the main Post Office for nothing. Maybe one or one fifty.'

'I don't believe you.'

'You calling me a liar?'

Rahul had the lunch of his life.

'Rahul, beta, come again,' Mrs Malhotra said.

'When?' said the fool. He shouldn't have. It meant he was dying to come. It was bad taste, not expected of a Kapoor.

'Next Sunday, shall we say?'

The net practice took place in a small clearing with a dis-used little clubhouse halfway up the densely wooded Mount

112

Jakhoo. Every afternoon, two college peons would bring the cricket stuff from a rented room nearby. They carried it on their heads - the matting and the net and the rest in a long trunk. The men would roll out the matting and nail it down, and stick the stumps in the hard mountain earth. Over them, they erected the net, a fifteen-foot tunnel of woven string.

While they were doing that, the surrounding foliage would part and there would appear fifteen players. Some wore full kit. Others came wearing whatever they had worn to college. Enveloped by pines and firs, the net had a rocky hill on its left, the broken clubhouse on its right, a narrow flat ridge in front and a bottomless gorge behind it. The boys wouldn't have exchanged it for Lord's. But those at world cricket's HQ might have swapped their nets' patches for this *Golden Treasury* containing all the sonnets, ballads and odes of the world.

Today everyone came wearing full kit. For today was a red-letter day. Today, the captain for this year was to be chosen, since all college appointments were made at the beginning of the first term. Cricket being cricket, college bigwigs who had never bothered with any other sport were coming today to make the selection - two college governors and Principal Khurana himself, along with the cricket President Professor Sharma, Head of History.

Today, one of the peons had fallen sick, so Bahadar Singh from the hostel had been drafted in.

'In the good old days it is Walker sahib's tennis courts, sir sahib.' said Bahadar Singh in English. 'Them lovely mems in white short skirt with up to there showing playing single and double. They drink gin and talk of balls. Of the Viceroy Ball. Of Bachelor Ball. They talk of shikar, of "Good old England". And the wind blowing their little skirties and showing the heavenly knickers. And after is dance and after is, you guessed it, fuckofying. Every night.'

'How the hell do you know?' barked the outgoing captain, looking unhappy - he didn't want to go.

'I am ball boy, sir sahib. So I see everything, hear everything and love everything. Only thing I don't like is them talking of "that naked fakir Gandy" our Mahatma-ji. The English were good but also very bad which I never understood.'

'OK, Mahatma Singh. Now get on with the net.'

The bigwigs arrived: Principal Khurana, governors Tandon and Bedi, and Professor Sharma. The players lined up for the handshakes. Then Principal Khurana, a boy-faced balding man of fifty-five and all of five foot five inches tall, waved his right hand. It was the signal for the net to get going.

It was a foregone conclusion who the new captain would be. The opening bowler, Final Year student Deepak, bowled with fire and hit the ball hard when he batted. But everything had to be seen to have been done properly. This was cricket.

Looking and standing like a captain, now retiring hurt, Ajit directed the net from behind the bowler's end. The two main contenders, Rahul and Deepak, were asked to bat first. Both played straight. They cut, drove and hooked well. Then they bowled. Deepak was really fast, the only genuine fast bowler in the side. He hit the stumps several times but he was also easily hit because he bowled short too often. No one, however, had an answer to Rahul's spin. Slow left arm, he spun the ball both ways. He didn't hit the stumps that often, but it was a snick here, a stumping chance there, now a flier at mid-on and a skier at long off, and sometimes a caught-and-bowled affair. A strike bowler was essential in any side - as was a good spin-ner. The almost fore-gone conclusion needed revising.

'Last round,' Ajit shouted when the first of the last six balls of the day was about to be bowled. Then he joined the dignitaries in the broken club-house. The five of them talked in whispers without looking in the direction of the players, nodding their heads gravely. The players hung around anxiously in Mr Walker's former tennis courts. At last Professor Sharma turned to face the boys.

'Tomorrow. Announcement tomorrow.'

The Simla College was a ten-minute downhill amble from the hostel. First, you went through the drab Lakkar Bazaar below the hostel. This bazaar began near the Ridge, where a milestone by the Odeon cinema said TIBET 200M. It ended where the road described a lazy turn around Mount Jakhoo. The road itself rolled gracefully on to Sanjauli, a Simla suburb.

Lakkar means wood. Lakkar Bazaar was made entirely of wood. Shops there sold only things made of wood. Rows of varnished walking sticks glistened along outer walls. Inside were Aladdin wonders of polished perfection. There was an exception, though, in Lakkar Bazaar: Imperial Cycles - a real bicycle shop seven thousand feet up in the Himalayas! It didn't sell bicycles, it only rented them out for trips to Sanjauli where it had a sister cycle shop. You hired a cycle for a quarter rupee and handed it in at the other end. On your way back, you rented another. Imperial Cycles were famous for being puncture proof, 'the only ones in all Himalayas'. This claim was 100% genuine, since it *was* the only cycle shop in the Himalayas.

The road to Simla College took off from the middle of Lakkar Bazaar. It was a very steep road, joining Cart Road at the local sub-post office. Going down this slope was fun, but coming up it a pain. Rahul had gone well past the steep bit, the sub-post office, and was right opposite the private road to the famous girls' school Auckland House on the peak of Elysium Hill - just before his college.

Rahul was free the first period that morning, as were Atom Lal and Chuba Ao. So they were going to college an hour late, arm-in-arm. Coming from the other side were none other than the 'sewage rats', also arm-in-arm.

And walking down the private road at the same time were a few beauties in their brown and yellow school uniform. All eyes were on the girls.

Rahul saw Kumar bend down and pick up a round stone. Rahul thought he was going to hit him with it. Kumar gave him a slanting look and pulled his arm back. But he aimed the stone with a bowler's action at the wicket gate of one Rose Cottage. Rahul then kicked a pebble for no reason.

Back in the college compound, Professor Sharma stood with Ajit, Deepak, Kishi and others.

'The appointment will be made after a match with the YMCA. Ajit will captain it,' Professor Sharma said when he saw Rahul. 'And I have just been on the phone to the YMCA. Its captain Mr Dass has given us a date. Sunday.'

What about Rahul's lunch invitation? He couldn't miss that, he said to Rishi later.

'Don't worry, Solan. We'll do something.'

'What can you do, Maharishi Mull?'

'I said we'd fix it, didn't I? So?'

'What will you do?'

'We'll work it out. A week is a very long time in Simla.'

The Presidential election was looming. Every year SCH fielded a candidate. Every year, SCH lost.

'No charisma.'

This year the hostel put up someone watertight – 'a master stroke'. It printed bills and pinned them to every tree on the road to the college:

Dripping with charm, armed with wit, and possessed of a heart which beats for you.

The 'master stroke' was Prince Atom Lal.

There were four other contenders.

Chaudhry was known as Cowdrey, like the English Test star though he did not play cricket. But he could score at a debate

Problem was, when he spoke, it was always from the top of Mount Jakhoo. And it was always a sermon. Being busy fitting Cowdrey with a loud-hailer, God had forgotten to bless him with looks. This made him invisible where the girls of the college were concerned. He was a jhuddu, an ignorable nobody. His looks were not his fault, but his character matching them didn't help. He was known to sneakily pursue easy prey – servants and untouchable bhangi girls. Even with such beings, success eluded him. Yet this final-year student behaved as if he was 'God's Gift', to Simla. He walked like a peacock in the mating season.

'God's Gift over-fancies himself.'

After Cowdrey came someone whom everyone fancied - Miss Moon Mehra, a Third Year science student. She was called .303 or Three Nought Three after the WWII rifle. She hit you with a shot from just below shoulder-level where there was always some absent-minded draping of the dupatta or the sari - oh, how she looked in one! She could have caused a riot on the Mall on an evening of her choosing had she been so evil-minded. She was good at physics. The college had already awarded her a Ph.D in it with a two-third majority, that being its gender ratio.

Having seen his father's fingers burned by democracy, Atom had been reluctant to stand. But the other prince had convinced him that he had to.

'We've got to show we were born to rule. So stand, you fool.'

Fever gripped Simla College. Money was being splashed around. Cowdrey and his 'best man', 16-stone mountain of flesh Joshi, had opened a register of free tea in a dhaba closeby. The other two held lunchtime meetings for 'policy and planning' over chaat for all. In Atom's case, there were crowded nightly meetings for 'strategy' at which a half bottle presided under the very nose of that One-Legga Prick!

The contest was really between God's Gift Cowdrey, Prince Atom and the to-die-for Three Nought Three. But Three Nought Three was not spending a penny – she thought it demeaning. However, Atom was shelling out through 'nose and arse' because he was not sure at all in spite of the writing on the trees. He was trying to buy out the remaining two candidates, neither of whom had 'a hope in hell', but were 'purchasable'.

Suddenly, in the middle of it all, Atom got fed up.

'Churchill was right. India is not ready for democracy,' he piped up.

This caused consternation in SCH.

'Fuck it. I'm not spending another pie,' Atom groaned when the price of the 'purchasables' was whispered at a strategy meeting.

'Politics, Prince, politics. You mean Kennedy didn't do it?' said the other prince.

'Kennedy's old man is sitting on a pile of sweet millions. Mine only on a heap of sour apples.'

In reality, his decision had nothing to do with money... only with the thought of having to stand up before the seven hundred and fifty members of the college and making a speech.

'Come, come, Atom. Cowdrey hasn't got the grass-roots support because he is a prick. And Three Nought Three only has tits,' said all SCH.

'I don't want to be President,' he confessed.

'You can't do this to us!' SCH hit the tin roof.

'You don't want an idiot like me to be your President, do you seriously?'

'Yes, we do.'

'People get the leaders they deserve. You don't deserve me.'

'You've got what it takes, Prince. The college crown is lying in the gutter. Pick it up with the tip of your sword like Napoleon,' Rahul said.

'Why didn't you stand, sunny boy? Why me?'

'Because you are royalty with lustre in your eyes.'

'True? But I am buying no one. OK?'

The thing which stood in Atom's favour was the fact that the 'purchasables' didn't like the way God's Gift walked. To teach him how to walk, they came over to the Atomic camp.

'Some are in this world to lead,' they said. They were not. Atom was, as the son of his royal father.

'Without doubting a shadow,' SCH agreed.

Now everything depended on the speech.

The man of letters Balbir wrote it. Rajkumar Chuba Ao and Rahul went over it with a pencil. Then the whole hostel did the same.

'Here is your instrument of delivery. Now disappear in the khud below and mug it up,' said the speech-writer. Atom did what he was told. Twice daily, he paced up and down the Teak Hotel's old tennis courts, addressing the tall pines covering Mount Jakhoo:

'Ladies and gentlemen. A house divided cannot stand . . .' Atom spent the next ten minutes telling the trees how he was going to turn the divided house into a one of harmony '. . .With dedication, self-sacrifice and tireless work, with your kind support and your kinder votes.'

On a sun-filled afternoon, Bahadar Singh gave Rahul a 'hand delivery':

Our dearest blaah blaah,
You've been here for how long and haven't yet found an hour to come to see your own loving aunt? Your mother may be angry with me - but why should you be? Blood is thicker than water, they say. I say it is thicker than misunderstandings, too ... blaah, blaah, blaah.
So come upon delivery. Or I come.
Your loving and dearest aunt, Savitri.

The cricketer was hit for six! How had she found out he was here? Rahul didn't even know what she looked like, his loving and dearest Aunt Savitri.

Rahul came out on the long veranda to read the note again, after which he intended to tear it up and feed the pieces to the wind. Whoever Mummy didn't like, everyone in the family liked even less. He had a bar of chocolate on him. As he broke off a piece, he saw the most beautiful dog he had ever seen, just like his own Terry.

'Where have you come from, oi?' Rahul's heart went out to him. 'Want a chocki?'

Yes, please. Yes, please.

Forgetting the letter, Rahul fooled around with him and missed Terry. Then the dog vanished and Rahul drifted downhill towards the Mall where anybody who had nothing to do went in the hope of finding someone to waste an hour with. Rahul found a legion of red faces and brown fur setting up a roadblock on the pathway with a near-vertical drop on his right – dangerously snarling monkeys. The scarlet-bottomed cheeky fellows had come from the famous temple of the monkey god Hanuman at the mountaintop. Rahul froze in fright. One wrong move and he would be torn to shreds. But luckily, the monkey brigade was more interested in itself.

Long ago, the wicked King Ravan of Sri Lanka had abducted Lord Rama's wife, beautiful Sita. With his monkey army, Monkey God Hanuman had helped Rama recover her after a bloody battle in which Rama's brother Lakshman became critically wounded. Rama's medics knew a herb which alone could save his life. But it grew only on the far-off Himalayas. Hanuman could fly. He took off. On his long flight to the Himalayas, the Monkey God had touched down at Mount Jakhoo for a breather, making it forever sacred.

These heirs of his went about their business as if they owned the mountain. Well, they did - they had been there long before Captain Charles Pratt Kennedy who had built the first English house in Simla in 1822, or any other man for that matter. Devotees from the depths of the wooded valley daily brought offerings of fruit and left them on the temple compound. These pink-faced creatures helped themselves without so much as a thank-you nod, just like the other pink-faced creatures that had built Simla. This mountain was theirs, as were its highways and byways. And they had made the traffic laws.

While Rahul waited for the roadblock to lift, he took out his aunt's letter and read it again to kill time. The address on it caught his eye. It had embossed printing with a crest of some sort. Humm.

When Lord Hanuman permitted, Rahul made his way down to the Mall. After some enquiries, he came face to face with a plaque: *Douglas Gibbs RIBA 1921.* A bulky house made of balsa wood stuck out in the air above a stupendous drop, peering down into a chilling void. Rahul was learning about the English. They were mad and liked living dangerously. They loved being at dizzy heights and playing at being God.

Rahul did not really want to see an unknown aunt he didn't care for. Then why the hell had he come here? He turned back. But unknown to him, Rahul had been spotted.

'Rahul. Rahoool!' Indians! They never speak, but they . . . Aunt Savitri had a piercing voice. A hundred heads swung around to behold he whose name had shaken the mountain – and Rahul had his first glimpse of his aunt. A large lady in white was standing on one of those balsa-wood balconies.

'Haa hai, and now you don't recognise us even!'

Seconds later, she appeared at the house's grand porch, followed by three children.

'Blood is blood. It is thicker than a misunderstanding.'

'What misunderstanding, Aunty?'

'Later. Later. Inside first.'

Inside was chaise longue and chaise short, marble-topped tables, ivory inlaid tables, carved chests, oil paintings of stags in Scottish Highland mist, tiger skins . . . ! Who the hell *were* these people? How come his mother had never said anything more about her cousin except that she was not on speaking terms with her? For her part, his mother's cousin seemed obviously sold on at least one member of her family – him.

'Where is Uncle?'

A stupid question. For on a table inlaid with ivory stood a large photograph in a silver frame of a good-looking man. It was hung with a garland of freshly cut roses. Now Rahul remembered his parents coming to Simla for a funeral a couple of years ago.

'You see? O, the day I meet Kamla . . . She made a mountain of a molehill. Telling you nothing of me.'

'Honestly, it's not that, Aunty. I just forgot.'

'Not blaming you. Sit down and eat and drink.'

'I just had lunch, Aunty.'

'Larka,' Aunt Savitri yelled at a door. 'Chai!'

Rahul knew he had had it. He had landed himself in a thick jam that was getting thicker by the moment. There was this impulse to stand up and just dash out of the door or even a window and see what happened. There was also this sudden curiosity to find out what that mighty misunderstanding was, between his mother and her cousin.

Larka, a boy of Rahul's age in crisp and colourful livery, brought tea on a large silver tray.

'But Aunty, I had a late lunch just now.'

'Late lunch - early tea. So what? So eat. Eat eat.'

After two cups, Aunt Savitri rose.

'Bathroom. Tea. Always.'

Now, Owl Rahul. Up, up and away… through that window. But that window opened to a vertiginous hundred feet of nothingness apart from the good Simla air. Other windows offered the same prospect. That door, then. And hurry, Rahul. A moment's delay can cost a fool his life.

Rahul got up to make a shameful exit. He did not run - that would have looked too disgraceful even in his own eyes. He rushed to the door and then the utterly unbelievable happened. But unbelievable things did happen to Rahul – history's gift to him.

This time they didn't collide. They just bumped into each other, literally. Which is to say, the fronts of their delightfully different torsos did so.

'I d-don't believe it,' he stammered.

'Idiot.'

Once was chance. But twice? Clearly it was fate.

But what was Miss Nath doing in his aunt's house? It was then Rahul noticed that she was not alone. She was with none other than the potential causer of riots on the Mall - Miss Moon Mehra. Moon Mehra? Three Nought Three? Could Owl Rahul be related to an apparition?

All this happened fast. Razor eyes inspected the interloper - what was *he* doing there? Then haughtily, the girls disappeared. Rahul could still make his exit. But now his seat pulled him back as if he had been tied to it with a rubber band.

Aunt Savitri came back. She shouted, 'Moon!'

Moon reappeared, alone.

'This is Rahul, your cousin brother, who won't come to see us. Is a liar Number One. Says he was too shy. Looks he the type to you? Ask him why he didn't come.'

'Hi.' Three Nought Three wore a night-blue sari.

'Hi,' Rahul replied and realised that he had the most kissable cousin in the world. For the first time in his life he wished he was not a Hindu, since Hinduism forbids cousins to get closer in any 'meaningful' way - she cousins are sacred, like sisters. Bloody Hinduism. An ancient dungheap of super-stition and mindless ritual. Yet Rahul would be returning to Balmoral.

'Ask him,' Aunt Savitri said.

'Why didn't you?' Moon looked deep into his eyes.

'Why didn't I what?' Rahul was mesmerised. But he knew one thing - he would be betraying his friend Atom at the poll.

'Why didn't you come earlier?'

'Oh. I was afraid.'

'Of what? That we might eat you?'

'Yes.'

'Mum, we have a joker in the family.'

'Who are you calling a joker, cousin sister-ji?'

'You. A total joker.'

'Why does everyone call me a total something?"

'Do they? Who?'

'How's the campaign going?'

'I'm going to win. Of course. And you are not going to vote for that pagal bewakoof, whatever you call him. He is not even a neutron or a proton, that Atom of yours. He's only a moron. You will vote for me and tell all your buddies to vote for me.'

'Is that an order or a request?'

'And you'll come here once a week. Or I'll make your life miserable when I become President.'

'What will you do?'

'I'll think of something.' Moon meant it.

Suddenly, seven-year-old Bachchu snatched the doll from his five-year-old sister Minnoo and jumped over a sofa and ran out. Issuing a loud wail, Minnoo chased after him. She collided with a chair and fell and howled deafeningly in pain. Moon picked her up and clasped her to her bosom, cooing. Then she gave the chair a smack – once, twice, thrice. That seemed to lessen Minnoo's pain and Rahul thought it was time to get going.

Rahul met his four-legged friend again.

'Chocki?'

Yes, please.

The dog turned up the following day as well for his chocki. Rahul still didn't know his name nor that of his master. But he learned it a little later the same afternoon. As Rahul rounded the bend in the densely-wooded pathway to SCH, the dog shot out of the foliage and barked and rolled on the ground.

'ROVER!' came a feminine shout. The speaker also turned the bend and Rahul's heart stopped.

'Rover,' Miss Nath said again, angrily this time.

Rover continued to mess around with Rahul.

'You must not feed my dog.'

'I don't.'

'You do. You give him chocolate.'

'How do you know? Did Rover tell you?'

'Idiot.'

'Don't call me an idiot. I am not an idiot. Ask Rover. Rover, am I an idiot?'

Rover said no.

'See? He loves me even if others hate me. You mustn't keep those apart who love each other. It's called heartlessness.'

'Total idiot.'

'Is that the only word you know?'

'Yes.'

'That is a very limited vocabulary for someone so charming. Will you permit me to introduce myself?'

'No.'

'Pray, why won't you?'

'Because I am not allowed to talk to any of you. Because I know all there is to know about you.'

'What?' The contortion on his face said all.

'That you are a drinking-dancing gallivanter. Always in the arms of beautiful girls.'

'You mean like the way we fall into each other's arms each time we meet? Can we go on meeting like this for ever?'

'Idiot.'

'If you continue to say that, I'll begin to believe in your unjust propaganda.'

This time Miss Nath could not suppress a smile. She looked away in order not to be seen to be smiling. 'Someone is coming. My father! Run.'

'Meena,' her father called from the foliage.

Terror struck Meena Nath. She ran and Rover ran with her. Terror struck Rahul, too, and he also ran - in the opposite direction, to the hostel.

Mohmi was on the veranda, looking at the far side of the valley, at the scores of wooded cones jostling each other in the distant haze and the sun pouring champagne on them. It was impossible to pass by and not taste the champagne and be intoxicated.

'Want to see a real beauty spot?' Mohmi said. 'A hill with a million Christmas trees?'

'Where?'

'Follow the leader,' Mohmi said and brought him to the hostel tennis courts. From there they took the slope down. Once past the road to Tibet, it became very steep, ankle deep in dry pine needles and very slippery. They had to hold hands to stop sliding. It was dangerous. It was exciting. They came to a bay-shaped clearing on the sheer slope. It was ringed with 40-foot-high rhododendrons like guardian angels. Rose bushes stood out in an all-pervading smell of rose attar and pine. A slim line of water trickled out of a crack in the rockface.

From afar they could hear the distant hum of the city and the motor traffic on Cart Road. Nearby, cuckoos sang and thrushes darted through the pine trees like little flying shadows. Mohmi's beauty spot lived up to its name.

'What did I tell you?' Mohmi pressed Rahul's hand and smiled. The boys put their mouths to the crack in the rock and had a long drink. The water was ice-cold, turning their lips purple. It was then Rahul noticed that Mohmi's lips were very red naturally, because colour soon returned to them. He was afraid Mohmi might make a pass which would be very embarrassing. But Mohmi did nothing of the sort. Instead, he talked about life in princely Bhopal. His mother was knitting him a grey sweater.

His elder brother was going to Balliol College in Oxford shortly. His younger sister was coming here to Auckland House next year. Did Rahul know that Lord Auckland was the first Governor General of India to live in Simla and that he had a sister, Emily Eden, who wrote letters?

The steep climb back to SCH was hard labour.

'Ah, there you are, Rahul-baba. Been searching up and down the mountain for you,' shouted Bahadar Singh urgently from the veranda.

'Why?'

'Rishi sahib came for you. Said it was a matter of life and death. Meet him at once in India Coffee House.'

Rishi sat in India Coffee House with a man of thirty five or forty, sipping coffee and eating dosas. The man wore a striped shirt, starched white collar, tie and the rest. The man was a man of means.

'Mr D.D. Dass - Prince Rahul. Rana Saheb of Solan's only nephew and heir,' said the builder and the decorator.

'Delighted. Delighted,' Mr Dass said, devouring Rahul with a lingering look. He had a bone-crushing handshake. 'Heard so much about you. Every bit an understatement.' Rahul needed force to pull his hand away.

'Mutual, Mr Dass.' Rahul felt he had to say that.

'You like Simla?'

'An understatement,' Rahul replied and the man laughed. He called the waiter and ordered another coffee and a dosa. They talked.

'I say, Mr Dass boss, the match on Sunday - can it be played on Saturday instead?' Rishi said.

'Why?' The man was taken aback.

Rishi leaned over and put a long whisper in his ear. It made the man beam the broadest smile ever at Rahul.

'Done.' The man then asked for the bill. 'Wish I had all the time in the world. Would spend every minute of it here. But… Anyway, we are meeting in the field. So? So see you then.'

'Who he, and why the life and death thing?' Rahul said after the man had left.

'D.D. Dass - the YMCA cricket captain. Better known as 3D.'

'What did you say to him?'

'None of your business. I promised we'd fix it, didn't I?'

At Simla College, English was compulsory. Then two arts subjects or science and maths, and one optional Hindi, NCC (National Cadet Corps), or Religious Studies. Rahul consulted Rishi about the optional.

'Hindi?' Rishi had said, pinching his nose - Rahul had lifted the lid of a manhole. Hindi was Indian. Hindi was common.

And Religious Studies?

'You must be joking.' Rishi knew all there was to know about God. He had Krishna by his side and that was what really mattered. Others: Mohammad, Jesus & Co, brainwashers all - didn't. There was French also on the syllabus. That would have been 'icing on the social cake', to be seen with a French book. But, alas, there was no French teacher in the college. So it had to be the NCC.

There had been a medical for the boys opting for NCC. Rahul and Rishi had missed it, being elsewhere at the time, somewhere more important. But they had to be cleared by the college doctor before they could get into the uniform. The doctor, Major Arjun Singh, IAMC, Rtd, lived in Sanjauli. Rahul and Rishi had nominated this day, today, to call on him to be inspected and declared fit of limb and mind. They agreed to meet at the barber's shop next to the paan wallah's in Lakkar Bazaar.

At the frontless barber's Rishi consulted a mirror, and roughed up his hair to look more dashing. Then they hired a bike from Empire Cycles 100 yards away. Rishi did his friend a favour and let him drive, jumping on to the carrier. They passed by none other than Cowdrey cycling from Sanjauli side. Cowdrey stuck up two fingers in the air as he passed.

'Up yours too,' Rishi barked.

'Why did he do that?' Rahul asked.

'Because Brer K once dunked his nose in mud over our helpless bhangi girl he tried it on with.'

At Snowdon Hospital half a mile on, Rishi jumped off as he spotted someone else known to him.

'Doctor sahib,' Rishi shouted at an elderly Sikh gentleman bicycling towards them. 'Most urgent.'

'What, Rishi, what?' the gentleman said, stopping.

'Our Medical, Major sahib?'

'I'm coming to the college next week.'

'Sir, Captain Sethi says he'll do some drastic surgery on our manhood if we don't have it done before tomorrow.'

'You mean. . . ?' The ex-soldier-medic chopped Rishi's manhood off with an imaginary knife.

'Alas, yes, Doctor sahib.'

'We can't let that happen. So clothes off then.'

The boys stripped to the waist. The Major made them open their mouths wide and peeped into their throats. Then he prodded their chests and their backs with his fingers.

A small crowd had built up. It watched the medical with mounting interest.

'Go away. Jao, bhai, jao,' the Major shouted. But no one moved and people stood on, fascinated.

'Now drop them,' the Major ordered.

'Major sahib?'

'Drop the trousers. And the underwear.'

'Major sahib!' The boys begged for mercy.

'*Drop them.*' It was an order. And an order was an order. The boys got out of their shoes, trousers, the underwear and laid down flat on the road.

'Hurry up, sir. Some college girls are coming.'

'I promise they won't rape you. I will protect you from them if it is the last thing I do. Promise.' The Major had a wicked smile. He hit their knees with a rubber-encased metal something, felt their feet etc and leisurely carried on with the medical.

'Hurry up, sir,' the boys whispered from the depths of the grave of shame. But the doctor timed everything right.

'Stand,' the Major ordered just when the girls were only ten feet away. The boys stood up, looking for their clothes. 'I didn't say dress.'

'Major sahib!' groaned the stark naked boys. But the Major was hard of hearing. He simply didn't hear them. Well, not till the ladies, themselves perishing of shame, had gone past. 'Very well – get dressed.'

It was too late. People clutched their stomachs.

'Fit,' the doctor wrote on two chits of paper.

'Doctor sahib, it was third-degree torture. Not a medical. I could have done it myself,' Rishi said.

'And saved me the bother of having to declare two healthy swine healthy,' the Major said, pedalling off.

'Boy, how that lovely bitch Goli was looking at our cocks. As if she wanted to gobble them. By the way, 3D thought you were damn good-looking. I said I was buying him glasses. No, he did say that.'

FIVE

Oh, what a week!

Simla College loved fun.

'What college life's all about, no?'

And there was plenty of it this week. Before the history-making cricket match on Saturday, there was to be the bitterly fought Presidential Election on Friday and the mouthwatering annual picnic on Thursday. A man would have given an arm and a leg for the picnic. The cost was steep – 2.50. But it included lunch and tea at the dizzy heights of a chosen mountain peak or at the bottom of a khud ravine the depth of which made one shudder.

Simla College stood in the shadow of Auckland House on Elysium Hill. The picnic march was to begin at ten. By 9.30, this side of the hill was awash with colour and glistening faces. Half the girls wore jeans and jumpers. Their tits stood out like those distant peaks, yum yum. In daily life the girls' tits were cruelly concealed under breast scarves which society insisted they wore at all times. Today, society was given a holiday.

The girls stood on one half of the green hillside, the boys on the other - them and us - two great magnets dying to succumb to what magnets are best known for – attraction. Two great magnets sadly unable to become operational because of the laws of Mum India. How they wished there was a loophole somewhere. Wherever there's a law, there's a loophole. Alas, not here. It was heart-breaking. Worse, Number Two always had her back turned to Rahul. Something about it alarmed him. Then he realised that she hadn't looked at him once for days. This began to eat him.

Atom - it was now taken for granted he would be the next college President - was chairman of the Picnic Executive Committee, a heavy responsibility. It became Atom's job to ensure the food was 'first class and piping hot'. Tradition required Atom to remain quiet about their destination. The college liked that. Not knowing where it was going added sweet suspense to fun.

'The Glen,' Atom announced at ten. 'More haunted and enchanted than your Coleridge's that holy place. Way down the valley through romantic jungle thick and dark. Past Annandale.'

'What's Annandale, boss?' asked a First Year fool.

'Used to be a racecourse till '47.'

'A racecourse in the Himalayas? Oh, yeah? Not a naval base - ships, submarines and things?'

Boss extinguished the fool with an atomic stare.

Intoxication hung in the air, thick and sweet. Simla College couldn't wait to get started, begin the great descent to the Glen past Annandale. Its heart was already there, far from the thorny all-seeing eyes of Mum India, there where, whispers said, 'pairings' would occur. The Elysium Hill began to return to its normal hue as lines of brightly coloured shirts and the rest began to move down. Commonsense dictated a walk down Cart Road and to keep walking till they came to a sign saying ANNANDALE 1M near Green Gables. From there began the sheer, waterfall-descent to the pre-1947 Atomic racecourse and to the Glen further down the valley.

But commonsense was not Simla College's best point. So Atom chose Lakkar Bazaar, the Ridge and the Mall, the route to the Malhotra villa. It added an extra mile. But so what? Simla College would be seen in all its glory by all Simla!

'An opportunity only an idiot would miss.' And Atom was not one.

At the Ridge, Rahul's cheeks caught fire when a black and gold painted rickshaw containing a large figure in white pulled up. Rahul hid behind Atom.

'Rahul . . . RAHOOL.' The college stopped. 'You didn't come all these days. You promised. Explain.'

Rahul could not explain.

'Not good, not keeping your word, neglecting your family duty, Rahul,' boss Atom rebuked him.

'Now make a promise in front of a hundred witnesses that you'll come to eat lunch on Sunday.'

'Promise in front of us all that you will go,' said Atom. It was the most embarrassing moment of Rahul's life. But he made the promise he knew he couldn't keep and the picnic wallahs moved on. From the Upper Mall they saw a hillside painted with wild geraniums. They passed by a huge hump embossed with columbines and pheasants' eyes. They went past a house named The Hermitage and heard the click of croquet clubs from behind the tall hedge. There were other houses with English names - Woodbine Cottage, Primrose Hill, Oakfield. Queen Victoria was alive and kicking loudly in Simla.

At last, they passed by the Malhotra house and arrived at the 1M sign on Cart Road. A jeep road, steep and wild, shot down from here to Annandale, but autocratic path-finder Atom rejected it in favour of a perilous pagdandi, a footpath cut in the jungle dark and deep. It was more exciting. It was romance writ in green and black. Colourful birds flashed in the trees above, ravenous crows croaked somewhere nearby, and kites and buzzards kissed the blue skies. High up from the branch of a majestic deodar, a langur with a white-fringed face took a disdainful look at the halla gulla below. He didn't like what he saw. He curved his long tail into a perfect circle and shot ten branches up. Down below, the collegiates kicked the pebbles in their path and, nimbly, on they went downhill.

Suddenly, there it was - a vast tabletop of turf lorded over by a lofty mountain embroidery of firs, conical pines and stately deodars 150 feet tall. At 7,000 feet, it was a sporting miracle complete with a pavilion and spectator stands. The last race had been run here over fifteen years ago. Cricket matting now lay spread in its middle with cricket stumps at either side. Men in white flannels practised slip catches. A cricket match was about to be played there.

'Wish I was playing,' Rahul said to Rishi.

But this game didn't seem to be getting off the ground. As the picnic-makers halted for a rest, Rahul and Rishi edged closer to the cricketers, mostly middle-aged flannelled fools.

'Himachal Secretariat versus Himachal Electricity Board,' Rishi said. 'But why aren't they starting, the old cocks?' A good question, it being past ten. 'Bala-ji?' Rishi shouted enquiringly at a pot-bellied chap.

'Let down, yaar. That fucker Jolly, the only spinner in the side, has taken to his bed.'

'With whom?'

'With flu. I've won the toss and put them in. Had the dogson been here, maybe we'd have a quick wicket or two in the pocket already. Morning moisture. The ball will turn in the fifth over.'

'What are you waiting for?'

'Sent for second-rate donkey Pathak. God knows when he is going to bray in. Where's Twinnie Two?'

'Discussing the Mutiny of 1857 with an Anglo merry widow from Meerut where it all started. Why not postpone the game?'

'Then we lose two points. And if I start the game with ten fucking men, it will have to be played with ten fucking men. Fucking league rules.'

'What's it worth if I solve your problem?'

'Name anything,' said the saddest man in Simla.

'An intro to that steno in your office, Miss G.'

'O, Miss G? She can take a whole battalion. One more idiot, she won't noice. Now solve my problem.'

'Meet Rahul Kapoor, Himachal Under-Eighteens last year. Off spin and leg. Even a googly.'

Bala-ji's face lit up like a 150-watt bulb.

'Oh yeah, yeah. The name rings bells. Welcome to Himachal Secretariat. Now I'll play with ten men.'

'But I don't work for the Secretariat,' Rahul said.

'Listen. You are my nephew, Rahul, no? So?'

'But?' Rahul wore jeans and a black poloneck.

'I'm fixing. I'm fixing. Oh Bhanot,' Bala-ji shouted at a worried-looking man. 'Get out of your kit.'

Bhanot was not a cricketer. Happily, he got out of his kit.

'One thing, though. Aren't you sad to miss your picnic? So much eye-opening beauty going with you,' the happy man said.

'No.' Rahul was a cricketer and he was only being given a view of her back garden today. 'Would you like to go in my place? It's only fair - I took yours, you take mine.'

Bhanot's eyes shone and the age on his face 'halved by half'. 'Maybe you are batting when we get back, hitting fours.'

Rahul *was* batting when the picnic party returned from the Glen. Long shadows of the tall mountain were sweeping across the ground. The sun had set on Annandale, though not on Simla. The light was still good and Bala-ji was pulling out his hair in the pavilion - his side was galloping towards defeat.

The Electricity Board had scored 183 for 7 in their allotted fifty overs. Playing with ten men, the Secretariat was 163 for 7. They were in their forty-seventh over with two balls to go - twenty runs in fourteen balls was a tall order with the number 9 batsman taking strike.

Upon hearing of the state of play, the merry-makers paused. They wanted to see the end - only two overs and two balls to go. They held their breath as the bowler, a tall lithesome electrician, ran half an electric mile to bowl. He bowled a bumper. The frightened batsman ducked and the ball went straight into the open jaws of the crocodile wicket-keeper.

Last ball of the over. Rahul walked up to the middle of the wicket. The other batsman walked over to him. There was a brief conference. Rahul told the frightened man what to do - take it easy and play forward defensive. The man played a forward defensive stroke. But somehow, the ball found the gate and the middle stump went cycling to Sanjauli. Still 163, now for 8. The tall order had become a skyscraper. In came the last man. But Rahul was on the striker's end. And his college shouted: 'Come on, Rahool!'

The bowler, a podgy little fellow, licked his fingers and trotted to bowl. An off break. But it was short-pitched and Rahul dispatched it to the mid-wicket boundary. Sixteen runs needed off eleven balls for a tie, or seventeen to win. Could Rahul do it?

'Easy, son. Easy . . . '

Mr Podgy, over the wicket, he bowled. It was a replica of the last ball. Rahul found the same gap in the fielding and Rishi did a somersault. Thirteen runs needed off ten balls.

'Easy, son . . .' Victory was within grasp. So was defeat. The third delivery lifted sharply. It got Rahul on the glove. The ball shot twenty feet up in the air and the college stopped breathing. But there was no close fielder. Rahul survived. Heartened, Mr Podgy bowled again. A good-length ball which Rahul pushed with a straight bat to mid-off. No fielder stood nearby. An easy single was there for the taking. Against his better judgement, Rahul took it. If the other batsman played out the next two balls, Rahul would have strike for the next over. Then anything was possible.

Another conference. Number 10 knew what he had to do. He played the fifth delivery with the patience and grace of Pataudi. Then, as the dragon came down on him for the last ball of the over, there was a sudden rush of the blood to his head and he lashed out and just ran, the ball flying to fall into the clutches of any of the four fielders who ran to catch it. Rahul had no choice. He ran as well. Two catchers collided and the ball fell to the ground to a deafening Simla College roar of delight. The batsman had run a single. It was bad news. The other man had the strike. Eleven runs off six balls seemed an impossibly tall order indeed now. There was yet another conference in the middle.

'For God's sake take a single,' begged Rahul. The tall fast bowler shot to the wicket and bowled - well outside the off stump. Number 10 missed. Ditto next ball.

Four balls, thirteen runs. Victory was out.

'Go for it, you fool!' Bala-ji screamed from the pavilion. The fool went for it. They got a single.

'Rahool . . . Rahool . . .'

Twelve runs, three balls. Three fours - highly unlikely. Or two sixes – 'even more highly unlikely'. Or two fours and a six – 'out of the question'.

The first ball Rahul received was very fast but very short and had just the right amount of bounce to be hooked. Six. The valley went mad. Six more runs needed. Two threes will do. Or a four and a two. But no, sir. Whack - another six.

The ascent to Simla was quieter than the descent had been. The girls were exhausted, the boys subdued. It had been a great day's outing. But who was the happiest of all?

'Say thank you.' Rishi wanted credit where credit was due.

'Thank you. Thank you,' said roly-poly Bala-ji.

'Davico's then?'

'Want to bankrupt me? There are eleven of us.'

'Twelve. Who gave you Rahul?'

'It'll cost me a month's salary. You crazy or loco?'

'This is not how a cricket captain talks, Bala-ji. Like a gentleman, he never talks of money.'

The college crowd dissolved as soon as it came near the Mall. What pairs there were, broke up for fear of the girls being seen and reported and having their legs broken by their fathers for dishonouring them. And the tearful gentleman took his triumphant team plus Mr Fixit to Davico's.

They got three tables at the far back on the left of the band. The bearer first joined the tables. Then he looked up and smiled at Rahul. It was the same bearer as last time.

'Baba sahib, will you come with me for a minute?'

'Where?'

'Just to the bill counter.'

Rahul followed the waiter to the counter.

'Narang sahib,' the bearer said to a burly man with a bushy moustache at the counter. 'This is the baba sahib.'

Rahul looked from one Simla specimen to the other in wonderment.

'Might you have dropped something here on the last occasion you visited us, sir?' The man spoke Simla English, perfect.

'My wallet?'

'If you tell me exactly how much it contained, it will be my pleasure to restore it to you.'

India a country of crooks, thugs and cheats? A nation of fools? No. It is a nation of the most beautiful men and women.

Rahul glanced at the sky through the vast glass wall. He saw Krishna smile.

Atom had an escort guard of thirty. It was his wish that Rahul be his 'Best Man'. It was a royal wish. It could not be denied.

'We'll dance on the Mall,' Prince Chuba Ao said.

'And dine at Davico's,' said Balbir with a princely smile.

The college did not have a hall of its own. It had hired one for today. The place was packed. In the mad pelemele, someone approached Rahul, Cowdrey's 'Best Man' Joshi. He put an arm around his shoulder and took him to the Gents for a 'hush-hush private word'. He offered him 'you name the amount' cash for changing sides.

Rahul was knocked over mountain and valley.

'These things happen all over the world all the time,' Joshi said. 'Victory won, you are Vice President. What more can you ask for? Yes or no?'

'No.'

The speaker's desk stood centre stage with a mike, three inverted glasses and a jug of water. On its right sat the Principal, the Vice Principal and Governor Tandon. On its left were the three contenders with Moon in the middle. Three of their closest supporters stood behind them – wrestler Joshi behind Cowdrey, Miss Nath behind Moon and Rahul behind Atom. Cousin Moon gave the traitor one icy look and that was it. After the intros, Mr Khurana called out:

'Mr Gopal Chaudhry, your opportunity to convince the house that you are the man it wants.'

The Peacock rose. Head held high, with the half-smile of someone who knows something important which the rest of the world does not, Cowdrey put his speech down. He began with democracy.

'It comes from the Greek word demos . . . Westminster is the mother of parliaments . . . 1789 Liberty, Equality, Fraternity. The Indian democracy is the largest in the world . . . Government of the people, for the people, by the people. But what is a government without the right leader? A bunch of nincompoops. What is a college council without the right man to lead it? A bunch of nitwits.'

Cowdrey paused for effect. Then he switched over to current affairs.

'What is happening in NEFA? How many of you know? How many of you care? Do you know Chinese soldiers have snow clothing and our jawans only the regulation jerseys? Are you aware that the Chinese have big mountain guns as against our World War Two mortars? Do you know that the Chinaman has automatic weapons and we only the pre-historic rifle Three Nought Three?'

The mention of Three Nought Tree brought the roof down with shouts of – '*Three Nought Three, Three Nought Three*.'

The bell rang. It was time for the next contestant.

'Miss Moon Mehra.'

'*Three Nought Three . . . Three Nought Three*.'

Miss Moon Mehra's intentions were clear - mass murder of willing victims.

'Why does it always have to be a man to lead a country or a council? We've been told that India is the world's largest democracy. But if the truth be known, it is the world's largest hypocrisy. What kind of democracy is it that treats half of its population as second-class citizens? Indian women are told to be obedient and servile. They are told they were born to serve, suffer and sacrifice. "Your karma", they are told. How convenient! What brainwash! What humbug! I know my sisters here will vote for me because they know what I am talking about. I also know most of my brothers in this hall hesitate because they don't like to hear what I am saying. But if you are the men you say you are, prove it by putting your votes where your mouths should be. Thank you.'

'Tikkoo Atma Lal,' called the chair.

'My knees,' Atom whispered to Rahul.

'Up, up. They'll be all right once you get going.' Rahul pulled Atom to his feet.

'I can't,' Atom hissed, clutching Rahul's hand. It became unclear whether Rahul was pushing Atom or if Atom was pulling Rahul. Both appeared at the mike and the hall gasped.

'Mr Chairman, ladies and gentlemen. Last-minute change, you can say. I took on more than I could chew, you can say. I give you the new hostel candidate – Mr Rahul Kapoor Esquire,' Atom said. Handing his speech to Rahul, he backed away.

The hush in the hall turned to astonishment. On the stage, with Atom's speech in his hand, Rahul didn't know what to do - run away. Or? Or what?

'Speech. Speech. Speech!' The hall exploded.

'Speak, Kapoor,' said Principal Khurana, encouragingly. Speak? Of what?

'SPEECH! SPEECH!' screamed the 'sewage rats' who longed to see him dragged in dust.

'You can't let them laugh at you like this, Kapoor. Speak.'

But words wouldn't come to Rahul. Then they did. A torrent of them.

'This is greatness being thrust upon me. Never for a moment did it occur to me that I might be standing here today - for I do not have any ambitions of becoming your leader. I feel like one of you. I *am* one of you.'

There was applause.

'I am not standing here on false pretences. I am standing here because of the bravery of one man, our own dear Atom. Don't say Atom has split.'

Deafening laughter.

'Atom has not chickened out. All he's done is realise he can't take the heat. So he has decided to quit the kitchen - and brave is the man who admits to himself his shortcomings. So, a hand of applause for good old Atom.'

There was a hand of applause for good old Atom.

'I don't have a speech prepared. Atom handed me his, but I don't want to read to you another man's speech. I want to speak to you from the heart. We have been given a lecture on democracy. We are told all of that by Professor Dyal of Political Science every day. I don't think there is anyone in this hall who will disagree with what the gentleman said. What most of you *will* disagree with is the manner in which it was said - as if everyone in this hall was a schoolchild and that speaker, the headmaster, a God's gift to us all . . .'

Laughter returned to the hall with shouts of 'God's Gift!'

'Would such an individual make a good leader? Arrogance in any individual is unpleasant. In a leader, it is dangerous.

'And as to what is happening on our borders - I will tell the first speaker what's happening there. My very own brother is among the jawans fighting in NEFA so that the gentleman can enjoy freedom of speech here and lecture us about democracy.

'Then we were told that India is the world's largest hypocrisy. I agree whole-heartedly. Until and unless India makes its women equal partners in every sphere of life, it cannot claim to be a true democracy. But to use this argument in order to make demands like - *put your votes where your mouths should be* - is emotional blackmail. It is misusing democracy, it is taking undue advantage of it, it is insulting our intelligence.'

Rahul woke up rather early next morning. He liked that, waking up early. It made him bubble inside himself. But today he felt a little different. Today he felt right on the pinnacle of Mount Jakhoo and like any of the primates - two-legged or four, red-faced or brown whoever climbed its steep slopes. But Rahul's happiness evaporated when he looked out of his large window, since a low cloud hugged Simla.

'The games's off if the sun doesn't shine.'

Rahul inspected himself in the bathroom mirror as he brushed his teeth. He liked what he beheld. Shedding his pyjamas, he made his way down to the dining room taking with him his napkin in a silver ring from home. He was too early - the long dining table looked lonesome. Coming from a fairly large family, though not too large by Indian standards, Rahul didn't like eating alone. He nearly beat a retreat. But he was there now. He decided to stay on - the others would soon be stampeding in for a long and leisurely Saturday breakfast of butter parathas. Rahul took a mug of tea from the kitchen and went and sat down near the far end of one of the long tables. Then in walked guess who?

'Good morning and congratulations, Rahul. What oratory, yaar! Mesmerising stuff,' Mahendru said in his syrupy voice, sitting opposite Rahul.

'You have done us proud, darling boy,' said Kumar, seating himself next to Mahendru. 'And at long last we have an opportunity to be alone, the three of us.'

'So sorry about that day. We should have been more tactful. We offended the very person we so adore. Very, very sorry,' murmured Mahendru.

'As we are alone at long last, we would like to repeat our offer with the utmost respect. And love.' Kumar made a deep bow.

'Now that you are President you are going to require our protection even more from bad elements in Simla society. And believe you me, Simla *is* bad. B.A.D bad.'

'Just two little words. Marry us. As a wedding present, you have five crisp ten-rupee notes on the first of every month.' Kumar whispered.

'No one need ever know nor shall.'

'We await your answer. Just say "I do" as in the church and have done with it. Please. We beg you.'

'If you don't, you should not hold us responsible for the consequences.'

Rahul trembled with rage. He wished he had a double-barrelled gun. He stood up, mug in hand. Next instant, he flung the hot tea at them, missing both their faces but drenching them.

The stampede. Suddenly the dining room was full. Rahul walked away. Several voices hailed him as boys milled around, trying to settle down. He went, got another mug of tea and sat next to Balbir on the other side of the table. In front of him sat Ajit, his forehead creased as the SCH dining room came alive with Saturday noise.

'What's wrong, oi?' Balbir gave Rahul a jab.

'Nothing.'

'Your mug is redder than the backside of a Jakhoo Bandar.'

'Is it?'

'Now that you are the bloody boss man of the Union, you should be happy, President sahib.'

'I bloody am.'

'You don't bloody look it.'

'Now that you are college President, must you also be the college cricket captain?' Ajit asked, looking sad. Broken.

'Not necessarily.' Rahul's paratha came. His appetite had vanished. But he began to eat, trying to look normal. It was not easy.

'Then you won't mind if the game is called off?'

'I would, because I like to play. Anyway, it's going to be sunny today. My forecast.'

'What's bugging you, Kapoor?' Balbir nudged him.

'Speech. Speech,' yelled a number of boys.

'Not on your belly button.' Rahul sipped his tea.

'Speech. We want a speech,' Atom shouted. 'A post-victory speech. All great leaders do.'

'Aah, the darling of the college! Look how elegantly he sips tea, little finger raised delicately. How dainty,' warbled one of the sewage rats. The bastards looked and behaved as if nothing at all had happened, in spite of their drenched shirts.

'And watch him use his napkin. What elegance, I say!' twitted the other rat.

'President yesterday, maybe cricket captain today and what tomorrow?'

'The Mayor of Simla.' Kumar laughed loudly, expecting others to join him. No one did.

Rahul fixed him with his eyes.

'But you wanted someone from the hostel to win.'

'Yes - Atom.'

'He put me forward. Like it or not.'

'We don't.'

'Hard luck. Five hundred people voted for me.'

'They can have you, with your little finger and napkin,' Mahendru said.

'Table manners maketh man, didn't you know?' Kumar sniggered.

'What would *you* know of manners, Kumar, when you don't know which end of the fork to shove in your big mouth - front or back?' Balbir said.

'That's very funny, Dumb Bells. What wit!'

'What did you say, Mahendru? Wit or shit?' Kumar laughed.

'So now that you've got the job, what wonders are you going to do for the college, Mr President? Have a common loo for ladies and gents?' Kumar said, sniggering at his own joke.

'Ignore him. He is jealous,' Balbir said to Rahul.

'I am talking to you, Pretty Boy.'

'Pretty Boy can't hear. Got rainwater in his ears.'

'Can't you talk?'

Rahul looked away in answer.

'I asked you a question.' Kumar stood up, kicked a chair and like a bull he came.

'It was a silly question.'

'You calling me silly?'

'Couldn't you think of something a fraction more intelligent than a common loo?'

'Now are you calling me a fool? Insulting me?'

'I can't bring myself to insult anyone. Especially those I consider beneath contempt.'

'You high-shit superior arsehole.'

'Look, Kumar, I only feel sorry for you – you're twisted and pathetic. So I won't be drawn into a fight. Go back to your place and eat your breakfast.'

'Kapoor, President, beware of jealous loonies.' Balbir spoke quietly, but audibly.

'You calling me a jealous loony, Egg Yolks?'

'Kumar, why don't you do what the man says? Go and eat your brekkie.' The body-builder rolled up his sleeves over those menacing biceps.

'I said: are you calling me jealous and loony?'

'You are a bloody loony and you can have a fight if you must.' Balbir stood up. He thrust his well-expanded chest into Kumar's, pushing him back and pinning him against a wall.

'It's not your fight, Egg Yolks.'

'It is nobody's fight.'

Kumar piddled out of the room, giving Rahul a 'we'll get you one day' look. Mahendru followed.

'Bloody wankers,' Balbir said. Table life returned to normal and he shouted at Ajit who was lost in thought, 'Oi, Handsome. Try and win today for a change. Your parting gift as captain.' But Ajit wasn't listening. He was at Annandale. 'What are you thinking anyway?'

'Of this YMCA, yaar. Full of fucking fuddy duddies but they play fucking well. This 3D fellow Dass. Hits up three figures every third game, believe it or not? That's why we've never beaten Y.'

'Always a first time,' Rahul said.

'You hit fifty and take three wickets, you have the captaincy in your pocket and dinner at Davico`s from my pocket.' Balbir made the offer again.

'Only if the sun does shine over Simla,' Ajit said.

The sun did shine over Simla and the match did get played at Annandale. But with only 141 runs in the bank, Simla College did not have a hope in hell. However, Y did worse - 129 all out. Rahul scored a lousy 11, though he took 4 wickets. All the same, it was his rival who put the captaincy in his pocket.

Deepak was out first ball. Determined to bowl out the entire Y, the angry fool bowled extra fast, losing all line and length. He was lashed mercilessly with just one wicket to his name. Yet the dinner at Davico's had to be dropped.

In the last over of the game, Rahul sprained his left ankle and tore a ligament. The murder-climb from Annandale back to the Mall made his foot swell up like a football. And now it became unbearably painful. He took a rickshaw to the hostel. Bahadar Singh threw a piece of rock in the fire. Then he dropped some water on it and wrapped it up in a towel. Rahul drank a glass of hot milk and went to bed with the hot stone under his ankle.

SIX

Things didn't look good next morning. Rahul could hardly walk - his ankle was obscenely swollen. On top of that, the hostel thermometer said 101 degrees.

'You can't go out like this, President,' Atom said.

'Can't I?'

'You'll catch pneumonia if you do,' Balbir said.

'You are a fool, Rahul. I made a mistake making you President,' Atom barked.

'Go in a rickshaw if you must go,' Rajkumar suggested.

Bahadar Singh was sent to fetch a rickshaw.

'But only fat people go in rickshaws,' Rahul said as he climbed into it. 'Or pompous arseholes.'

It was an afternoon steeped in romance, with love leaping out of every nook and crevice in the hillside carpeted with pine needles. Simla breathed a vapour of freshness. Leaves glistened and dew drops dripped from ferns. Far away, an avalanche of corrugated iron and collapsing woodwork clung to a near-perpendicular slope. And the sun shone so.

Two minutes from the hostel, Rahul saw pal Rover and Miss Nath coming up. Rover shot from the side of his mistress and jumped on his friend. But Miss Nath did not see Rahul. She just did not see him. Neither did she call Rover back. Rover loved the rickshaw ride for 20 yards. Then, just like that, he decided to race back to his mistress.

Rahul dismissed the rickshaw at the Krishna temple. But today the temple door was shut and bolted from the inside. He put his eye to a crack in the door and had the shock of his life. A naked young woman stood in the light from the earthen lamp, hands folded on her shapely bosom. A red line of sindhoor in the parting of her hair meant she was a married woman. She was praying for a child. She had bared her all to the God. Rahul withdrew instantly out of silent respect.

The Malhotras were bowled over. But she wasn't among them.

'Captain and President. My Oh my,' said young Bobby. 'You know what happened at school on Friday? We were doing clocks and time when we had a visitor – the Bishop of Simla, the big pundit-ji of the English church. Breathless, we stood up. We sat down. He asked the Sikh boy next to me, "What's your name, young man?" "Jaspal Singh, Your Grace-ji." "How old are you, Jaspal?" "Half past twelve, Your Grace-ji." The Bishop thought for a bit and said, "Ah, so you'll be one in exactly half an hour then." The penny dropped, the class roared and Miss clutched her tummy.'

Rahul roared and clutched his foot because it hurt to laugh.

'Very painful?' Mrs Malhotra's was the voice of concentrated concern. 'You look very pale. You shouldn't have come walking.'

'I didn't.'

He saw *her* flit past the door, only her backside.

'Then how did you come? Flying?' Bobby said.

'Yes.'

'Funny boy. You should have taken a rickshaw. Young men don't think these days. I wonder where their brains are. In their cricket boots, I suppose,' Mr Malhotra said. 'Devi, give him lunch jaldi jaldi and call him a rickshaw.'

154

'Uncle, I am fit as a fiddle. And I am not hungry at all.' But where was *she*? He dared not ask. It would spell out his intentions. Then he'd get the boot.

On the way to the dining room, Rahul wangled a moment with Bobby.

'Didi has a headache,' Bobby said. 'But it is not a real one.'

'What do you mean, Bobby?'

'She's furious.'

'With whom?'

'Don't know.'

The panelled dining room spelled glamour. The varnished long table shining mirror-like had twelve chairs. As they sat down, Rahul saw her outside in the hall, again only her back garden.

'Darling, aren't you coming in to eat?' Mrs Malhotra called out.

'No, Mummy. I've a splitting headache,' came the reply with her back to the room.

'Liar,' yelled Bobby.

Mrs Malhotra was all smiles: 'So how many acres have you, Rahul? You were saying.'

Rahul's temples were on fire and his ankle throbbed with pain. Yet he knew why he was being asked these questions. He let his hostess hear what she wanted to hear and doubled their acres.

'And property - houses, I mean?'

'Besides the Sun House and the Moon House, we have only two more.' Rahul invented these just to see the effect. The effect he saw was good. 'Please don't mention this to anyone. Daddy would beat me black and blue if . . . You understand, Aunty.'

155

Of course Aunty understood. She felt his brow.

'You are unwell and you haven't eaten a thing.' She checked his pulse. 'Ram,' she shouted. 'Drive Rahul baba to Lakkar Bazaar and put him in a rickshaw there. He should go straight to bed.'

Outside, Bobby whispered, 'Guess who Didi is furious with?'

'Who?'

'Not telling you though.'

'Why not?'

'She'd kill me if I did.'

Only when Rahul set foot in his room did he remember.

'Fool Rahul.'

His body ached with fever. His foot throbbed with pain. But before he buried himself under his quilt, there was this little thing he had to do. Otherwise?

Very dear and highly respected Aunt Savitri,

I trust you are all well and flourishing. I am neither one nor the other. In the historic cricket-match yesterday your loving nephew sustained serious injury and had to be carried all the way from Annandale to the hostel. I rose this morning with a high temperature.

The college doctor Dr Arjun Singh came and gave me a lethal pill that put me to deep sleep. I have just woken up and am sending you one hundred and one apologies about lunch. As soon as my foot stops to hurt and my body to ache, as soon as my fever goes, I will present myself to you in person. Then you can scold me as much as you like. In the meantime, allow your generous heart to continue to shower affection on me.

And please, beg Cousin Moon on my behalf not to stop talk-ing to me. What happened in the hall on Friday was not of my making. With the hysterical crowd yelling 'Speech. Speech,' what could I do? I was pushed into the jaws of victory against my will, or liking. Honest. Cousin Moon would have done the same had she been in my shoe.

I am waiting to get well so that I can come and eat that lunch. Yours affly

Rahul gave the letter to Bahadar Singh.

'Don't tell her I've been anywhere. Only that I'm dying. Add a bit of mirch-masala spice.'

Time - three o'clock. Rahul put the SCH thermom-eter in his mouth. 105. Humm. He laid down in his bed and passed out like a light. He had a dream, a meaningless dream - hushed noises and people milling around in a dense haze. Balbir towered over his bed like a kindly big brother. Rajkumar and Mohmi stood guarding his feet. Other boys just hung around. Atom was whispering something to someone. A woman, not Rishi, was inspecting his wardrobe, pulling clothes from it.

It couldn't be?

'Aunt Savitri?'

The unthinkable had happened. But before Aunt Savitri could answer, a sweet face whispered in his ear with a per-fumed breath: 'You were marvellous.'

'So you are talking to me?'

'A lot. The better man won.'

'Pity we are cousins.'

157

The whispering stopped. The sweet face with a perfumed breath faded in the haze. Aunt Savitri came and felt Rahul's forehead and held his wrist.

'Silly boy. Very silly boy. Why did you go out?'

So some son of a bitch had betrayed him. This hostel was full of low-grade snakes in the grass.

'Is Cousin Moon still talking to me?'

'Come home and ask her yourself. Two rickshaws waiting outside to take you home.'

'To Balmoral?'

'No, to Buckingham.'

At home, Aunt Savitri picked up the phone.

'Don't, Aunt Savitri,' Rahul yelled - he didn't want her to phone Solan. But Aunt Savitri was not phoning Solan.

'Doctor Chatterji . . .'

While Aunt Savitri shouted the plight of her nephew at the family doctor, Nephew Rahul talked to Cousin Moon in whispers.

'I'm sorry I won.' For the second time in his life Rahul wished he was not so brilliant.

'What sorry-worry? The better man won. That's all. After I heard you speak I didn't want to win.'

'Honest? So you are talking to me?'

'Not till I know: A, why did you go out at all in just a shirt when you had fever already? B, where did you go to lunch, who with, that is? C, why didn't you come here as per your public promise?'

Rahul was saved. Aunt Savitri came back.

'Doctor Chatterji says take two saridons, drink a glass of hot milk and get a lot of sleep. He'll come in the morning.'

There was a discussion about booking a trunk call to Solan.

'No, no, no,' Rahul said.

'I will drink my pride and speak with Kamla.'

'You will do nothing of the sort, Aunt Savitri. It's only a little temperature, for heaven's sake.' Rahul didn't want his mother to know he was staying with her cousin. His mother would cry her lungs out to know he was ill. She would want to fly to Simla that very instant. It would shame her to come to her cousin when she was not on speaking terms with her.

'OK then. We'll wait one-two days. Now take the milk and sleep till the doctor comes.'

'UK-returned doctor - MBBS and MRSP,' Aunt Savitri said when the doorbell rang next morning.

Dr Chatterji was an ageless sparrow of a man. He wore a three-piece white linen suit and a khaki solar hat. 'Humm,' he said at the end of his examination. He wrote out a prescription note. 'Humm,' he said again. He put his stethoscope in his bag and walked to the door with Aunt Savitri.

'Two-three days and nephew will be climbing mountains like a Jakhoo monkey. Let him sleep and sweat. Diet? Toast, milk and fruit.'

Rahul slept through the day. He woke up at four in the afternoon. Aunt Savitri sat beside his bed in a deep chair, knitting. Little Minnoo and Bachchu played 'doctors' on the floor. Twelve-year-old Dolly in the brown and yellow Auckland House uniform stood against a wall, reading a comic. The September sun shone sweetly on Simla. But it felt dark in the room. And damp. Rahul blinked - *where am I? Who are these people? Why does my body ache? Why am I sweating?*

'Sleep. Sleep,' Aunt Savitri said.

Rahul had slept for more than twenty hours. He couldn't sleep any more. He was thirsty.

'Water? Larka, water glass.'

Rahul sighed - he wished he lay in his own bed in his own room in Solan. He longed for his mother and Shobana and . . . A noise and he saw an apparition in a sari, college books in one hand. It was only then Rahul recalled that he was in Simla, that he was a collegiate and this was Cousin Moon and Aunt Savitri and these her other children. His bed had brass knobs and a brown and cream counterpane. The curtains were made of silk and satin of the same colours. There was a marble-topped table by his bedside.

Larka brought a glass of water on a lace-covered silver tray and said to Aunt Savitri, 'Phone.' And Aunt Savitri went away.

'How's the celebrated patient?' Moon asked.

'Celebrating.'

'Celebrating what?'

'Being in Buckingham.'

'Balmoral, actually. Let's take your temperature.' Cousin Moon first felt his brow. Then she held his wrist.

'Don't touch me. You make my temperature shoot up.'

'Shush.' Moon took his pulse. 'Normal.'

'You lie, Doctor sahib. My pulse is racing. And you should listen to my heart.'

'Have you eaten anything? Open your mouth.'

Cousin Moon stuck the thermometer in Rahul's mouth and went away. She came back a couple of minutes later, wearing the ordinary salvar kamiz, and pulled the thermometer out of Rahul's mouth.

'Oh, my God. I'm not sure if you are going to. . .'

'Let me see. Let me see.'

But Cousin Moon didn't let him. She went away again and returned carrying a silver tray with a silver dome, a silver tea service and two cups and saucers. She lifted the dome to reveal a plateful of scrambled eggs. The sight of it had an instant effect on Rahul. His stomach made its presence felt as being hurtfully empty.

'You can't leave us like this. You have runs to score, speeches to make and ladies to kill. Do you know what the girls call you?'

'I know.' He didn't want what Miss Nath called him spelled out.

'No, you don't. Just as well. Or it won't be the clouds, but the stratosphere itself.'

'What on earth are talking about, cousin-ji?'

'What on earth indeed?'

'A clue would be helpful.'

'Don't talk. Eat. Mr James Dean goes to lunch in a rickshaw! But where? That's the question.'

Aunt Savitri was back, talking to herself.

'Mummy, do you know how your dandy nephew goes about town? Who was on the phone?'

'That Mrs Brigadier. Says give the boy green tea. That woman is herb fanatic. Would make you eat grass and say it was good for you.'

'What I want to know, Mummy, is where did this boy go for lunch instead of coming here?'

161

'Suggest you ask your Sherlock Holmesy friends.'

The doorbell rang and Cousin Moon went to answer it. Rahul heaved a sigh - the Spanish Inquisition was temporarily over.

'Mummy, it's Auntie Devi.'

'Bring her in here.' Aunt Savitri couldn't be bothered to get up from the chair again. 'Bring her here to see Rahul.'

Rahul squirmed - had he become a tourist attraction then?

'Rahul?' said the visitor from the door.

'So you know this rotter, Auntie Devi?' Cousin Moon put one, two and three together and gave Rahul an *I`m never going to talk to you again* look.

When Rahul was well again, he wished he was ill again. But he did not want to outlive his welcome. And he wanted a whiff of the Mall. So on Friday afternoon, feeling in the shape predicted by Dr Sparrow, he decided to return to his mountain. A hundred yards from Balmoral he saw two familiar figures sitting on the wooden railing of the road. There was much hugging. But what were the Twinnies doing there?

'How did you know I was coming?'

'Been waiting here every day. You had to come out sooner or later.'

Arm-in-arm, they walked. Passing a small eatery, the twins stopped. Kishi tapped his tummy.

'Empty. Mice running amok in it.'

He pulled out the corners of his pockets. So did Rishi. Well-fed Rahul had no money on him either. He asked his friends to walk back with him to SCH where he would give them hostel tea and a bun. Nearing it, Rishi suggested they entered Rahul's room from the balcony at the back.

'So that we don't run into the One Legga Lunn.'

They climbed the hillside to get to the balcony.

'Look!' cried Rishi, hiding in the bushes. Professor Nath stood in his room talking to a dashing army officer, his own brother Pithi! There were Mummy and Daddy and Shobana and Bimbi and Shoki and a wonderful smell of the Sun House.

'Sorry,' Rahul said to his friends and hurried.

'Mummy. Pithi.'

Rahul bowed down to touch his father's feet first. Then he crushed his mother in his arms. Now he hugged Pithi - he hadn't seen him for months - and Shobana and the boys. What a surprise! What delicious joy! But how come they were in his room? And why did Daddy still look unwell? It was September now.

'Waiting for you. Mrs Mehra said on the phone you were hale and hearty and on your way here,' Professor Nath said and, realising that the family wanted to be alone, left them.

'Pithi arrived yesterday and your mother couldn't wait a second longer to see you,' Daddy said. He was short of breath.

'Daddy, sir!' Rahul said.

'Nonsense. I'm fit as a fiddle and fresh as a cucumber. We are booked at the Cecil and want to make a move to check in.' They were parked on Cart Road under Lakkar Bazaar. Mummy wanted to change. They had a dinner date.

'With Aunt Savitri?'

'No. The Malhotras.'

'The Malhotras?' But the Malhotras were hardly known to them.

'College captain, eh? And President too! Jolly good show, I say,' Pithi said. He looked very dashing in his uniform. More hugging. More laughter.

'Mummy, why didn't you ever tell me anything about Aunt Savitri? And what's the big misunderstanding?'

Mummy's sparkling face became cloudy. She exchanged a quick glance with Daddy.

'Ask your father.'

Prakash Kapoor laughed and said nothing. Usually, when Prakash Kapoor chose to say nothing, his children dared not ask.

'Please tell us, sir,' Rahul insisted.

'Some other time.' Prakash Kapoor had an apologetic smile which radiated guilt. This made everybody want to know.

'Your Casanova father and Savitri . . . '

'What?' Five pairs of eyes popped.

`You must be joking, Mummy. Have you seen Aunt Savitri?'

'I only wrote a few letters. That was all. I swear,' Prakash said. 'And pray when was it? Twenty-five years ago. Before I had even heard of your mother.'

Kamla and Savitri were first cousins. Kamla lived in Peshawar, Savitri in Lahore where Prakash was running the family estate. They had met during one of Gandhi's Civil Disobedience marches. They met again at a Congress rally. And again at another meeting. A few letters were exchanged.

'All full of patriotism and nothing else. I swear.'

Foolish young Prakash kept Savitr's letters neatly tied with a ribbon in a purse made of straw. Years after their arranged marriage, Kamla chanced upon them during a Diwali clean-up. That was back in `42, the year of the Quit India Movement when Pithi was three. Kamla burned the letters in their purse and did not speak to her cousin ever again.

'Mummy, that was nearly twenty years ago.'

164

'Twenty years or thirty. Your father was about to be engaged to me and she was affairing with him, writing him love letters. I never want to see her again. Finish.'

'Remember two things, begum mine,' Prakash said. 'A, they were letters about freedom fighting. B, our families, yours and mine, hadn't arranged anything yet. So why are you still so sore?'

'Aunt Savitri has been good to me, Mummy.'

'Maybe she still thinks of him - and sees him in you. That's why she's been so good to you.'

'Not fair. She sees in me a nephew. That's all.'

'That's not all. I know Savitri.'

'Mummy, she has four children of her own. Anyway, how can you blame her if she saw Daddy and was slain by his charm? Who wouldn't have been smitten by it then?'

'What do you meant then, boy?' Prakash laughed.

'Stop it. Both of you, father and son,' Kamla said and started crying.

'*You* stop it because you are being unreasonable, begum. Not fair, that.'

But Kamla couldn't stop it.

'Mummy!' Shobana also started crying. She hugged her mother. The boys knew that their mother was not being very reasonable. Yet they all wanted to put their arms around her.

'Twenty-plus bloody years, begum. For heaven's sake.' Prakash sounded angry. His breathing became heavier.

'Mummy, it's time you made up with Cousin Savitri. She thinks so highly of you. Even wanted to telephone you. Please.'

'I told you then and I am telling you now, woman there was nothing to it, in it, about it or what have you. So stop torturing yourself.' Angry Prakash raised his voice. 'Savitri has been good to your boy. Looked after him when he was sick.'

'True, Mummy.'

'If you can't say thank you to your cousin, be graceful enough not to hold anything against her, OK, begum mine of yesterday, today and tomorrow?'

Begum Mine blew her nose. Then she smiled. It planted rose bushes on Mount Jakhoo.

'Okay. We will call on her tomorrow. Now, we have a date to keep,' Kamla said, standing up.

'Mummy, you are the best mum in the world,' Bimbi said.

'Of course, she is. But what about your dad?' Prakash laughed.

'Numero Uno, sir,' Shobana said.

A typical Simla September evening - magical. And so light, a man could walk on the air. Father and sons sat on the manicured lawn of the Cecil. A burra peg in one hand, Prakash looked worried.

'I don't trust the blasted Chinese, Pithi - they are vipers. I trust our Krishna Menon even less. He's nothing but an inflated windbag.'

'Sir, the feeling in the army is that they won't get up to any hanky-panky. And though Menon is not much loved, he is a good Defence Minister.'

'But will he prove to be a good war-time Defence Minister like Churchill? He talks too much, Pithi.'

'So did Churchill, sir, if I may say so.'

'But Churchill had style and substance. Wrote some of the best prose of our times. You must read him. Every Indian must.'

'He was such an awful imperialist. He hated us.'

'He loved himself more than he hated us. But this Menon? No style and certainly no substance. A politician who talks too much has little to say. Menon should be preparing instead of talking. He's hiding behind Nehru's prestige - as if that could be a shield against that Chou.'

'I wouldn't worry, sir. It won't come to war. We are sure of it.'

'Well, I am not. And I can't help worrying. You are there at the naked front facing Chinese guns. I can't sleep. I wake up with a cold sweat in the middle of the night and look at maps.'

'The Chinese are jolly nice chaps. We can see them across the River Namka Chu. When they are felling big trees, they let us know in advance so that we are not alarmed by the noise.'

'Oh, where are the girls?'

The father and sons were sitting around a table, waiting. Mummy and Shobana had been in the dressing room of their ground-floor suite for ages. Suddenly, a light veil of silver materialised in the air.

'Getting chilly now, sir. I'd better take you in.'

Inside, the ladies were still at it.

'Are you going to the Viceroy's Ball or something, Mummy? It's only the Malhotras', Rahul shouted.

No, it seemed more than that, as it became clear when mother and daughter appeared. The officer and a gentleman whistled most unofficer-like. The other boys gloated at what they saw.

'Mummy, you look a million dollars,' Rahul said.

'And Shobana, you look half a million dollars minimum,' Shoki said.

'No, my Shobi. You look a million pounds sterling,' Daddy said, kissing his daughter on the head.

'But you are not looking so well, puttar Rahul,' Mummy said, caressing her son's cheeks.

'Maybe he should not come with us after all, begum. It'll get cold at night and he'll have to walk back all the way by himself. Maybe you should go back to your hostel, Rahul.'

'Daddy, I'm fresh as a fiddle and . . .' Rahul said and the younger Kapoors stuck their tongues out.

And so the Kapoors went to the Malhotras'.

The Green Gables was a house of light in that lush fairy-tale setting. It had the curtain backcloth of a million incandescent pinpoints of All Simla behind it, and the dark drama of the deodar-soaked Annandale Valley beneath it. The house was floodlit, as was the garden.

'Looks as if the Malhotras are expecting someone tonight,' Rahul said.

'Yes, they are,' Shobana replied.

The Malhotras met the Kapoors at the door.

'Come in, come in. And welcome, ji. Welcome,' Ramakant Malhotra said, taking Prakash's right hand in both his, 'Namaskar, sister Kamla. Good evening, Captain Prithvi.'

Mrs Malhotra did something Rahul had only heard of and dismissed as nonsense. She poured mustard oil from a porcelain milk jug on both sides of her threshold. This was the age-old way of welcoming important guests, so old no one remembered why it was done.

'Is it to lubricate the door-hinges?' Rahul said to himself. 'Why so much fuss? We hardly know them.' He sensed Mr Bull turning in his grave at the way his property was being treated.

168

Inside, there were flowers everywhere. Servants brisked about, seen but not heard. The large chandelier-lit drawing room shone like a Mughal court. The Malhotra ladies were all eyes. Big eyes. They glittered like Mughal jewellery. But one of them glittered more - Sushma. While other eyes were glued to the shiny soldier's face, only she looked nervously at her chapliencased toes. In that instant Rahul knew.

'Sit, sit, sit, ji. Please.'

There was the usual, kick-off small talk. Everybody seemed somewhat nervous, although everybody smiled a lot.

'So where are you posted in NEFA, Captain Prithvi?'

'We are manning forward posts thousands of feet high, sir. Fifteen, sixteen thousand feet high. I've just come home on leave from a forward-most position called Dhola.'

'Where exactly is it on the map?'

'It is so tiny, it is not on any map, sir. It is located at the tri-junction of India, China and Bhutan.'

The ladies found the conversation tedious. Sensing this, the chief guest changed it.

'What a wonderful chandelier! Venetian?' Prakash asked politely.

'I think it is. Mrs Bull said it was very old.'

'Ram,' Mrs Malhotra shouted at the door and in came Ram and two servants carrying silver trays. Ram had two glasses of Scotch on his for the chief guest and the master of the house, the other two contained soft drinks and titbits. Indira and Padma stood up. They took the trays from the servants to serve the guests personally. Sushma was left on her own. She gazed at her toes.

'Come and sit by my side, Sushma,' Kamla said.

The ten-foot walk to the sofa on which her possible future mother-in-law sat was the longest journey of the young girl's life. But she made it. While Kamla talked to her, Indira and Padma went around the room, serving. Pithi and Rahul didn't take any. Rahul felt heart-broken because Indira was behaving as if he didn't exist. Pithi just didn't feel like it. This alarmed Mrs Malhotra.

'Take something. You have to. Try our home-made rhododendron squash,' she pleaded. 'Doesn't it look like Campari?'

Pithi took a glass of this ruby-red transluscent liquid from Padma's hand. Rahul from Indira's, making sure their hands touched.

'So how long is your leave, Captain Pithi?' Mrs Malhotra said.

'Three weeks.'

'And Rahul, are you fully all right now? Bobby darling, why don't you show Rahul the cricket gear you bought from Janki Das today.'

This was a godsend - Rahul wanted a moment with the boy. He followed him upstairs to see the cricket bat and the rest. Made in India. Awful. But the conversation was made in heaven.

'So is your didi still furious?'

'As a matter of fact she is.'

'But with whom?'

'With you. Don't you know?'

'With me? But why?'

'That I don't know.'

Some time later, Rahul came down, alone. There were only two people in the vast drawing room - Sushma and Pithi looking at her oil paintings of hilly landscapes on the walls, their backs to the door. Humm. Rahul tiptoed away.

Dinner.

Dinner was chaos, lovely chaos. The great dining room was smiling - the chairs, the crockery, cutlery ... everything. Nobody knew where to sit on the very long table. In the end Ramakant and his wife sat in the middle facing the windows. Opposite them sat Prakash and Kamla with Sushma between them. Captain Pithi sat on Mrs Malhotra's right. Others fended for themselves. Rahul found himself at the bottom of the table sandwiched between Shobana and Bobby. This left Indira standing. There was no room for her. Nor a chair.

'Bobby!' Ramakant chided his son.

'Rahul!' Prakash scolded his. Both the boys leaped to their feet. But Ram appeared with a chair and squeezed it between Bobby's and Rahul's.

Rahul had read about it happening in novels. He had seen it happen in films. Now it was about to happen to him - the joining of thighs and legs and hands under the table - and there was a monumental uprising in his groin to prove it.

'Down, boy, down,' Rahul ordered. But nothing happened. Not even a miserly, fleeting accidental brushing. Nor a single glance at him. While everybody ate and talked and laughed the laughter of 'success of the special occasion', Saint Indira touched not a morsel, but she fumed a lot with her back always turned to him. This nearly persuaded Rahul to do ditto about food, but he saw no merit in being a martyr without a cause.

Dinner finally over, everybody marched into the great Malhotra garden. It was a carefully planned move by the lady of the manor to give Sushma and Pithi a few minutes to gaze at the stars from behind a wall of flower bushes. Ramakant Malhotra and his wife took Prakash Kapoor and Kamla for a walk around the garden. Padma led Shobana by the hand to the swing. Shoki, Bimbi and Bobby got involved in a discussion of great importance. Rahul and Indira found themselves staring at each other under a rhododendron behind the morning room.

'Why are you mad at me?'

'You made a total fool of me, sending me to the General Post Office.'

'You didn't?'

'Yes, I did.'

'What - to buy a poetic licence?' Rahul laughed. He laughed like a lunatic - so loudly, the rhododendrons shook. The other Kapoors hastened to see what the matter was and Indira flew away, a terrified bulbul. And Rahul got a mouthful from Shobana for his loutish laugh.

'Owl Rahul. Can't take you anywhere,' Shobana spoke with those eyes of hers. 'Breakfast is at eight,' she said.

SEVEN

Professor Lall didn't notice Rahul in the classroom. He lowered his glasses and raised his head when Rahul answered his number.

'Ah! The invalid is back with us then? Stand.'

Rahul stood up, colouring.

'Humm.' Professor Lall studied Rahul with interest, nodding to himself. 'To tell you the truth, it's done you good.'

'What has, sir?'

'Being ill. You look healthier now, if you ask me.'

Rahul coloured more. The Kapoor mercury rose.

'I don't recall asking you, sir.'

This didn't go down well with Professor Lall. But he chose to ignore Rahul's insolent reply.

'Must be the hostel air and water. It was the Teak Hotel, after all.'

Teachers. Did God have to make them? He made millions of species. Couldn't He cut this lot out?

'As a matter of fact, I was staying with my aunt at the Balmoral, sir.'

'Ah, the Balmoral. Did you know it is a famous castle in England?'

'Scotland, not England.'

'Same thing. Both in the UK.'

'No, it's not, sir.' For a fucking professor, this Lall knew fuck all.

'And did it occur to you to look at a book or books while you reposed in bed?'

'No. I mean, yes.'

'Which books?'

'A novel, sir. War and Peace.'

'Ah! You read it in one week!!'

'No, sir. I only looked at it, as you said.'

Loud sniggers said the class liked that. The teacher did not. He ground his jaws, knowing his moment was at hand.

'I see . . .' Professor Lall extended his study of this specimen of a rare species. 'When do you propose to fall ill again? I don't suppose you have taken a decision yet.'

Now Rahul's cheeks burned. His nostrils flared.

'I am very touched, sir, but why are you so interested in my health?'

Professor Lall exploded. 'It's not your physical health I'm interested in, you brainless arrogant fool. It's your mental health which is cracking up. Next time around, read books that concern you. Not novels. Novels are for idlers. Sit.'

'Fancy reading the Swiss Constitution with a thermometer in your mouth,' Rahul groaned. The class laughed and Professor Lall gave the specimen the dirtiest look in the teaching profession.

'Insolence will take you far in life. SIT. Number Nineteen . . .' He went on with the rollcall. Rahul remained standing. Professor Lall stopped.

'Unfair to treat a member of the class like this, sir. It's demeaning. I had done nothing nor said anything till you provoked me.'

'Hear, hear,' shouted ten boys.

'Apology. Apology,' hissed another ten.

'Number Twenty . . .' Professor Lall went on.

Rahul gathered his books in his hands and was about to storm out of the classroom. But something happened to him. He sat down.

Rahul fumed all day - his first day back at college. But he had the class's support - apology, apology. That must have hurt Lall. Yet Rahul felt he had to get Lall out of his system, exorcise him.

Cricket! He wanted to hit the ball. Hard.

Come the afternoon, Rahul got changed for the net. Then he realised he was rather early. But he was restless. So he came out of the hostel. Now he felt foolish. He had nowhere to go. No, there was that mad bookshop on the Mall.

'I knew it,' said someone the moment he set foot in the shop. 'I knew we would meet again.'

'Hi.'

'I bet you've forgotten my name.'

'I bet you've forgotten mine.'

'I'm ashamed to say that I have.'

'Rahul. But I haven't forgotten yours, Lin.'

'I'm flattered. So how have you been keeping and behaving? Me, I've been good as a Peking duck, you might say.'

'And I have been reposing, relaxing and rewarding myself with pamperment by others.'

'I like that - pamperment. New word? Your invention? Put it here.' Lin laughed, his eyes narrowing to mere lines. The two had a good shake.

They spent twenty minutes looking around the treasure-house of words. Rahul bought a second-hand novel. Lin bought one too. But when it came to paying for them, Lin wanted to pay for both.

'But why?' Rahul was taken aback.

'Because I was here before you.'

'This is the barmiest thing I've ever heard of.'

'My pleasure.'

'Balls to your pleasure , Lin.'

'You can be as rude as you like. But you are not paying.'

The young men had a fierce wrestling match of words. The proprietor, gentle Mr Maria, watching, solved their problem.

'All right, boys. The books are yours.'

'WHAT?'

'A present from Uncle Maria. Now go and come back next time.'

'Uncle Maria, you want to liquidate yourself?'

'I said go. Go, go, go. Come back next time. I'll charge double.'

The boys went muttering:

'Crazy man.'

'Lovely man.'

Out on the Mall, Lin took Rahul's hand in his.

'Take tea together at Kwality sometime?'

'Why not now, Lin?' Rahul still had time.

'I'm taking Gran to the optician. She's going blind. Next time. So your cricket net is by the Ladies' Mile on Mount Jakhoo?'

Rahul didn't know that. He liked the name.

'Is there a Gentlemen's Mile somewhere?'

Lin laughed in answer and went away.

At the net, Rahul hit the ball hard and he sweated a lot. That got Lall out of his system. He said no to the daily dose of loafing on the Mall with his team-mates and went straight back to the hostel, where he was greeted not only by the mouthwatering whiffs of roasting garlic, but also the sounds of a sizzling row. The cook was on fire in the kitchen.

Rahul saw Mohmi coming down the stairs. The two ran to see why the cook was belching fire.

'Son of a hilly whore. How many times have I told you? How many?' Khansamah roared at Bahadar Singh, whacking him on the head. Bahadar raised his hand to cover his head. This drove the dragon insane - how dare he protect himself! 'Put your hand down. What's the matter with you? I'll tell you what the matter is with you. A donkey climbed on your mother and the result was you - Bahadar Singh best only for the worst,' he shouted.

'All right, Jhandoo,' Rahul yelled and took hold of the temperamental chef's hand. But Jhandoo's foot still found a target - the poor mundu's backside.

'How many times I not tell this hilly whoreson?'

'What did you tell him, Jhandoo?'

'That in the kitchen it is ten things at the same time. And he can't do one properly.'

'What has he done?'

'Am away fifteen minutes and he's burnt the masala for the meat, fucked up the gobi, and the dal is piss all. So what am I giving for dinner?'

'But Khansamah-ji . . .'

'And would you believe, Mohmi sahib, this hollow-head is getting a wife? And he can't fry masala properly.'

'It's unfair to treat him like this. Anyway, what's masala got to do with marriage?' Rahul said.

'A lot. If he can't do a simple kitchen thing well, how will he do that properly with his wife?'

'True, Bahadar? Are you getting hitched?'

Bahadar's fair face coloured.

'Speak, bandar-arse. Tell sahib when you are getting married.'

'Week today, sir sahib.'

'Personally, I'm already feeling sorry for the girl,' the cook went on.

'How old is she, Bahadar?'

'Sixteen, sir sahib.'

'This old cock of twenty-eight getting a girl nearly half his age,' grunted the cook.

'It's perfectly legitimate. Our boy is handsome.'

'Our boy is a fool, sahib.'

'Where is she from, Bahadar?'

'Mahasu, sahib. Fair as a princess, the beautiful bulbul.'

'Have you seen her?'

'Not yet.'

'Then how do you know?'

'Everybody says, sahib. The whole village.'

'And her father is the village headman, believe it or not, Kapoor sahib. Should have his head examined for giving his girl to this dunce head.'

'Stop it, Khansamah. Bahadar is a good boy.'

'Good boy, my arse. Sleeps all day, eats like a horse, thinks like a mule and acts like a donkey.'

'So you are getting a wife, eh? Are we invited to the wedding?' Rahul said.

Bahadar Singh looked down at his feet.

'Not nice, that, Bahadar Singh.'

'What use would it be, sahib sir? You wouldn't come anyway.'

'Why wouldn't we?'

'Because you are heavenly born and I a mere. . .'

This put Rahul and Mohmi to shame. Both realised for the first time that Bahadar was several years older than them and yet they still called him *mundu* - boy.

It was half twelve. Rahul was debating. A masala dosa at the tuck shop or lunch proper at the hostel? He saw Rishi hurrying towards him. Rishi wore a dull grey sweater and a bright dolphin grin on his mug - he obviously had something up his sleeve.

'You won't believe this,' he said.

'I am very gullible.'

'You are invited to a party.'

'By whom and where?'

'Does it matter?'

'As a matter of fact, yes.' Rahul had never been to a party in Simla. And a party was a party. So he didn't really care. 'But when?'

'Now. It's a lunch 3D is hosting to celebrate. He's been made the MD of his firm - Himachal Construction. I don't know what he sees in you, but he's insisted I bring you along.'

'Is it because I am my uncle's nephew?'

'I told him I was pulling your leg. And his. I think he fancies you.'

'You mean . . . ?'

'Yeah. I would let him have it.'

'Why don't you?'

'But 3D fancies you. He thinks you've got class. My arse. He needs glasses. Let's go.'

'What, this minute? Sounds like a shotgun invitation.'

'None of your smart-arsery, son. Let's go.'

The next lecture was at ten to three. So . . .

'But where are we going?'

Without answering him, Rishi took Rahul's hand in his and dragged him along. He stopped at the openfronted barbershop in Lakkar Bazaar under SCH. All the shop's four mirrors looked on to the roadside. Rishi pulled out his pocket comb and gave his hair a deft dab, inspecting himself in one.

'Squire, can I change into something decent? Can't turn up at the Clarke's in this gear.' Rishi spoke through clenched teeth and pulled Rahul up the slope to his hostel. In the borrowed finery of Rahul's blue suit and polka-dot tie, he brought him to the Clarke's half a mile away.

'Voila!' Rishi said, sounding triumphant.

Along with the Cecil and the Grand, Clarke's was the last of Queen Simla's top three hotels. Tourists didn't mind paying through their 'nose'n'arse' to stay here, as Rishi would put it. Not as expensive as the other two, the Clarke Hotel's front was a lot of delicate woodwork. Its back was all wall, a very high wall pock-marked with tens of windows. The party was being held in a part of the large dining room. Some thirty people, mostly men, stood around, drinking beer or Coca Cola. Rahul knew not a soul among them.

3D came and greeted them with his fearsome handshake, and said, 'Hello and welcome,' in response to their congratulations. He whispered a compliment in Rahul's ear with a strange look. Then, mercifully, he left them to circulate among his guests.

Beer arrived promptly. One glass. Then two. Then Rishi spotted someone he knew, none other than Bala-ji himself. Bala-ji looked unrecognisable in a brown striped suit and a paisley tie. It meant so much to the boys to meet someone they knew. Laughing their lungs out, they sat down at the edge of the party. The captain of Himachal Secretariat went over that historic win at Annandale the other day again and again, laughing. Suddenly, he shut up. He had seen something. In fct, he had seen a family of five arrive and sit at a nearby table, but away from the 3D party - Papa and Mama, two little girls and their big bosomy sister of eighteen. They all had a pinkish-greyish complexion. Mummy wore an elegant two-piece suit, the little girls flowery frocks and and Sweet Eighteen had on blue jeans and a polo-neck very heavenly. Eyes popped.

'Christians. From Bombay,' Rishi mumbled.

'How can you tell?' Bala-ji said.

'I can read tourists like an open guide-book.'

'What is the difference between a Bombay Christian and a Punjabi Christian?'

'Bombay Christians give,' Rishi winked.

Rahul became aware that the young girl's eyes were on him. Food, a feast. The 3D lunch got going with three dozen beer-loosened tongues wagging all at once.

'Oi, don't look at her too often.' Rishi nudged.

A little later, Rahul stole another glance and his heart missed a beat - the girl had smiled at him. He heard Bala-ji say, 'I say, Rahul, what magic have you done to the poor girl?'

'Son, smile back next time she looks.' Rahul did. Time passed. They ate and talked. Lunch was over at the other table and the girl rose, her eyes on Rahul.

'Son, follow her. Talk to her.'

'Maharishi Mull . . .' Rahul's knees!

'Go after her.'

'I can't.' He felt like Atom in that hall.

'Are you a man or a mouse? Move.'

'Yeah. Go. Move,' whispered Bala-ji.

Rahul moved, his heart pounding. He followed the girl to the long wooden balcony jutting out of the side of the hotel and overlooking the valley. The girl leaned against a wall to admire the Himalayan drama unfolded before them. The question was, did Rahul have the courage to speak to her? The answer was, he did not. 'Say something to her, Owl Rahul. Or turn back.' But that would make him look a fool - after all, she was there only for him.

Suddenly, the girl looked him straight in the eye.

'May I have your permission to speak to you?' he asked nervously.

'What do you want to say?'

Her eyes were blue-green.

'I just wanted to say hello.'

'Hello.'

'I'm at the Simla College here. I live in its hostel.'

'Oh. I'm from Bombay. I go to Saint Xavier's. It's lovely here.'

'Breathtaking.'

'So you are not from Simla. Where do you come from then?' The girl was fully in charge of the conversation.

'Solan.'

'Oh, that sleepy little town.'

Rahul felt apologetic. 'I'm afraid it is rather.'

'But it is a nice little town. I like it. We stopped at the Khalsa Hotel for tea. What's your name?'

'Rahul. Rahul Kapoor.'

'Betty. Betty Sinclair.'

'You have the most beautiful eyes I have ever seen.' Rahul hadn't meant to say that - they had only just met.

'You are the most beautiful boy in Simla I have seen.'

Rahul's heart missed a beat to hear her say that.

'What colour are they?' he said.

'What do you think?'

'Blue? Green? Blue-green?'

A little girl came running.

'Betty, Mummy wants you. We are going shopping.'

'Tell her I'm coming.' Betty sent her little sister back. 'Rahul, do you want to go for a walk?'

Rahul's heart stopped. What about his lecture?

'Wait here.' Betty left and Rahul looked at the valley, and the valley said, *forget the lecture*. Five minutes later, she was back. 'Where shall we go?'

'Where would you like to go?'

'Far from the madding crowd.' Betty laughed. Her laughter sounded like that of an old friend.

'We are reading it, would you believe?' Rahul said.

'So where then? Somewhere nice.'

'I know just the place.' Rahul did – Mohmi's beauty spot. 'It's bit of a walk. But you'll love it.'

'How do you know?'

'I guarantee you will.'

'What if I don't?'

'Then you can take out a law suit against me.'

Going to Mohmi's beauty spot meant going through the Mall, the Ridge and Lakkar Bazaar. Rahul would be seen and tongues would wag. But it was only half past two and the valley whispered, *Everybody is still at college, you will not be seen.*

By the Odeon cinema and the TIBET 200M milestone, a V2 rocket fell on Rahul - Professors Lall and Dyal in mufti today.

'Humm,' they said, walking past.

'Do you know these men?' Betty asked.

'Never seen them before in all my life.'

In Lakkar Bazaar a Panzer tank blocked his way Professor Nath talking to the barber. But he managed to tap Rahul on the leg with his walking stick, making it look like an accident.

'That lame man has no manners,' Betty said. 'Didn't even say sorry.'

'The lame man has lame manners.'

A hundred yards further, Rahul saw Eichman himself coming his way with Bormann - Cousin Moon hand-inhand with Meena Nath.

'Rahul, tell me the story of your life,' Betty said, and Rahul did a quick Eyes-Left to avoid eye-contact with his cousin. 'Are they from your college?'

'I don't know. I've only been here a few weeks.'

'They looked at you in a sort of curious way, as if they knew you.'

'Mistaken identity.' Rahul smiled as he imagined the grilling he would get when he met Moon again.

'Why do you smile?'

'Someone mistook me for a fruit vendor once.'

'That someone must be dim.'

'Actually she was a Colonel's daughter.'

'I hope the Colonel's brighter than his daughter, or God help us - what with the Chinese massing troops on our borders.'

Ajit and Deepak in full cricket kit passed, waving to Rahul.

'Cricket in Simla? Is there a mountain version of the game?'

The hill with a million Christmas trees.

The rhododendrons were loud in welcome, and rose bushes breathed on the valley an intoxicating perfume. The steep slope today was very slippery. More dry pine needles covered it, making it more dangerous. The question arose in Rahul's head - should he venture to take her hand in his to help? With the question rose something else in him, or rather in his fly. But would it not be taking advantage of a helpless girl in this savage setting?

The helpless girl solved the problem for him.

'It smells like Christmas,' Betty said, offering him her hand. Rahul had only to hold it in his and . . .

Down, boy, down. It was shame sweet shame.

Rahul didn't know Christmas had a smell. He had never celebrated Christmas. Only the holidays it brought.

'Gosh. How frighteningly deep is the gorge! What if we slip?'

'Shall we go back?'

'No. I want to see your famous beauty spot.'

At last they were there.

'Wow!' Betty put her other hand to her mouth.

'Are you still suing?'

They placed their lips onto the crack in the rock and drank the ice-cold water. Then they sat down on a rock. And very suddenly the colours of the valley changed. From very green, it became very dark as a dense grey cloud settled on it. It became cold and Betty shivered and edged closer to Rahul.

'I'm frightened. There's going to be a storm.'

'Looks like it. We should go back.' Rahul began to feel guilty - he never should have brought her here. What an idea.

'Yes, let's go back.' But Betty didn't make any effort to move. Instead, she leaned over and placed her head on his shoulder. 'You've been drinking.'

'I had a glass of beer. I am sorry.'

'I don't mind. You know, when I saw you I knew I had to get to know you. Didn't you?'

'Two hundred per cent.'

'It was sort of fated.'

'Divinely ordained.'

'What a shame we are going back tomorrow.'

'You are not.' Rahul's heart - it fluttered like a bird. An urge rose in him to put his arms around her. But that would be taking advantage.

'You are very quiet.'

'Am I?' Rahul took a deep breath.

'I bet those girls fancied you, those two. Look.'

There was a blinding flash followed by a deafening roar. Betty clung to Rahul for her life. The heavens broke open.

'Run.' Rahul took her hand and ran to a dent in the rock-face. It was a six-foot-wide hollow, a perfect shelter. Lightning struck again, and thunder shook the valley and then the waters came - loud and thick and fast. It was like standing behind a waterfall, a fast-slipping curtain of liquid glass.

'Oh, my God!' Rahul said.

'Can't hear a thing.' Betty put her arms around his neck and nestled her ear at his lips. 'What did you say?'

'I said Oh my God.' Rahul pressed her into him. He had taken advantage, shameful advantage. He felt ashamed of himself. Betty turned her face into his. Their lips touched and Rahul went berserk. He shut his eyes and sucked her lips. It was pulverising. His hands were now inside her polo-neck. This was exploitation at its worst. The poor girl was in his hands, at his mercy in this jungle wild. And he was behaving in this most unnameable way. He wanted to withdraw his hands. But how could he when her own hands had found their way inside his shirt? And now they were travelling down. Soon . . . And the rain fell.

The rain still fell, a mere spray now, when Rahul left Betty at the Clarke's. He ran the moment they parted. He had lost that which he had been dying to lose. He should have been over the moon and on the way to the next heavenly body. In one way he was. In another, he was ashamed of himself - he had taken advantage.

Rahul ran on urgently. At Scandal Point, he took the Upper Mall and hurried on towards Green Gables. He stopped only when he came to the temple. Here, he covered his head with a handkerchief, got out of his shoes and went in. The small statue of Krishna today was lit by a tiny earthen lamp at His feet amidst some flowers, an astonishingly beautiful sight. Rahul had five ten-rupee notes on him, nearly a fortnight's mess bill. He pulled them out from his pocket, placed them on the flowers and hung his head in shame.

'You aren't really sorry, are you?' Krishna said.

The fire of shame still burning in him, Rahul walked out. At the popular paan booth by Scandal Point stood Rishi. Rahul didn't want to see Rishi. Not just now. Not for some time. Pretending he hadn't seen him, he hurried to the Ridge.

'How did it go, son?' Rishi ran and caught up with him. Rahul did not answer. Words had dried up in him.

'Somethig happened, son? Something bad?'

Asking Rahul questions was useless. But Rishi being Rishi, he persisted.

'Her father had you beaten up? What happened?'

'I took advantage of an innocent girl.'

'What? You fucked her? Come on - tell Dad what happened and how.'

Rahul did. Rishi laughed and laughed, loudly, thumping Rahul hard enough to break his back.

'You didn't fuck her, you peacock prick. The nympho fucked you.' Rishi took his hand and ran.

'Where are you taking me?'

'Think with your pea brain. And hope the fucking temple pundit hasn't got there before us.'

At the temple, Rishi kicked off his shoes and darted in. Next moment he darted out.

'Serves you fucking right.' Rishi was empty-handed.

Rahul tossed in agony all that night, reliving the rainy afternoon. Everything had happened so fast. He wished he had had some control over what had occurred. Betty had to get back. That and his guilt had made him bring her back to Clarke's as soon as he could - in silence. Now he wished he had talked, exchanged addresses. What a fool! What must she think of him?

'Here you had a Bollywood-Hollywood prize in the palm of your hand and you let it go, you peacock prick . . .' Rahul soared through the night with an erection so hard, it hurt. 'You peacock prick.'

A four-page letter came from home. Its authors were Mummy, Shobana, Bimbi and Shoki. They all said the same thing. Daddy had approved of Sushma. Pithi had accepted her. The letter ended in a telegram-style PS in Pithi's hand.

CHINAMAN BOWLS A GOOGLY. LEAVE
CUT SHORT. BIG HUGS FROM SOLDIER
IN HURRY. LOVING BRUV P.

Front pages had begun speaking seriously of Chinese troop concentration on the NEFA border. Its timing was baffling. Its scale - several divisions - threatening. New Delhi requested an explanation. Peking said it was a matter of national security. At an NCC parade that afternoon, Rahul felt a commotion inside him.

'China's never won a war. It won't fight. So have no fears about your brother,' said Captain Sethi, the NCC supremo.

After the net, Rahul bumped into the Malhotras on the Mall. 'What news from Solan?' they asked.

Rahul told them. A look of mortal fear overcame Mrs Malhotra. 'Hanuman maharaj!' she appealed to the Monkey God, folding her hands towards the Jakhoo peak.

'Chou En Lai is bluffing. He is testing us. So don't worry, rani. And why haven't you been to see us, Rahul? Do you need anything?' Mr Malhotra said. He pulled out a few ten-rupee notes from his wallet and tried to push them into Rahul's top pocket. Rahul stepped back, throwing his hands up. 'All right, then. Come to drink tea on Sunday, OK?' the well-meaning man said, moving on.

Rahul stood opposite Lajpat Rai's statue, holding the wooden railing and looking down at the darkening valley below. Someone came and thumped him on the shoulder - Lin.

'Eating the good Simla air? Eat, eat, eat. It's free. The only thing in Simla that is. Everything else has a big price-tag.'

'I am going back to the hostel to eat dinner. I'm starving.'

'Come and eat with me at home.' Lin took his hand and led him to a Chinese shoe shop with a large glass front by the Fire Station, one of several on the Mall. 'Wait here a sec. I'm just checking to see if Dad wants anything.'

Once back, Lin led Rahul down the steep road going to the Novelty cinema. Lin lived above Hotel Blessington in a long two-storey building with a wooden veranda. He ushered him into a pleasant room with a large painted mural of the Great Wall of China snaking over mountains.

'Back in a sec,' Lin said and left him again.

Minutes passed, but Lin did not come back. Rahul picked up books; he put them back. There was a Murphy radio set. Rahul turned it on. It didn't work.

Some time later, Rahul got this funny feeling he was being watched. It was just a feeling. There were two doors. One opened to the veranda. The other had a curtain. Then he noticed the curtain ripple as if a gust of breeze had breathed on it. Rahul saw a doll-like face. It belonged to a girl of around fifteen. She ran away as their eyes met.

'Sorry, sorry, sorry.' Lin came back. He carried a tray with two bowls of hot water and two Chinese spoons. Hot water? Chinese hospitality! It turned out to be a clear soup. Rahul had never eaten a soup so delicious. He told his friend so.

'Tell me about your country,' Rahul said.

'This is my country. I am Indian and I love it.'

'I thought China was your country.'

'Never been there. My parents neither. I was born here, in this house. Never been beyond Tara Devi.'

Lin went away with the empty bowls. He returned with boiled rice and two dishes - chicken with cashew nuts and round, black slippery mushrooms on a bed of boiled cabbage leaves and soy sauce. Rahul did not know cabbages could taste so divine. Nor anything cooked without spices. This was by far the most delicious meal he had ever eaten. Again he saw the curtain ripple.

They had just finished eating when an old lady came in. She was almost bald, with a few strands of long hair pressed down carefully. She wore thick glasses and carried herself with dignity. She spoke perfect English. And she giggled.

'Grandma, this is my friend Rahul. He liked your cooking.'

'An understatement. I loved it.'

'You did?' Grandma giggled. She took a good look at Rahul and sat down. It was clear she liked him. She also liked to talk. She talked.

'Most of the Chinese people of Simla came here during the Second War. But we came here soon after the First, and ours was the first Chinese shoe shop in Simla. We came from Calcutta. In the year 1919. In the month of April. India was in a turmoil. It was on strike. Every city. At Gandhi's orders. Punjab was the worst. In Gujranwalla and Multan, Governor O'Dwyer had aeroplanes drop bombs and fire machine guns. Law and order had broken down. But Hindus and Muslims were one - like this.' Grandma clenched a fist. 'The government of the English was afraid it was about to lose India.

'Then General Reginald Dyer fired bullets in Amritsar on the thirteenth. He shot thirteen hundred innocent protestors at Jallianwalla Bagh. Curfew was imposed on Punjab. The Raj was saved. Church bells rang on Simla Ridge. There were balls here every night to celebrate. You should have seen. Balls and dinners and fetes. Though it was not the season proper yet.

'But Simla had always been a swinging city. The Indian Mount Olympus, the Capua of India as they called it. A mountain of celebration. Of music, dance, drink and bubbles of joy. When the Englishman and his mem went to a ball or to a moonlit picnic party, they forgot that they were married.

'You see, I was governess to Mr and Mrs Hodson's daughter Abigail. One night there was this big Bachelor Knights and Black Hearts Ball at Peterhoff. I dressed Mrs Hodson, a lady so radiant, chandeliers dimmed when she entered a room. She was so fair, you could see red wine going down her throat.'

'Oh, Grandma!' Lin burst out into a splutter of laughter. 'You are such a liar. You shame me before my friend.'

But Grandma wasn't listening.

'They went. She in a rickshaw pulled by hillmen with the Hodson crest on their chests and he on the back of this beautiful but unruly mare, Begum. At two a.m Mr Hodson came back. Alone. And drunk. He took his revolver and remounted Begum. He never got to where he was heading to do what he was intending to do. For Begum threw him into a deep ditch, head first. Murder was prevented. But there was a funeral nonetheless, attended by all Simla. Poor Elizabeth. She was devastated. But she recovered. Three months later, she re-married.

'Then I was with Mr and Mrs Singleton. They had separate bedrooms. Mr Singleton was sixty, a rich box wallah. He drank. One bottle of Scotch every evening if there were no guests, more if there were, and Mrs Singleton liked having guests every other night. He ate little at dinner. At eleven he left the guests and came and sat on the veranda, looking at the valley, a man asleep with his eyes open. An hour later, the khansamah and the khitmatgar carried him to bed. And Mrs Singleton was in the party, laughing, with a glass of champagne in one hand and the cigarette holder in the other. She was forty. She was beautiful. She didn't drink, but she took champagne when Major Rodgers came. He was often the last of the guests to leave. Sometimes he didn't leave at all, but only the staff knew of that. And Mr Singleton snored upstairs. Late one night it rained very heavily and the roof of his room sprang a bad leak - Simla has always been a city of leaks. Water fell thick and fast like from a drain. It fell directly on his face and Mr Singleton woke up. He took out his Purdy from the case and went to his wife's chamber and shot them both. Then a third shot was heard - Mr Singleton had put the nozzle of the gun in his mouth. We ran up to see. Lying by Mrs Singleton was not Major Rodgers, but Captain Hardy who was new to Simla.'

'Grandma, you should write a book about Simla. It'll sell like hot samosas,' Lin laughed.

'Oh, the things I know,' Grandma said, and as she giggled again, her slit eyes narrowed to a line and Rahul thought she looked like a naughty little girl with a million wrinkles. Grandma stood up to go. 'But it changed suddenly. And all fun stopped,' she said, her smile disappearing.

'How? When?' Rahul said.

'When Mountbatten came. In '47,' Grandma said and sat down again. 'Simla became world news. Not for flirtation, but for India's future. It was being decided here. The Cripps Mission a year before had failed. Attlee had sent Mountbatten to sort things out for Independence. He called Nehru and Jinnah here to talk, to keep India united. I saw Nehru riding a horse on the Mall, a rose in the buttonhole of his achkan, looking beautiful, and I fell in love with him. I saw Jinnah in a starched white suit and co-respondent shoes, dreadful shoes - our shoes are much better, more tasteful - in a rickshaw, looking dry and stuffy like his suit and I fell in hate with him. My God! It was something. You should have seen. The contrast. They disagreed to agree. Simla loved Mountbatten. It loved Nehru. Even the English loved him, believe it or not. And now he wants to wage a war against us. I can't believe it.'

'Grandma, Pandit Nehru doesn't want war. It's your Chou En Lai who wants to invade us, eat up our land the size of England, Grandma.'

Lin's father and uncle came in at this point. With them were two other Chinese men. They were all pale-skinned, short, small-boned and gentle-looking, with quiet faces. So this was the kind of opposition his six-foot brother and his seven-foot Sikh warriors would be fighting if it came to that. Rahul felt sorry for the Chinese. He hoped it wouldn't come to that.

It was time for him to go. He stood up and happened to see the curtain ripple again. And he had another fleeting glimpse of that doll-face.

'Lunch with me tomorrow, Lin?' Rahul was free in the afternoon.

'I'm taking Gran to Snowdown tomorrow. How about the day after?'

That was fine. Rahul had Lall then. He would bunk off and serve Lall right.

Being a Thursday - Lord Hanuman's day - the hostel lunch was strictly vegetarian. Veg, dal, and chapattis. It was humble. Rahul felt embarrassed, but Lin said, 'Fingerlicking,' and Rahul thought maybe it was, for a Chinese. This made him feel better. That feeling flew out of the window, however, the moment he saw the 'sewage rats' walk in.

There were only half a dozen lunchers around, First Years all. The 'rats' first bowed to Rahul with the grace of a Lucknow nawab, to Lin after, smiling like watermelons sliced in two. Then they went and sat down at the far side of the very long table.

Rahul's temples began to throb with a mixture of fear and anger. But Kumar and Mahendru ate quietly without once looking at Rahul.

The meall over, Rahul took his guest to the Odeon to see a Hindi oldie-goldie, an all-time great weepie *Do Bigha Zamin* with Balraj Sahni. The packed hall sobbed throughout the film. The two friends also cried their lungs out. But they burst out laughing as they stepped into the light of day, thumping each other on the back.

'Guess what?' Lin said.

'What?'

'She's fallen in love.'

Rahul nearly stumbled. Did he mean . . .? But Rahul couldn't permit himself to think further.

'She who?'

'Grandma.'

'Who with?'

'With you, you fool. Who else?'

'Tell her me too.'

'And she says you have to come to eat what she's cooking tomorrow after your net. Now don't say no or she'll rap my knuckles. You don't know her.'

They embraced and parted company. The thought of another Chinese meal put Rahul on the aeroplane to the Land of Delights. When you live in a boys' hostel, the prospect of a home-cooked meal is nearly as delicious as the thing itself. Rahul wished tomorrow was today. Or vice versa.

The second Chinese meal out-excelled his first.

'Guess what we are eating, Rahul?'

'I can't, Lin.'

196

'Chicken feet.'

'What a treat.'

'And guess what this thing is?'

'Chinese baby chicken?'

'How strong is your constitution? It's frogs' legs. Simla frogs caught by guess who.'

'Grandma, I'm coming again. Every day.'

'Come again. Every day.'

'Now tell us more Simla stories.'

Rahul didn't want to leave. But he had a pain-in-thebackside essay to hand in tomorrow. Otherwise, Professor Nath would boil his balls like Grandma had boiled chicken feet. At nine he rose and again saw that curtain ripple, and again he had a fleeting glimpse of that doll-face.

Outside, the magic mountain glittered with starry lights. The air was fresh and clear and the steel-blue sky a riot of luminous pinpoints. It was going to be a cold night.

Rahul turned up the collar of his jacket and began the climb to the Jakhoo Mountain, feeling at one with the mountain - he had struck a gem of a friendship. Rahul hadn't gone ten paces when a little rock hit him on the back. A shout followed:

'TRAITOR!'

EIGHT

Hollywood hit Simla. *Psycho* came to town. The ticket queue for the opening Sunday morning show stretched from the Odeon to the barber's shop. Simla College was its star. The hostel alone occupied a length the size of a cricket pitch.

Professor Nath and Captain Sethi were seen walking up. The former slapped his forehead in disgust on spotting his hostel boys. The latter shook his head gravely, similarly overcome.

'I am ashamed of you boys,' Professor Nath said.

'Why, sir?' SCH was shocked - what did the old fool mean?

'Why? Why?' Professor Nath was beside himself.

'Sir, it's no ordinary film. It's Psycho.'

'So?'

'And it is Hitchcock's. His masterpiece.'

'Who's he?'

'Never heard of Hitchcock? Sir!' SCH cried in pity.

'Never. And have you heard of the McMahon Line?'

Only Rahul and Rajkumar Chuba Ao had. The McMahon Line was the boundary line between India and China. 'And of Thagla Ridge in NEFA?' No one had heard of Thagla Ridge either, except these two.

'Go and paint your faces black.' Professor Nath slapped his forehead again. His disgust was profound. It was etched with painful clarity on his otherwise handsome face. He unfolded the newspaper he carried. Its headlines howled:

CHINESE CROSS MCMAHON LINE
THAGLA RIDGE TAKEN
7 Brigade Ordered to Throw Them Back

Gory details followed of a surprise attack by a large Chinese force. A heavily outnumbered Indian position had suffered heavy casualties. There were maps with dotted lines and arrows.

'Shame on you, boys - enjoying yourselves while your brothers are dying. You should be queuing outside the recruitment centre.'

'Not to worry, sir. The Chinese are yellow, garrison soldiers. One look at our Sikh seven-footers and they'll press their tails between their legs and run to Peking,' Atom said.

'Kapoor, isn't your brother with the Seventh Brigade?' Captain Sethi asked.

Rahul didn't reply. As the two men moved on, Rahul, a lump rising in his throat, realised he wouldn't be seeing Hitchcock's masterpiece after all. He slipped out of the queue.

Rahul took a disused pagdandi pathway. Remote and smothered by thorny bushes, it was dangerously steep. Nobody ever used it for those reasons, only the monkeys. But feeling as he did with that lump in his throat, he preferred it to the usual way.

Halfway up, he saw the 'sewage rats' coming down the same pagdandi. Rahul had known all along that something like this would happen sooner or later. He had mentally prepared himself for it. But now that it was about to happen, he felt the earth slip from under his feet in fear. There was an alternative - he could make a run for it. But that Rahul could not do. He was a Kapoor.

'Welcome, Mrs Kumar. At last,' Mahendru said.

'A hearty welcome, Mrs Mahendru,' Kumar said.

The eyes of the two had widened with lust. Their faces were lit with disbelief at their good luck. They had found Rahul in jungle thick and desolate. The pair bowed like Lucknow aristocrats.

'Let bygones be bygones,' cooed Mahendru. 'Forgive us for our past mistakes. To err is human, to forgive divine. Let's start afresh.'

'You see, Rahul, we love you. It's only human that we do. Nothing wrong in that. True love.'

'And we have loved you from the moment we saw you,' Mahendru went on.

'Be ours, Rahul. We'll love and cherish you. My money order came from home yesterday. So here's the fifty we promised.' Kumar pulled out five crisp tenners from his pocket and held them out.

'So let's have a quiet ceremony. This place is just right. Mount Jakhoo can be our Best Man. What do you say? Just say "I do",' Mahendru purred.

'We'll have a poetic honeymoon here in nature wild and beautiful.'

Rahul picked up a stone the size of a cricket ball and aimed it hard at middle stump - Kumar's face. The rat ducked.

'Rahul, darling boy, you don't understand.'

A smaller rock got the bastard in the side.

'Come with us like a good Indian wife - willingly.'

'We don't want to force ourselves on you.'

'Of course we don't. Never.'

Saying that, Kumar leaped across to Rahul and took his right elbow in an arm-lock. Mahendru jammed him against the mountain face. Rahul was done for.

'Let go, you bastards,' he screamed.

It was only when they tripped him down to the ground and tried to pull his trousers off that something happened to Rahul. A sudden surge of adrenalin transformed him into an engine of strength unknown to him. In a single movement, he pushed the two rapists away, landing a full-blooded blow on Kumar's left jaw.

'Son of a Solan whore,' Kumar yelled as he and Mahendru fell on Rahul. Rahul was struck in the shoulders. As he reeled back, there came a violent push of four hands and Rahul fell. Then came the rain of kicks.

The drop from the path was sheer. If pushed off it, Rahul would go rolling down to a rocky bed fifteen feet below. Rahul's only thought now was to prevent himself being pushed off the track, his head hitting naked rock, followed by a cracked skull and certain death. But his enemies didn't seem interested in having his skull opened up. Their only aim now was to keep him down and do to him what they were determined to do. They were no longer humans. They had become beasts in the vice-like grip of the vilest of instincts. Their transformation was sudden because they knew that luck was on their side today - the time and place were right to quench their murderous thirst. It was not now or never. It was now.

As boots of hate and lust rained on him, Rahul caught a foot and twisted it with all the force he possessed plus that extra amount generated by the extraordinary circumstance. The result was that the owner of the foot, Kumar, fell on him. In an it's-either-you-or-me struggle for life and death, Kumar got pushed off the path. Rahul's hands now caught hold of Mahendru's right foot. In the same struggle for life, Rahul gave it a twist. Maybe he twisted it a bit too fiercely. Rahul had no idea that by doing so, he was sending Mahendru the way of his accomplice. He stood up and looked down the precipice and saw two cracked skulls and blood.

What had Rahul done? It was serious what he had done, very serious. But it was done in self-defence.

Rahul's lips were cut. His face and head throbbed with pain. His ears rang with noise. His eyes were wide open in an empty stare. Rahul sat behind bushes to think. He thought and thought - what to do? Then he knew what – he must go to the police station and confess. What about his family? More than for himself, Rahul felt sorry for them. So sorry, it made him numb. He could think no more.

SCH mess was shut and the hostel almost empty, everybody having gone out for their Sunday lunch. Reaching his room, Rahul emptied a bucket of ice-cold water on himself in his English bathroom. He dressed again, this time in his favourite navy suit, the one he had worn to Simla on his first day and which Rishi had returned only yesterday.

He was leaving his room for the last time in his life and he wanted to look his best, like a true Kshatriya warrior going to the battlefield, knowing full well he wouldn't be coming back.

He had been forced to do what he had done. Now it was up to the forces of society to do what they would to him. Would it mean a life sentence in prison or a hanging even? India believed in capital punishment. The police station on Cart Road was only half a mile downhill. Then . . . it didn't matter any more. Nothing did. Nothing at all. Nothing mattered at all.

Rahul left his room for the last time.

Rahul did not want to see anyone from SCH on his way down. Fortunately, he did not run into anyone known to him till he reached the police station, where he asked to see the Superintendent. Only an Inspector aged about thirty was on duty. Rahul went straight to the point.

'Sir, I have a confession to make.'

'Of what sort?'

'It's rather serious, sir.'

'Is it? Tell us then what you've done. Firstly, what's your name? What caste are you? Father's name? What does he do? Speak.'

Rahul spoke.

It was the young man's English. The inspector gave him a long hard stare. High caste. Upper class. Well brought up. Well educated. Highly agitated. The policeman knew how to sum up people with one look. He summed up the tortured man in front of him.

'You sure, Rahul Kapoor?'

'Yes, sir. Or I wouldn't be here.'

'I think we'd better look into this - visit this spot of double murder. I shall take you with me instead of putting you inside. Tejpal, jeep,' the man shouted.

'Yes, sir,' came the reply from an open door.

Next instant, the Inspector and his driver, two police constables and Rahul were on their way. Motor traffic on the Simla Mall was forbidden. So they went via Cart Road and up the steep Lakkar Bazaar and the steeper climb to the old Teak Hotel. Rahul's ears burned, ringing deafeningly:

DOUBLE MURDER! DOUBLE MURDER!

Mourning his own end, his heart racing, head throbbing, Rahul had no feeling. Only:

DOUBLE MURDER! DOUBLE MURDER!

At last, the jeep came to a halt in front of the SCH porch. But lo and behold, who should Rahul see on the hostel veranda?

The very two wild rats he had killed.

They were admiring the stupendous view! There was not a trace of blood on their faces nor a hint of guilt for what they had tried to do to Rahul - rape him. They chose not to look at Rahul.

Rahul coloured deeply, crushed by shame for wasting valuable police time. But the Inspector was a man with a heart. He had known the truth all along anyway.

'Best use of time, closing the shortest criminal case of my career. So, it's no jail. Only a free ride back for you. Not bad, that, eh?' The man with a heart knew all about boys' brawls.

It was astonishing that no one other than those two had seen what otherwise would have been the scandal of the century, a police jeep at SCH!

The empty shell began to resound with life. The day of shock and horror had also been one of disbelief. But instead of a feeling of triumph, shame engulfed Rahul. Why? He didn't know. It also made him feel desperately lonely. Walking away from the hostel again, he started crying. He cried and cried without knowing why he was crying. Then he started walking downhill again because that was how the road track was constructed.

Down on the Mall, Rahul put a hand in his pocket and found a piece of paper with Rishi's address on it, somewhere below the Middle and Lower Bazaars. Rishi hadn't once asked him home for a meal or something. This was odd. The first thing Indians do after meeting you and the how-do-you-do is say, 'Come to dinner tomorrow.' And Rahul had known him for how long? It seemed from the cradle.

A broad flight of stone steps led down to the Middle Bazaar from the Gaiety Theatre on the Mall. There were rows of cloth shops and grain shops and spice shops and bookshops and toy shops and shoe shops and other shops, punctuated by dungheaps. Open sewers flowed under the thresholds of the shops, with leaking drainpipes adding their contents from latrines, bathrooms and kitchens. Houses above and below them seemed to elbow each other down the steep slope. It was a miracle that they still stood there, and had for decades.

At the far end of the Lower Bazaar, Rahul stopped at a wooden shack to ask for directions. The shop was clogged with sacks full of flour, rice and dals, chilli powder, haldi, hing and other spices. The man had tied a piece of white cloth around his nose and mouth like a Jain monk. He spoke through it and pointed to a flight of rather steep steps leading further down towards Cart Road.

'First door on second floor of that third building.'

Rahul couldn't believe the twins lived here, in this gutterland, Simla's 'runny nose'. They dressed like lords and spoke lordly English.

'You sure, Lala-ji?'

For no reason, the man's neighbours from the right and left - the oil merchant and a cobbler joined them. They looked at Rahul as if he was a curiosity, a foreigner. Rahul felt that he was indeed a foreigner. He and they were one and the same people. But there were crucial differences. Their ancestors two thousand years before Christ had emerged from different parts of the body of their God. The twice-born high-caste Kshatriya warrior-kings had come from His arms. The others had made their appearances in this world from the God's lower parts – His middle, legs and feet.

The grainseller removed his Jain-monk's mask, revealing a mouthful of sparkling white teeth.

'It's those two you want, the Mull boys, no? They are good lads with good hearts, but they have a cruel stepmother who won't give them food. India. Our Mother India.'

Rahul took those stairs and found himself on a long wooden balcony somewhat like his hostel veranda.

'Rishi,' he called out.

Rahul heard loud shouting from a room. An old woman in white lay on a charpoy bed inside the dark interior. She was yelling:

'Snakes will bite you. You will burn in hell. All you want is my son in your crutch. You want me dead. You want his sons dead so that you can stuff the faces of your own. Why don't you take the gun from the almari and shoot me?'

Rahul had come at the wrong time. He should turn back. 'Rishi,' he shouted again.

'I gave this whore everything. All my gold, all my heera moti. And look how she treats me now in my hour of need.'

Did Rahul understand what was going on? He thought he did. Maybe not. Then he saw a face at a window of the adjoining room, that of a young girl.

'Rishi,' Rahul shouted for the third time, making eye-contact with the face at the window. The girl said with her look: *Can't you see we have problems? Go away*. Rahul went away.

Once again, Rahul had left it too close for comfort. He had to hand in another pain-in-the-arse essay tomorrow at noon or Dragon Dyal would roast him alive. He had had a whole week, but Rahul hadn't written a word yet. It was 7 p.m now and he was still eating the air on the Mall.

Rahul walked arm-in-arm with Balbir and Rajkumar Chuba Ao. They were heading for India Coffee House to round off the evening with a cup. At the 'world famous' Gaiety Theatre which had lit up English Simla's naughty summer nights in days gone by, classmate Mohan came lumbering up the steps from Middle Bazaar. He thumped Rahul's back in greeting.

'Just done Dyal's torture.' Mohan had a look about him which said he had been inside for a year. 'Seen the Twinnies? Haven't for days.'

'Think of the devil.' Balbir pointed a long finger.

And there they were too, coming down the Mall. Between them walked two middle-aged ladies of some girth and foreign looks.

'The ladykillers of Simla. Captains of our tourist industry with their khana-peena nourishment and pocket money for a week or two.' Mohan said what everybody knew.

The twins stopped. Rishi did the intros:

'Dashing Mohan, cricket star Rahul, Rajkumar Chuba Ao of NEFA and college heart-throb Balbir from Kashmir. Bertha and Ludmila.'

The four men bowed to the ground. The ladies were charmed. They smiled graciously and moved on. Rishi looked back.

'Stop farting around with these time-wasting loafers, Solan,' he shouted at Rahul in Punjabi. 'Go and write Dyal's obituary.'

'So you can come and copy it?' Mohan barked.

But this did it for Rahul. Without a word, he set off back to the hostel. From the Ridge, Rahul half ran. At exactly the spot where once he had nearly been torn apart by the red-faced landlords of Mount Jakhoo, he saw something that made his heart race. Two waif-like girls were coming down a wild and lonely side-track. Close behind them walked two goonda louts, one of them huge in size. They were making dirty talk loudly and trying to snatch the girls' dupatta breast scarves, unaware of Rahul, it being very dark.

'The one on the right is mine.'

'The other one will do nicely for me, thank you.'

'Don't make pulp of her under your weight.'

This sort of lewd-mouthing was called eve-teasing, and was a serious offence. But in that wilderness it could become a serious crime. The evening had turned sinister.

The girls quickened their pace when they saw Rahul. It meant help of a sort. The men fell back, but they continued with their filthy mouthing. Rahul moved fast. In the dim streetlight he thought he had seen one of the girls somewhere - he couldn't quite tell when or where. But it didn't matter. For the girls, his appearance was a godsend. They started running towards him.

Rahul roared: 'POLICE! POLICE! POLICE!'

Frightened by Rahul's bellowing, the goondas slid down the densely wooded slope and disappeared in the pitch-black foliage. It took a minute for the frightened girls to recompose themselves. Then Rahul walked them down to the safety of the well-lit Ridge. There was hustle and bustle here. The girls were grateful. They hurried away. Only after they had gone did Rahul realise he was quivering.

Reaching the dark huddle of the hostel, he had a quick bite and dashed upstairs. Once in his room, he changed into his 'battle dress' - pyjamas - and sat down at his table. By nine he had the first draft, all one thousand words of it. He didn't like what he'd written so he tore it up and began again. An hour later, he had another draft and thought he had got it right this time. There was a knock on his door. It was Atom. Rahul gave him his essay to read. Atom lay down on his bed and read it in five minutes flat.

'Not bad for someone with a pea brain.'

Rahul read his essay again and tore it up again.

'Why did you do that?'

Rahul shrugged and sat down to start again. He was still only halfway through when there was a tap tap tap on his window. The twins. They stood on the balcony. Rahul knew why. Rishi had come to copy his essay.

'I've come to borrow something,' Rishi said.

He already wore one of Rahul's jackets. Rahul was not lending him any more clothes, not even a sock.

'It wouldn't be something to wear by any chance?' Atom said.

'As a matter fact, yes. But not clothes.'

The twins looked different from the way they had on the Mall earlier. They looked glum. Something was the matter. Was it cash they were after?

'We've come to borrow two cricket boxes.'

'What? Having a midnight cricket match on the Ridge then?' Atom said.

'We need them for the morning.' Rishi opened Rahul's wardrobe. Rahul being the cricket captain, it was always stuffed with cricket gear. Rishi pulled out a couple of brand new abdomen guards and put one over his trousers.

'How do I look?'

209

'Irresistible. You must go to college like this tomorrow and see the result. A mass female fainting fit.'

'Can we or can't we borrow them, Kaptaan?'

'Only if you tell me what for.'

'No questions. If you really want to know, meet us under Gandhi's statue on the Ridge at eight thirty in the morning,' Kishi said.

'As a matter of fact, I would like to know.'

'Me too,' Atom said.

'Then be there. Eight thirty on the dot.'

'A bit early, Mr Wicket-keeper. No?' Atom said.

'I have a brilliant idea,' Rishi said. 'Why don't we sleep here tonight? We can talk late and go together in the morning. The four of us.'

Rishi's logic was irresistible. He helped Atom bring his bed into Rahul's room. Rahul knew that version three of his essay would not get completed tonight. So be it.

The four slept two to a charpoy, Rahul's essay-writing postponed. They rose early next morning and left SHC just before eight thirty. It was furiously cold. The mist clung to Simla like a possessive mistress. Visibility was poor. It was not cricketing weather.

From above the Ridge, the twins took the Ladies' Mile on Mount Jakhoo that led to the Himachal Secretariat. Rahul and Atom followed.

'Where to, Mr Mull sahib?' puzzled Prince Atom asked. 'The suspense is pulling my balls apart.'

'We said no questions. So no questions.'

A few minutes later, they stopped at a sharp bend in the road. Below them was spread the whole of Simla in a sea of woolly mist. Rishi selected a boulder the size of a bus to sit on. They watched men on their way to the Secretariat.

'What the fuck?' Rahul, too, had run out of steam.

'Wait and see. Not long to go now.'

Two familiar figures cut the bend in the mountain road. They were Cowdrey and his 'best man' Joshi. They lived near there and were on their way to the college. Old enemies, it seemed, Rishi and Kishi jumped down and blocked their way.

'Cowdrey, your innings is over,' Rishi growled. 'Yours too, fatso Joshi.'

'Oh yaar? What are you going to do, Mr Mull-Mull?'

'You wanted to be College President, cheapo? You will be, after we've beaten you into the shape of a peacock's arse. A President peacock's arse.'

'Oh yaar? What, four against two?'

'No, Prince Atom and Rahul will spectate while we do some wicket-keeping on your faces,' Kishi said.

The two men moved fast. They rammed their heads into the twins' midriffs. Then they went for the ultimate, their balls.

'This whoreson is wearing something,' cried fatso Joshi.

'This bastard too,' yelled Cowdrey.

Now Rahul understood. He jumped down, laughing. A crowd of passers-by with morning-fresh faces built up, cricketer Bala-ji and half his team among them on their way to work. They formed a circle around the arena. Rishi and Kishi hit out like prize-fighters with amazing speed, flooring their enemies within minutes.

'Why are you beating Cowdrey and Joshi into the shape of a peacok's arse, Twinnies?' Bala-ji said.

'Ask the shits themselves,' Kishi panted.

Rishi whispered something to Bala-ji.

'You did that, Cowdrey?' Balaji put his boot to the man's backside. Then his team-mates took over. It was a good thing for the failed presidential candidate and his 'best man' that they did not wear cricket boots to the office.

'Now beg apology.' Bala-ji gave Cowdrey one more kick, the loudest of the morning.

The goondas mumbled their apology.

The show was over. But the epilogue had yet to come. It came in the shape of the twins embracing Rahul. It puzzled him. What had he done? Only lent them the guards. No big deal.

'Thank you, Squire. Thank you for helping our sister last night,' Kishi said, and explained.

With his arms around Rahul, Rishi whispered in his ear, 'It's only nine fifteen. You still have plenty of time to finish Dyal's essay . . .'

'And for you to copy it?' Atom said.

The morning sun shone sweetly on Simla. But sighs filled Rahul's room. Kishi, Ajit, Deepak and the rest of the cricket X1 sat there, looking tense. It was a matter of life and death. They had 'a make or break' game on Saturday, their annual fixture with India's Eton, the Bishop Cotton School. They had to win this time. If not, a mass cremation pyre would be lit. Rahul's door was ajar. Boys popped in and out to see what was going on. Atom breezed in, talking to himself. He had just had a bath. He smelled of Lux soap and wore only a towel around his waist.

'I am furious and I am curious,' he announced. 'I am so furious that I don't know whether I have any right to be curious at all.'

No one asked him who he was furious with or what he was curious about - it was just a way of being noticed. Atom stopped in front of Rahul's Raj-time wardrobe mirror, admiring himself. Then he walked out of his bathroom to the sun-drenched balcony, muttering, 'But strange things happen at the borderline of curiosity.'

'Oi, specimen! Come back,' Rahul yelled. But Atom wasn't listening. With the sweet sun falling on his near-naked body, he walked up and down on the balcony, mumbling to himself. Lord Hanuman suddenly materialised from nowhere and the two found themselves face to face. Lord Hanuman disagreed with Atom. He bared his fangs angrily. That made Atom shut up and turn back. But before he could reach safety, the Lord of Mount Jakhoo did something quite unforgivable. He just whisked the towel off Atom's waist with one flick of his hand. A fierce tussle began between man and beast for the possession of Atom's towel. All this happened in full view of the Nath family basking in the sun in their garden. The ladies quickly turned their back on the rude spectacle and Professor Nath slapped his forehead. But he continued to watch with interest this contest between man and monkey.

Then the beast did something even more unforgivable. Atom's towel in hand, he took an elegant leap off the balcony, landed gracefully on the corrugated iron roof of the kitchen out-house, leaped again and disappeared in the wooded ravine below. And Atom, his hands around the royal jewels, ran for his life to Rahul's bathroom door, only to find it firmly shut.

'Let me in. PLEASE,' Atom begged.

Nobody heard him. The life-and-death talk went on. Finally, Rahul took pity on him. But not before Professor Nath had witnessed for the full length of a Bollywood drama what Mrs and Miss Nath had refused to watch even for a minute.

'Son of a bitch,' Atom snarled, monkey-like, and ran to his room, his hands still clamped around the crown jewels.

No sooner had he left than the talk in Rahul's room changed from cricket to something a little more important – SIZE!

A 12 inch ruler appeared, all the twelve flies got opened and twelve angry-looking erect penises popped out proudly. They were measured meticulously and their lengths recorded in a notebook and compared with the last reading. *No Change* was heralded as a good sign and an ejaculation competition followed – who would last the longest and whose 'man butter' would fly the farthest. It was Rahul's first time. He hesitated.

'Cap'n Kapoor, rise to the occasion and lead by example from the front,' Keeper Mull grunted.

The Captain rose to the occasion all right, but he only reached the upper middle order. It was the keeper himself, however, who came first triumphantly, his hand still at it, piston-like.

September-December was the cricket season in Simla. In the plains of India, cricket was played till the following February and March. For Simla College, it usually finished with their first varsity fixture late in November because it never got beyond the first round. And Christmas brought snow and winter hols. But before that was this 'make or break' yearly game at the end of September.

Bishop Cotton School was founded by a Bishop of Calcutta called Cotton a couple of years after the Mutiny of 1857. (His Grace did not live to see his handicraft flourish, for he drowned soon after, while crossing a river). It was meant for the sons of

British army officers. Now it was for any 'silver spoon boys', sons of snobby super-rich. It was famous as ever. It was expensive as ever. Ex-pupils called each other Old Cottonians. Old Cottonians were among the 'best top dogs' of India – 'in business, army, IAS, IFS or what have you'. And the young Cottonians were known to be 'damn good cricketers'.

Although they were only schoolboys, the buggers were unbeatable. They had a ground attached to their school. Being boarders, they had all the time in the world to practise. More importantly, they had a secret weapon - an ex-Oxford Blue as a coach, the beautiful Englishman Mr Brown. Brown taught them how to keep a straight bat and made them practise slip catches in the half-dark. No Simla side had ever beaten BCS, not even the 3D's YMCA. Simla College played BCS annually. It got beaten annually.

'We won't be this year,' it said this year. It said that every year.

'Rahul, the college expects,' Principal Khurana had said.

'Sir, he expects the college to expect,' non-cricketer Rishi had replied.

'Separate the men from the boys. Show them who's who.'

And this was what was being discussed so hotly in Rahul's room before Atom made such a damnfool of himself - how to separate men from boys and show them who was who. It seemed a tall order - for everyone knew who was who. The boys in question had always beaten the men in question. But still the talk went on. It went on all day - in the college, on the Mall, in the nets and in India Coffee House - till it was time to part for the night.

But at night, Ajit could not sleep. He turned up in Rahul's room again to 'talk tactics'. Atom also turned up, just for a chat.

Then Kishi appeared at his balcony window. He knew now what they had to do to win. Was there anything to eat? And could he pass the night there? It was too late to go any-where.

The team was announced the next day. Copies of it were posted around, inviting all to the historic duel, especially the ladies.

No college boys except Rishi turned up to watch. But a few girls did, for the morning session only. Moon, Meena and Indira were not among them. Rahul felt as if he had been kicked in the box area. It hurt even more when he learned that the girls had come not to watch them, but the BCS boys.

Their purpose-built Bishop Cotton School was a vast huddle of half-timbered structures with open spaces. Being a Sunday, boys of twelve to eighteen swarmed around. But no one took any notice of the visitors, the 'ordinaries' as they called them.

'Effing snobs,' Rishi quipped as some Cottonians passed within earshot.

'The silver spoon has not gone to their heads, it's got stuck up their arses,' piped Kishi loudly. He did so intentionally – to get heard.

Everything about the school was impressive. It even had a small swimming pool. The tennis courts served as the cricket ground. This ground had a sliced hill on one side topped by a small pavilion and a downward slope on the other. It was a four if the ball hit the hillside without a bounce. Otherwise, it was two runs. The long on and long off boundaries were reasonably good.

The BCS XI's Captain was a tall Sikh. His name was Bhandari but he introduced himself to Rahul as Ben his team-mates called him Big Ben. Like his team, he wore off-white flannels and a light blue blazer with an embroidered school badge on the pocket. He was beautiful - and he knew it. The college girls only had eyes for him. He expected it. But his style was not affected. He walked tall and never once looked towards where the girls sat or stood. He won the toss and played a straight drive with his left hand to his team watching the two captains from the pavilion. This meant they were batting.

Exactly ten minutes later, Ben was back on the matting with the other BCS opener, another Sikh boy. This chap was half Ben's height. But he stood as if he was just as tall - chest thrust forward and his backside puffed-up like a turkey. They put on 61 cavalier-style before lunch, which was taken in a palatial dining hall with something of an army officers' mess feel about it spick and span, polished parquet floor, glinting silver and glinting brass and panelled walls. The Simla College boys were agog. After the meal, they were taken on a conducted tour of the school.

'Fuck me rigid,' Rishi cried out in the library. 'So many books. Are they for reading?'

'No wonder the bastards come up top dogs,' said Kishi when they saw the school science labs.

They were called to the field to resume play.

Ben and his partner went in the first over after lunch run out, the cocky fools. Their numbers three and four put on a brave twenty before being trapped LBW by Ajit in the next few overs. From there on, it was downhill all the way. Invincible BCS fell to something unknown to it - panic. Deepak wrapped up most of the remaining wickets in great style. The great BCS was all out for 151.

It seemed a left hand job for Simla College - beating the brats. And the college did - in the fifteenth over after tea with skipper Rahul and keeper Kishi at 46 and 47 not out respectively. It was tragic that no college girls remained to share, or even witness, their moment of glory.

'Bloody bitches,' the college boys called them.

Big Ben took the visitors to complete the tour of the place. The school hall stage had a painted set for a play. It looked unbelievably real. There were other wonders too, such as their art room. The star attraction, however, was the swimming pool, the only one in all the Himalayas. Though it was no longer in use - too cold - it had not yet been drained. The college boys looked at it with longing. Then they looked at each other - some of the hill boys had never seen a swimming pool.

'Feel like a swim?' he who had scored the match-winning forty-seven runs asked his captain.

'You are mad,' said Big Ben. 'The water is freezing. Have a heart.'

'Benny,' Rishi gave the BCS captain a new name. 'Haven't you heard of Englishmen swimming in the frozen Serpentine in London on the twenty-fifth of December? Or is it the first of January?'

'But they are mad Englishmen.'

Rishi, Kishi and Rahul stripped to their underwear and dived in. Then their whole team stripped and jumped in. The hundred odd BCS boys big and small with rosy cheeks watched.

'I say!' they said to each other. 'Golly!' They could not believe their eyes. They had never seen so many common twits all in one place. In this instance, within their own freezing pool.

The college boys did not feel the cold. They had a good swim. It had been an exceptional day - history had been made.

They shivered. It was time to go. With blue lips, the swimmers did a lap of the cricket ground to dry their bodies. Then they looked for their clothes. They found them where they had left them - by the poolside. But where were the twins' clothes? The college boys refused to put their clothes on till they were found.

Big Ben was embarrassed. But he also laughed in his throat. The other BCS faces were not embarrassed, and they laughed loudly, enraging the twins. Big Ben summoned the school bigwigs.

'Astonishing,' said one of them, School Captain Parmar, throwing his chin up in the air like Nawab Latti Khan. 'Then he spoke to the schoolboys. 'Go and find them.' It was an order. Minutes later, a fat little boy of twelve found them lying in a ditch fifty yards away.

'A silly place to undress. Awfully silly,' he said snootily.

'But we did not undress there, smart-arse Twiglet. Promise to write home that you are losing ten pounds this month and every month for the next twelve months,' Rishi said.

'Then you'll become weightless. Then you'll be able to fly home to Mummy,' Kishi added.

'Don't have a go at the boy, Twinnies,' said Parmar. There was hostility in his voice.

'The school had a go at us.'

'Obviously they don't like you here.'

'Tough shit. We don't care for them much either.'

'I'd clear out then if I were you.'

'We'll clear out when we are good and ready. If anyone here wants to hasten our departure, they can try,' Rishi said loudly.

A bombshell. Then pin-drop silence - twelve near-naked fools challenging a hundred plus!

Rahul thought fast. What to do to save their skins? He put an arm around Parmar and Big Ben. He wanted 'a little word'.

'*Noblesse oblige*,' he whispered. 'So just cool it. Let them get dressed. I'll take my team away.'

'You know we can't touch them here because it's our school. So take these two away before we do something to them that we might later regret,' Parmar hissed, and turned on his heels. He addressed his schoolmates in a loud and clear voice: 'Dismiss. Back to your dormitories. Our guests are leaving.'

The collegiates took their time getting dressed.

'Not very good losers, are they?' the team muttered loudly on its way out.

NINE

The NEFA story started to move like a fast-forward film reel. Indians had not expected this to happen. The sleeping giant next door had never been a problem. For 2,000 years, it had imbibed India's message of peace and non-violence as preached by the Mahaguru Buddha. How could it possibly want to harm the land of the revered Preacher?

Yet, daily Chinese incursions ended up in serious armed clashes claiming more and more Indian lives. Land-grab, as yet of inhospitable Himalayan tracts, became the order of the day. A patient lot, Indians gradually became impatient, then enraged - what the hell was their government doing about it?

'Bugger all' was the answer.

Indians had been told time and again that their British-trained army was one of the best in the world. The world's fourth largest, it was strong – and if the Chinese ever set foot on Indian soil, they would be given the thrashing of a lifetime. Indians wanted to know what their government was going to do now that their 'Chini brothers' were resting their yellow backsides on thousands of square miles of the sacred soil of Mother India. 'Delhi is between the goat and the cabbage,' they cried. They meant the indecisive Indian government was shilly-shallying.

But one morning in early October Indians rose to hear just what they they had been waiting for. Newspapers said:

Special Task Force Created To Oust Chinese
Gen Kaul Leaves for NEFA To Assume Command

221

One paper described this famous Indian, a Nehru favourite, as 'a soldier of extraordinary courage and drive'. Another paper wrote what was music to Indian ears:

Indian Army Poised For All-out Effort

People up and down the country kissed the papers they were reading. They wished Gen Kaul with his matinee idol's looks godspeed.

But soon, too soon, that music began to turn sour. Exactly a week later, a fierce battle was fought in the unheard-of jungle Tseng-jong at 15,000 feet. General Kaul was in charge. Instead of his seven-foot fire-eaters giving the yellow pygmies the lesson of a lifetime, Indian soldiers were thrown violently back. Very heavy casualties resulted this time! War being war, this setback was considered as one of those things that happen. However, what followed confounded the Indian braves. While the battleground was still smoking, General Kaul flew out of NEFA that evening for consultations with Prime Minister Nehru in Delhi 1,600 miles away.

This caused much consternation in the press and the country - the general leaving the field mid-battle! But as it happened, Nehru had a long-standing state visit to Sri Lanka, then called Ceylon. Nehru liked being seen on the world stage. He left for Colombo the day after, a Friday. So things couldn't be that bad.

To the world this might have seemed as if it was business as usual, but not so to Principal Khurana. He felt it necessary to bring his college together. He urged the Union President to arrange a special college assembly to be held at the end of the day in the college compound, the original hotel dining room being too small. Rahul had an URGENT notice typed and placed in the THOUGHT FOR THE DAY glass case. But, as the last period of the day began, blak clouds blanketed Elysium Hill and it started to drizzle.

This threw the assembly into jeopardy and Mr Khurana into a pool of panic. He telephoned all around Simla to see if a public hall could be had at such short notice. None was available. He convened an emergency session of the college union. Captain Sethi and Professor Nath also attended. The issue was - what to do? Call the whole thing off?

'Sir. . .' Rahul whispered in Mr Khurana's ear, pointing a finger towards Auckland House.

'Humm. I don't think it'll work. But there's nothing like trying,' Mr Khurana said, and went on the phone again. 'It is a bizarre request, Miss Atkinson, but . . .' Mr Khurana spoke for five minutes. Then he put the receiver down. 'Ladies and gentlemen, we have a hall. Auckland House at five-thirty, on this very hill. The Headmistress, although English, fully understands.'

Rahul had another notice typed. The Principal signed it and a college peon ran with it from classroom to classroom. Alarmed professors read it out aloud to their classes. There were murmurs of astonishment, there were ripples of excitement. For the first time ever, the ex-palace of the first British Viceroy to reside in Simla, Lord Auckland, was to open to outsiders.

Auckland House, managed mostly by British nuns and British teachers, was a boarding school for the daughters of the heavenly born who remained invisible to the outside world.

Simla College, run entirely by Indians, was very visible to the world.

The late hour and the rain said not many would turn up. But in no time the 1830s elegant wooden hall in which the Viceroy's sister, Emily Eden, had thrown balls and danced the waltz with gay hussars and held theatrical soirees, got packed from wall to wall. Not an inch of standing room remained. All senior girl boarders also attended, fodder for the college boys' devouring eyes.

It was a College Union do at which a few teachers would also speak. Everybody realised they had a war on their hands. Yet nobody knew what it meant - Indians had not fought a war for over a hundred years, not since the so-called Mutiny of 1857. They had forgotten what war was. But suddenly finding themselves caught in one, they felt euphoric, confident and united.

Rahul found it filled him with bubbles of excitement to be chairing this meeting. He felt directly linked to the danger in those far-off places. For the first time in his life, Mohmi felt that he was an Indian first before he was a Muslim. The girls in the hall felt that the boys in the hall were not what they had always thought they were ogres and oglers - but brothers.

Principal Khurana spoke first. India and China had been good neighbours and brothers for centuries. For no reason, Chinese soldiers had recently crossed the border - the McMahon Line - and occupied large parts of Mother India. This was neither neighbourly nor brotherly. To make matters worse, the Chinese had advanced into Indian territory on the false grounds that the time-honoured McMahon Line was a bogus boundary. Something had to be done about it. India had everything going for it - an army to be proud of and great leaders like Nehru and Krishna Menon. Moreover, it had worldwide respect and sympathy: to date, thirty-nine nations had condemned the Chinese aggression. The time for talk was over - you couldn't talk to the Hitlers of this world. India's phony war was over. Our soldiers had a job to do. Give them the tools and . . .

Captain Sethi, wearing his medals, spoke next. So what if the Chinis soldiers had snow clothing and our jawans didn't? Wars were not won by what soldiers wore. They were won by determination and dedication.

Could the young men of a Communist regime forced to serve in its army match the determination and dedication of our freedom-loving jawans and their love for Mother India?

Professor Nath said, 'Our troops are out-numbered, out-equipped, out-weaponed. Even out-kitted. But they won't be out-witted.' He aimed a finger like a pistol at the girls, 'Daughters of India, your country needs you. Go home and start knitting sweaters and socks for your brothers fighting in Himalayan ice to protect you. Raise funds. Collect jewellery and say ORNAMENTS FOR ARMAMENTS.'

The motion was now thrown open. Speaker after speaker came from the hall and thundered for full five minutes. Lastly came Moon.

'It all began here in Simla fifty years ago, believe it or not. The seeds of our troubles with China were sown here then. So China thinks it has a point . . .'

It was a shocker - it had all started here in Simla! But NEFA was more than 1,500 miles away. And what was that about China having a point?

'In October 1913 a conference was held here between British India, China and Tibet to settle the border between them. Foreign Secretary of the Indian Government, Sir Henry McMahon. . .'

Moon stopped. She wasn't getting good vibes - the boys didn't like it that she, a girl, knew more about Indian history than them. Dissenting voices arose in the hall. What point did China have? China had no point.

The whole bloody world knew it didn't. So what was Tits on about?

'Sod them and carry on,' the chair whispered. But Moon wasn't listening. She was enraged. And when enraged, Moon Mehra was matchless.

'They say *know thyself*. To this may be added - *know thy enemy as well*. I'll go further and quote Matthew from the Bible and say *Love Thy Enemy* so you know him better . . .'

Love thy neighbour OK, but love thy enemy too? This was too much. Tits had gone bonkers, loco.

'Boooo . . . Boooo . . . Boooo.'

The fragrant Auckland House Hall had become a stink house, as if all its male occupants had issued a collective fart: 'Boooo . . . Boooo . . . Boooo . . .'

'DO NOT INTERRUPT THE SPEAKER,' the chair shouted.

'Let me return to the conference,' Moon resumed. 'The talks went on for an incredible six months. Finally, there was an agreement. McMahon drew the boundary on the map which has since borne his name. A three-way treaty was drawn up and initialled in April 1914. Then the Chinese changed their mind about the whole thing. But they did observe the McMahon Line as a border for fifty years. Why suddenly do they now say it is bogus? And why, after such touching declarations of friendship for years, do they inflict these stabs in our backs? It is here our enemy's perfidy becomes clear. It is here my Know Thy Enemy comes in. Our enemy is trecherous, selfish and ruthless. He will stop at nothing. Let us prepare ourselves to meet him and defeat him. Thank you.'

First Rahul stood on his feet, then Mr Khurana and finally the entire hall. It erupted volcanically.

The rain had stopped and the sky was clear. It was pitch dark and cold. A full moon reigned on Simla. Cousin Moon stood in the grand wooden porch with Meena Nath and some other girls. Out on the gravelled drive stood Indira and her sister under the wrought-iron lamp-post. Bobby and their servant Ram were also there, come to fetch them. Bobby waved at Rahul and came running.

'Mummy says come ASAP. Tomorrow. Okay?'

While leaving, Indira gave Rahul a sleep-wrecking look. Rahul almost walked away but Cousin Moon gave him an arresting stare. He heard the girls make plans for getting home. Moon lived the farthest away towards Chotta Simla.

'You must feel very proud of yourself, Cousin-ji.' There was pride in Rahul's voice.

'And you must feel very ashamed of yourself.'

'What have I done?'

'You haven't bothered to show us your face for how long is it since Aunty Kamla came and you ask what have you done? Wait till Mummy sees you.'

'How are you getting home?'

'I'm flying. General Kaul is sending me his helicopter.'

'Hasn't he got better uses for his helicopters? I suggest you walk. And if you promise not to be so angry, I'll walk you home.'

Cousin Moon turned to her friends. 'What do you think, Meena? Shall we let my part-time cousin walk us home? Protect us from Chinese invaders?'

They walked, the girls in front of Rahul, like a shield. The girls were talking of one thing only – Moon's speech. They had found her a job: MP for Simla come next general election. At the sub-post office two of their friends broke away. They lived near Hotel Blessington on Cart Road to the right. Two other girls lived nearby before the steep climb to Lakkar Bazaar began. That left Cousin Moon, Meena Nath and Rahul. Now they walked side by side with Cousin Moon in the middle. They walked in silence. The climb at nearly 35 degrees was tough going. Rahul was thinking, We are not cousins really. Our mothers may be. Not us.

'Why didn't you speak, Meena?' Moon said.

'Me do public speaking? You are loony, Moon.'

'Cousin Moon, you were matchless. Is it true what you said about the Simla Conference?'

'No, Cousin Rahul. I made it up.'

'I thought so. But you pulled it off all right, though. Everybody believed you. But then they are such nutters, those boys.'

'Don't forget you are one of them.'

'Are you calling me a nutter?'

'Yup.'

'That's not a very nice thing to say, Cousin-ji. What do you think, Miss Nath? May I call you Meena-ji?'

'I think Moon is too generous in her estimate.'

Kicked in the backside, Rahul slipped on the wet road and found himself between the girls when he stood up. The climb here was at its steepest, leaving them breathless. By some chance, Rahul's hands touched both the girls' and he had a premonition that something was about to happen. It happened. Their hands touched again. Then again, and this time

Rahul took their hands and kept them in his and heaved them up the slope. Their hands were soft and delicious. It surprised him that the girls made no effort to pull them away. The effect on Rahul of holding the hands of two of the most beautiful girls in Simla?

'Down, boy. Down.'

Rahul held on to their hands till they came to Lakkar Bazaar which was well lit and where they could be seen and recognised. What if they had already been seen and recognised? It would make headlines more sizzling than the Chinese soldiers had succeeded in capturing.

At the barber shop, from where the hostel road took off, it was time to say goodbye to Meena. Atom and Balbir stood at the paan booth next door, listening to the news on the paan wallah's radio and smoking. They waved to Rahul - they were bowled over. Meena said goodbye and the two cousins walked on - Balmoral was still a good fifteen minutes away downhill. Rahul didn't know what to say. He just felt foolish. They passed the Gandhi statue and came to Christchurch. The wet surface of the Ridge glinted in the moonlight. It was quiet and deserted apart from their own two moving silhouettes. Rahul wished he had the necessary courage to take her hand in his again.

'What are you thinking?' Rahul spoke at last.

'Nothing. What are you thinking?'

'I was only wondering.'

'What about?'

'I was wondering which moon is more heavenly - the one above or the one by my side?'

'You're going to get a black eye if you talk like this.'

'Only answered your question.'

The necessary courage came.

'I'll never talk to you again if you ever say things like this. And let go of my hand. The whole world can see.'

'There's not a soul in sight. How wonderful it is just to hold your hand.'

'Don't talk. Just walk.'

'What, in silence?'

'In intelligent silence. Don't forget who we are.'

'I have worked it out. We are not cousins.'

'We are walking together because we are. If we are not, you have no business to be with me. So scram.'

They came to the Mall and Rahul let go of her hand. But only a few people walked here tonight. It was October. The season was long over and the tourists had been washed down the hills.

'You are my responsibility and I am walking you home.'

'Shhh . . .'

'But I like talking to you.'

'Is that why you disappeared from the horizon for so long?'

Rahul had no answer. But he improvised one:

'Yes.'

'You disappeared because you like talking to me?'

'Yes.'

'You expect me to believe that?'

'Yes.' It was a loaded yes. It had an effect on them both, bringing that silence back between them.

From Kwality onward, the Mall was completely deserted. Rahul could have taken her hand without the fear of being seen or recognised. But he couldn't. Past the Clarke's Hotel, it was jungle all, with sparser street lighting. And now they walked closer to each other, his right arm brushing her left breast accidentally now and then. The silence deepened - exquisitely. Well past Oak Wood House, they came to a lordly deodar tree and they stopped under it by some silent agreement. Here it was moonlit jungle true with no sound other than that of their thumping hearts. Divinity had come down to earth.

Moon knew Rahul was about to pull her into him. She could feel it in her limbs. Any minute now. She was afraid, afraid of her own self.

'Listen, Mister,' Moon said at last. 'It's useless.'

'How?'

'A, we are cousins. B, it's wrong. C, we are the same age.'

'So?'

'So it's no good. So we stop here. Full stop.' Moon ran - Balmoral was only fifty yards away.

Next morning, yesterday's clouds returned, blurring Simla, making ghosts of walking figure - ideal weather conditions for someone who had some thinking to do, deal with a few blurs in his own head. It was the way she had said *we stop here full stop*. It sounded so hopelessly final.

Clouds stuck to Simla all day. To Rahul too.

'Oi, you!' Rishi barked. Rishi was a reader of the human mind. 'Why do you look like a lidless bidet?'

'Do I?'

'You should be on top of Mount Jakhoo after your triumph last night.'

'What bloody triumph?'

'All those bitches dribbling. Tell Dad all.'

This was one matter Rahul couldn't confide in his friend, in anyone, because it involved a cousin. So Rahul fobbed Rishi off, saying: 'It's something you won't know. It's called thinking.'

Only someone older and not from his world could help. But Rahul knew no one older and from another world. He saw Bahadar Singh on the veranda by the newspaper stands by himself. He was scanning the pages of script he couldn't read.

'Bahadar Singh . . .'

Bahadar Singh heard him out. His boyish face acquired a statesman-like look.

'Rahul baba, lady saying fuckofying is wrong and cousins never should and girl must be at least five years younger for marriage.'

Marriage? Rahul was knocked over Mount Jakhoo. What was he going to do? What could he do? Nothing. Only read his books, hit the ball hard, score runs, take wickets and never look at a girl again. NEVER.

Strangely, the Krishna temple was full today. Yet Krishna spoke to Rahul loud and clear:

'Injured innocence. Hurt pride. Dark chamber of rejection. Get out of it all.'

'Meaning what, Sir?'

'Meaning there's more to life than is available at any given time. Go for it. It's there for the taking.'

'Promise, Sir?'

'I only say what I mean. On your way.'

The morning room again. Only the three sisters sat there, their eyes sharp as needles made in Japan. Rahul felt like a nutter, an utter nutter. Who should he address his greetings to? It was easier to stand before 500 in a hall than this triad. Rahul folded his hands on his chest in namaste to the eldest, Padma. It would have to do for the other two delicacies as well. Again, there was that leg-glance and that leg-cutter. But to what bloody use? Rahul should quit, go, get lost.

'Uncle and Aunty OK? And that Wonder Boy?'

All three came in just then.

'So you beat us? Incredibilous,' Bobby said.

'Beating BCS was a left-hand job.'

'Everybody says it was a freak result.'

'They would, wouldn't they? Bad sports.'

'But we hear they stole all your clothes and that you all had to get back half naked. True?'

'Only half true. We had to walk back stark naked and got half arrested. Namaste, Uncle. Namaste, Aunty. There's going to be a storm, it looks like.'

'I don't suppose you have news from Captain Pithi? Things don't look good,' Mr Malhotra said.

'Hanuman-ji Maharaj,' muttered Mrs Malhotra to herself, folding her hands to Mount Jakhoo.

'Only a border skirmish, Aunty. Don't worry.'

'Chinis are not fighting with chopsticks. We are.'

'Not true, sir. We have a professional army. British trained. And Pithi said his Brigade is one of the best.'

' It's also a question of leadership.'

'Pithi also said that his CO, Brigadier Dalvi, is a World War Two veteran. An astute commander, loved and respected by his men.'

'Our only real weapon and leader is Nehru.'

'And he has the whole world behind him, sir.'

'We'll see who comes to help him if that Chou chooses war. Devi rani, give the boy a cup of tea. He's come all the way from Jakhoo,' Mr Malhotra said. 'And I wouldn't mind one myself.'

Tea came. Tea was drunk and Mr Malhotra stood up he had 'a lorry-load of work' to do. Suddenly, Rahul remembered the mountain of homework he had to do before Monday. The storm timed its arrival with his announcement.

'You can't go out in this storm. Sit down. Have a game of cards or something,' Mr Malhotra said and left the room. Mrs Malhotra also stood up - she had much housework to do.

'And us,' said Padma and Sushma, standing up.

Left on her own with the boys, Indira twisted and twirled the end of her breast scarf. She was in a fix - to stay or not to stay. It would look odd, not to say shameless, if she did stay. Half blushing, she just walked out on the boys. The storm had come with a vengeance. Rahul wanted it to pelt down on his back. With a vengeance. The storm obliged.

The 10 a.m. Simla sun in mid-October was 'Fortnum & Mason honey to taste, not waste'. Simla wallahs did the tasting without any wasting. They sat the mornings out in the heavenly gold in their private gardens, on public benches or wherever grass graced a slope. From half-closed eyes, they watched the petals of blood-red peonies, having now bloomed to mature handfuls, fall.

But these mornings could also be hellishly windy. It was both that morning, and Bahadar Singh was in a whirlwind of a hurry. He had to get home. Now. This very instant - to be indoors with his bulbul, his new wife of a few days. He had done his share of the morning's work - the breakfast, the clearing up and the rest. All he now had to do was put the newspaper stands

234

out in the sun from the veranda - the boys liked to read while basking in the sun. Feverishly, he put the stands out. Free at last, he raced up to his little hut fifty feet above on the hill and slammed the door on the world. Ten minutes later, there came a loud bark from the hostel kitchen.

'Oi, where have you buggered off to?' It was Jhandoo. He aimed his bark up at the hut. He knew perfectly well where Bahadar Singh had disappeared to and for what. And that was why he had shouted for him. He didn't want him to be where he was. 'Put the stands back inside, you hear? Or should I come and pour some mustard oil in your ears to clear them?'

Bahadar Singh did not hear. He was doing what he did most of the time when not working. He lay on top of his bulbul under a quilt. Both were fully dressed. His hands were inside her blouse. His mouth was fastened to hers and he was fully inside her. Jhandoo shouted again. Again Bhadar Singh did not hear. But his bulbul did.

'Lord-ji, boss is calling you,' she murmured. The sixteen-year-old Hindu bride had been told that her husband was her lord and master on earth.

'I'm going to bust the Angrezi-speaking boss's angrezi gaand one of these days.'

'Mundu Bahadar, come hither at once!' the voice bawled. 'Or I'll come up there and drag you down.'

'Cruel bastard. What does he know of love and marriage? Just when . . .'

'Never mind, Lord-ji. Go and come back soon soon,' his bulbul said, coming to the door.

'Langoor off-spring,' Jhandoor roared as soon as Bahadar Singh appeared in sight. 'Can't you see?'

235

'See what, Khansamah-ji?'

'The wind.'

'No. Who can see the wind? Can you?'

Jhandoo didn't like to be spoken to like that by a mere mundu. He feigned to whack him.

'Don't try that in front of my wife.'

'Then prove you are a worthy husband.'

'I don't have to prove anything to you.'

'Because you are not. Because you are worthless.'

'Anyway, how would you know, Khansamah?'

Bahadar Singh had dropped the all-important ji. Jhandoo's nostrils flared.

'What do I know of what?'

'Of being a husband? Nobody ever gave you a wife. Your pidgen Angrezi has swollen your head and gaand.'

Had Bahadar Singh gone mad, talking to his boss like that? But the Khansamah was not really his boss. His boss was Nath sahib. His boss was Khurana sahib. Good married men both. They would understand why Bahadar spoke like that.

Jhandoo went double mad.

'Dog, I am going to beat you into a chutney,' Jhandoo screamed and aimed a mighty kick at his backside. Bahadar Singh leaped aside and caught Jhandoo's foot in his hands. Bahadar Singh had had enough of being screamed at all the time, and of now being called an unworthy husband. He wanted to put a stop to it, once and for all. He could do it now. He had the man where he wanted him - half on earth, half in his hands. A good little twist and a few kicks up his arse would do the trick. And no one was looking.

But someone was looking - Mrs Bahadar Singh.

'No, Lord-ji,' she yelled and raced downhill to stop her husband from busting his boss's arse. Jhandoo's honour was saved, albeit by she of the unworthy husband. 'No, Lord-ji.'

The sudden appearance on the scene of a lady had an unexpected effect on both men.

'All right, Khansamah-ji,' Bahadar Singh said, as if they had been playing a game, and let go of his foot. Restored to both his feet, Jhandoo nearly fell. For he had never beheld such unearthly beauty – a butter-white face with a rose in her cheeks, red, red lips and very large blue eyes.

'Yes, all right. Let's put the newspaper stands inside. Or the wind . . .'

But the wind had already done its job. All the four papers the hostel had delivered daily were flying around. *The Times of India* flew into the faces of Rahul and Rajkumar Chuba Ao coming from around the side of the hostel. Atom, Mohmi and Balbir turned up at the same time and chased the leaves of *The Tribune*. But they all stopped in their tracks when their eyes fell on the new wife of their mundu. And she on her part turned the deepest pink as she felt the gaze of so many well-dressed young men on her. Like a shy child who had walked into a roomful of strange grown-ups, she turned on her heels and ran. Her Lord-ji ran after her and Rahul looked at his friends, his forehead creased.

'We should be ashamed of ourselves.'

'Why?' the other four said, shocked.

'We never gave Bahadar Singh a wedding present.' This had an instant effect on Rajkumar. He pulled out a pink two-rupee note. Rahul, Atom and Mohmi did the same.

'Balls. What are ten rupees going to buy?' Balbir said angrily, producing two of those notes. 'It should come from the whole hostel, a present for Mr and Mrs Bahadar Singh.'

'Atom, job for you. Make a collection,' Rajkumar said. 'You are the right man for the job, dripping with charm, saturated with style. Settled?'

'That's better. Any hopeful news?' Balbir asked.

'They are at their favourite past-time in NEFA – wanking with words. That's as hopeful as it gets. Kaul is back there and Menon had a useless conference with him in Tezpur yesterday. Why? Because like this they are seen to be doing something. It keeps Delhi happy. And the editors,' Rajkumar replied. He had been through the papers earlier. He did so every morning as soon as the papers arrived from the plains, pruning them for news from home, NEFA.

'What does it mean, Strategy Prince?'

'Things are going from bad to worse at Thagla Ridge. And along the Namka Chu. It's going to flow with blood. Our blood. We should pull right back.'

Leave the battlefield without giving battle?

'Why bloody should we?'

'Because it is 16,000 feet high. Because winter is coming. Because you won't be able to send even a toy gun up there, let alone a cannon once it is snowed up. Because we don't have snow clothing.'

'So?'

'So our soldiers will freeze before they can fire a shot. So we must pull back to Lumpu and consolidate massively to give ourselves a chance.'

'Where is your Lumpu, Field Marshal Chuba Ao?'

Rajkumar Chuba Ao raised his pencil-thin eyebrows and rolled his eyes in despair. He put an arm around Rahul. 'We are surrounded by idiots. Never want to see them again.' He took him away.

But they saw the idiots again in the evening at the paan shop in Lakkar Bazaar. Paan shops remained open till late. They had a radio on at all times. People converged to this one for a cigarette and a paan. And to listen to the radio.

There stood a good hostel crowd around the tiny shop, discussing what to do with the forty-one rupees Atom had collected.

'Give Bahadar an envelope at breakfast with a speech from the President,' Balbir said when they saw Rahul and Rajkumar coming up – it was time for the news.

'Field-Marshal!' Atom yelled, holding aloft the yellow packet of Gold Flake like a football referee. With the cigarettes came the newscaster Malcolm De Mello. The news was all about continued Chinese troop-building along the River Namka Chu. It also said that General Kaul had returned home in Delhi, sick. 'A bronchial allergy . . . respiratory infection, stress and exertion.' The General had gone *home*, not to a hospital.

'Oh, really? Bronchial allergy . . . respiratory infection, stress and exertion too! But why fly back to Delhi? NEFA has a first-class military hospital at Tezpur,' Rajkumar shouted.

'How do you know, Field Marshal?' Atom asked.

'Bloody fool, I know because I come from there.'

'Then why did he leave? Has he chickened out?'

'YES. The great General prefers bed to battlefield. How could he leave likethat? What bloody use is an army without a leader?' Rajkumar's handsome face became darkly distorted. He was crying inside. The boys understood – NEFA was his home. It had been left unguarded. They also knew why Rahul looked like him. They gave them hugs. These were hugs reserved for would-be mourners.

TEN

A loud thud on the corrugated-iron roof above his bed woke up Rahul. A four-foot giant towered above his skylight, swishing his tail around - Lord Hanuman Himself? There were more thuds, though not as loud the young ones of the giant. Rahul had been dreaming. He couldn't remember of what, only that it was a sweet dream. He tried to get back to it. But he couldn't.

'Hanuman-ji maharaj, maybe you own this mountain, but . . .' But there was a time and a place for everything. Lord Hanuman understood and moved on. Rahul looked at his timepiece. Five thirty. It was light, but very murky.

Simply unable to sleep, Rahul left his cosy comfy bed and did what every Indian does upon waking up in the morning – he washed his face and brushed his teeth and the rest. Rahul got dressed and came out on the balcony through his bathroom to look at the world. But the world could not be looked at. Thick mist shrouded it. The mist was so thick, Rahul could feel it on his cheeks like a caress. It felt strangely good to be standing there in a cloud, as if he had never seen mist before. A smile broke out on his face. Someone watching would have said, 'Ah, here is a young fool who is happy for no reason. And this happy-for-no-reason fool wants to make a further fool of himself.'

Rahul walked to where the balcony cut a corner. With the agility of his roof invader, he lowered himself to the ground. Something reminded him of Solan, a fragment of the forgotten dream. It produced a sudden ache of longing for home.

Rahul started walking downhill. Visibility was less than six yards, adding to the mood he was in. Lakkar Bazaar was a wall of white wool. There wasn't a soul or a smudge of one in that wall. Nor was there a sound of any sort. Rahul turned up the collar of his jacket and quickened his pace. He walked past the Odeon, the roller-skating rink, Mahatma Gandhi's statue, and came to the Ridge. The Ridge, too, was deserted except for a solitary walking blur - his own Principal Khurana out for his morning stroll. Only at Scandal Point did he hear the first sounds. An invisible dog barked in the mist and a feminine voice shouted sharply in English English: 'Oh, shut up.'

Next moment, a beautiful Irish setter came running to Rahul, making him cry, '*It can't be?*' It wasn't.

'Rex, Rex,' the voice said indignantly and a young English girl came face to face with Rahul. 'Please don't mind him. He doesn't mean any harm,' she said in faultless Hindi, and then became mist herself with her dog. Rahul took the Upper Mall. He stopped at the little temple.

'Ah, Rahul?' Krishna said, as if He was expecting him. Then He waved him on his way - the God was busy today.

Green Gables looked a huge milky hulk in the woolly mist. Nothing beyond the gate was discernible, the flower bushes, etc.

Rahul had no idea why he had come here, nor any expectations, great or small. He thought of turning back, but decided to walk down to Cart Road, which was a natural turning-point as it cut the mountain in two Simla above it and the Valley of Annandale below.

Near Cart Road, something caused him to almost stumble - the sound of muffled laughter. Next moment, he stopped dead in his tracks as he saw two smudges advance towards him.

'Look!' yelped the smaller of the two smudges.

The surprise was total and totally shattering.

'I thought I was seeing things. What on earth are you doing here at this hour?' Bobby said.

Rahul knew about the power of hypnosis. But he did not know it could turn an above average smart-arse into an instant imbecile. But a smile on her lips came to his rescue.

'I'm out for a walk,' he managed to say.

'What, here? At this hour?'

'Why not? I do so every morning.'

'Don't lie. We've never seen you.'

'I hope the shock hasn't been too much?' Rahul asked Indira.

'What if it has?'

'Then I'll go away.'

'Go away then.'

'But I love this mist.'

'What's there to love about mist? It's only vapour. Next you'll be saying you love steam too.'

'I'd adore that – to have a Turkish bath on the Mall or the Ridge for free.'

'I'd advise against it. It might get in your ears. Like rain.'

'Come on, let's walk, dammit,' Bobby said.

'Can we walk together?' Rahul asked.

'If you promise to walk intelligently.'

'I promise. I know how to walk intelligently.'

'Move, then,' Bobby said impatiently. But before that, Rahul had to do something, come up with some 'whizzkiddery' - make them turn back, downhill, not uphill which would soon bring them home. And to get rid of the boy for a few minutes.

'Bobby, how fast can you run?' Rahul said.

Indira gave Rahul a look one gave to an idiot.

'Pretty fast. Why?'

'Just wondered. How long will it take you to run down to Cart Road and back? Ten minutes?'

'It's only a furlong. I'll do it in five. Want to bet?'

'Yes. Name your price.'

'Never mind. I'll do it for the heck of it.'

'Referee-ji, say ready, steady go,' Rahul said.

Indira looked at her watch: 'Ready, steady, go.'

Bobby dissolved in the mist.

'Indu-ji. Did you really go to the Post Office?'

'Have you come here at six a.m to ask me this?'

'Yes.'

'I'll never believe you again. Never ever. You made such a total fool of me. The man went and brought his boss. And that bloody fool said due to heavy demand they had sold out. But he said he would give me one hand-written for free. The Post Office went up in hysterics and I cried and cried.'

'Miss Number Two-ji.'

'What?'

'So much to say. So little time.'

'Then cut it short. Tell me the gist of it.'

'The gist of what I want to say is . . .' Rahul didn't know how to put it. 'It would help matters if I could hold your hand.' He took her hand.

'No.'

'And put my arms around you.' He put his arms around her. It led them both to shut their eyes.

'What are you doing?' she murmured.

'Thank You, Divine Krishna.' Rahul addressed his prayer to her divinities.

'What? Thank Krishna for what?'

'He kept His word.'

'Is this the gist of what you want to say?'

'I . . .' Rahul said and took her mouth in his.

'Stop it. Stop it!'

Running footsteps!

'Bobby is coming back.' Indira tore herself away.

'May I come again tomorrow?'

'Public road.'

Bobby showed up, breathless.

'How many minutes? How many?'

'Oh.' The timekeeper had forgotten her job. 'Five.'

'Oh, golly. I did it.'

'Yes. You should have taken me on that bet,' Rahul said.

'What would you have given me?'

'Bobby!' Indira chided her mercenary brother.

'No, no. Bobby deserves to be rewarded, the more so because he refused the bet. How about a reward for the time-keeper, too?'

'No,' Bobby said, looking at his own watch. 'Didi, you cheated. You patronised me. I did it in seven minutes.'

They laughed. Gradually, the mist began to lift and they started to walk.

Then suddenly, the goodbye gate. From across it, the Malhotra dahlias smiled. And now Rahul could smell their roses.

'I hope tomorrow is as misty as today.'

Mother Earth had obviously ceased to exercise her chief quality - gravity. For Rahul remained afloat in air all day long. He lived and re-lived the misty morning and felt the taste of her lips on his and those heavens in his hands. This created a permanent state of semi-erection, resulting in unbearable sweetness. Life had suddenly become too wonderful to be true. But it was wonderful and it was true.

After cricket, he bought four comics from Maria Bros. At 8.45 he turned up in Mohmi's room.

'Coming to the paan shop?'

'Why?'

'To listen to the nine o'clock news.'

'Oh!' Mohmi understood. He was at his writing desk. He wore pyjamas and a dressing gown. The former were made of purple satin with black piping, the latter of yellow silk. In front of him on the desk was a large mirror. Mohmi had to have it there while studying or he could not concentrate.

He threw away the dressing gown and put a polo-neck sweater and trousers on top of his pyjamas. Then hand-in-hand, the two friends came down to Lakkar Bazaar. A small crowd stood at the paan shop. Rajkumar was there. Atom was there. Balbir and Ranbir were also there along with others, chewing paan and smoking, even the Sikh! The news came on. It was the usual story - clashes here and there along the Namka Chu, heavily out-numbered Indian troops standing up to better-equipped Chinese intruders. Defence Minster Menon was quoted, saying how determined the government was 'to throw the Chinese back until Indian territory was free of all aggression'.

'But when, Mr Talk-Talk?' barked Rajkumar.

'Depressing bakwasi,' Balbir said.

'The Peking Duck Chou needs a good roasting,' Rahul said. 'Or a good ducking in the Namka Chu.'

'For the moment he's giving us the roasting and the ducking,' Rajkumar groaned.

'Come on, Kapoor,' Mohmi said, pulling Rahul by the sleeve. They had heard what they had come to hear. 'Let's get back. I have something to finish.'

But Rahul had not heard everything he had come to hear. He was not too worried about his brother. Pithi was in no danger. Rahul had seen the Chinese - they were no match for Pithi and his Sikh warriors. He wanted to know tomorrow's weather.

The radio said tomorrow would start misty with a touch of frost. Afraid that he might not hear his alarm clock, Rahul kept waking up every half hour to see if it was dawn. Finally, it was not his alarm clock which woke him up, but hail-stones as large as a golf ball hitting his flimsy tin roof. The storm of the century had unleashed itself on Simla. Gone was Rahul's walk. But the fool got dressed anyway. He put his raincoat on and stuffed the comics in the inside pocket. On second thoughts, he put them back on the table and hit the golfballs-lined road.

'Man proposes and God disposes. O, Krishna-ji, You like playing games.'

This was ridiculous. The storm of the century said Rahul was a bewakoof nut. But he still went. And today Rahul didn't feel like going in the temple as he passed it - he was angry with Krishna. The Green Gables looked grey and unwelcoming. It said, 'You are a fool, why have you come? Go away.'

Perhaps tomorrow will turn out to be like yesterday, Rahul thought.

It did.

The mist was opaque and lovely as Rahul glided down to Lakkar Bazaar. He remembered something when he reached Mahatma Gandhi's statue - the comics. He had to go back to get them. It would cost him another fifteen precious minutes. But he simply had to get them. He had promised. Rahul first ran uphill to his hostel. Then all the way down to the Green Gables. He walked past it, expecting the sound of laughter. He walked up then down.

'She came, she saw, she went back - disappointed.' Rahul crumpled up the comics and turned back. Krishna, knowing how the young man felt, called him out from His temple.

'No good, this, Rahul. The world is full of girls.'

'What do You mean, Sir?'

'You haven't got Moon out of your system yet.'

'You mean I can love more than one girl at the same time?'

'I did when I was your age. Resoundingly successfully too.'

The whole world knew of the Divine Lover Krishna and the many sexy gopis He made love to at the same time in his perfumed arcadia.

'But You are God, Sir.'

'Who made me God? Who gave it all to me? You chaps did. So I'm giving some back.'

'You are giving me the poetic licence, aren't You, Sir? O Krishna-ji, sometimes You make me laugh by what You say.'

Something sweeter than Fortnum & Mason honey laced the morning. Rahul walked up the Elysium Hill to go to college. Indira walked in front, hand-in-hand with her friend Manu. She looked back. She smiled. It made his day.

'Wish I could go up to her and walk with her.'

That would blow her reputation to bits, to be seen walking with a man and talking to him. Bring shame and dishonour to her family. Render her utterly worthless on the marriage market.

'And they say India is the world's best country! Its culture the greatest.'

At the begining of the first lecture - English and Keats's 'Ode to a Nightingale' - she happened to look at Rahul. He tried to hold her glance, hoping she would understand that he was trying to say something. But she shied away. For the next lecture - Indian History with Professor Lall in that room with a view - Rahul remained waiting outside for her. She came, accompanied by Manu. Seeing him stare at her like a mug made her realise he wanted to say something. She darted her eyes around to see who was looking. Nobody was. Everybody was inside, waiting for Lall. Manu moved on, having understood the situation.

'You didn't come, Indu-ji?'

'Where? When?'

'Yesterday.'

'In that storm? You came in that storm? Professor Lall!' Indira ran away, a frightened rabbit.

All through the lecture, Rahul stared. Then suddenly, he stood up to leave the classroom.

'And where do you think you are, One Eight? In a come-and-go-when-you-like waiting hall?'

'Not feeling well, sir.'

'I think we know the nature of your malady. I'm afraid there's no known cure for it.'

The classroom and the valley resounded with laughter. 'Bastard,' Rahul hissed to his neighbour, Rishi. 'I'm going to amputate one of his legs like Nath's. His balls, too, if he's got any.'

'Mr Kapoor, if you want to say something, say it coherently. Don't mumble. Mr Mull, what did he say to you? Stand.'

'Frankly, I haven't a clue, sir. He was mumbling, as you rightly noted. What did you say, Mr Kapoor?' Rishi asked Rahul and the class laughed again.

'I asked if you've heard the test score from the West Indies.'

'And have you, Mr Kapoor? Stand.'

'No, sir. That's why I asked. Do you know it, sir?'

'You will see me at four after college and I'll tell you what the score is.'

'I can't. I have an important net.'

'You will have to forego the net then, won't you. NOW SIT DOWN. No, remain standing and make a summary of what we've discussed.'

Professor Lall sat back to see the president of the college union and captain of its lousy cricket team make an ass of himself. For he knew Rahul hadn't listened to a word of what he had said about the downfall of the Mughal Empire.

Trapped, Rahul looked at the cinemascope screen of wooded embroidery, blue skies and high altitude ice-cream unbelievedness. It was an odd moment to acknowledge that the English had made the right decision to locate themselves here.

'Problems?' the Profesor sneered. 'But you are good with words.'

'Problems? I see no problems, sir. What you said in a whole hour can be put in a few simple words. That the main reason for the collapse of the Mughal Empire was that zealot

Emperor Aurangzeb behaved as an orthodox Islamic ruler ruling an orthodox Islamic state while he should have ruled India as an Islamic ruler ruling a largely non-Islamic state, taking notice of people's wishes.'

'So you were listening? So you should have been. I'm letting you off the hook this time - but next time? Watch out.'

After the lecture, Rahul spoke to her for a quick second: 'Meet me tomorrow morning?'

'Can't. Tomorrow is Saturday and it's Mummy's birthday, the twentieth of October.'

'Tomorrow evening then?'

'If I can. But where?'

'Same place?'

'What time?'

'Six.' This was serious - it would be dark at six - his suggestion of meeting him in the dark. Indira looked down at her feet. They saw Professor Nath coming. Indira took to flight.

'Rahul Kapoor. Watch your ways, young man.'

But Rahul Kapoor also flew away - to tomorrow evening.

Tomorrow evening came dressed in light mist. Rahul first heard footsteps and then he saw shadows approach him. There were three, not two, and his heart sank. The third shadow was bad news Sushma. This put to the winds his well-laid plans for a long walk, for getting rid of the boy, for taking Indira behind the bushes.

'Oh, hello there. Are you all right?' Bobby said.

'Fine, I think.' Suddenly, Rahul felt more than fine. For it was not bad news Sushma, but good news Manu.

'Your reward.' Rahul handed Bobby the comics.

'Gosh, so many? Thanks awfully.'

Rahul looked at Indira and she at him. His eyes asked - *Why have you brought Manu*? Hers replied - *You know*. They moved, Manu and Bobby in front.

'You frightened me yesterday. Everybody saw us talking. The girls made my life miserable,' she said.

'I had to talk to you. Otherwise . . .'

'Otherwise what?'

'What happens to a fish out of water?'

'How do you feel now?'

'Splash! The fish has been thrown back in water.'

This brought a bubbly smile to Indira's face. They slowed down to place a little more distance between themselves and the other two and walked in silence towards Cart Road. It was maddeningly beautiful, the silence. The mist echoed it back.

'What are you thinking?' she asked.

'Of you. I am missing you.'

'But I am here. With you.'

'You'll be gone soon. Then I'll become that fish,' he said and took her hand. It was the greatest thing in the world for him, just to hold her hand. A question arose should they go on down the Annandale Road into jungle, or . . . ?

Bobby and Manu decided for them. They kept walking down the dimly lit road. This was jungle real of shapes black and silence deep. Rahul placed her hand on his aching heart.

'What does it say?'

'Nothing.'

Rahul opened his shirt buttons and put her hand inside. 'Can you hear it now? What does it say?'

'It says you are the craftiest so-and-so.'

Rahul pressed her cold hand on his chest and felt her fingers grip his warm flesh gently. 'You lie, Indu-ji. It says I'm only beating for you.'

'One Eight, you are good with words.' Indira tried to withdraw her hand. But Rahul didn't let her.

'Calls for a reciprocal arrangement.'

'It does nothing of the sort.'

Rahul pulled her behind a boulder.

'May I kiss you, Miss Malhotra?'

'You may not, Mr Kapoor.'

'Would the earth move if I did?'

'This here is a mountain.'

'Would the mountain move?' Rahul placed his lips on hers.

'Don't . . .'

The mountain moved and they were in this world no more. One thing, though. Rahul must not open his eyes. Or all that would vanish in thin Indian air.

From the TIBET 200M sign in Lakkar Bazaar Rahul saw a crowd bulge at the paan shop: they were there for the news in a few minutes. He rushed to join the fifty men gathered there, an unusually large crowd. There were bazaar men wrapped up in shawls with mufflers covering their heads, ears and chins. There were office clerks in jackets and ties. And there were the hostel boys. They stood in silence, looking mournful, His heart in his throat, Rahul ran and put his arm in Rajkumar's.

Looking grave as Rahul had never seen him, Rajkumar merely shook his head.

The newscaster came on punctually, unfolding horror. In the pitch black of 5 a.m. mountain jungle that day, the mammoth Chinese dragon had begun roasting alive 7 Brigade with its volcanic fire. Great Chinese mountain cannons blew the peaceful morning apart by hurling hell on Indian positions all along the fast-flowing Namka Chu, wiping them out. Holding a twelve-mile line of defence, ill-equipped and heavily outnumbered, 7 Brigade had fought bitterly to the last man. But it was all over in a mere four hours. Communications were cut. It was not known how many of the Indian soldiers, if any, had survived.

The news removed the earth from beneath the feet of the paan-shop crowd - a whole Indian brigade wiped out just like that? Indians had been expecting news of a glorious victory. The government had promised not one, but many.

'My brother Pithi?' Rahul shuddered. His heart jammed in his throat. He wished he was at home, in Solan. What must they be going through, Daddy and Mummy? Rahul agonized: 'What if Daddy has a heart attack?'

Of course he wouldn't. And Pithi was safe. Of course he was. 'I know he is. Nothing can happen to him.' But what was an army position 15,000 or 16,000 feet up in snow? A trench, a bunker? Could they breathe there? Rahul wanted to be with Mummy and Daddy and Shobana and Bimbi and Shoki - that very instant, as if by an act of magic.

Rahul tossed and turned all night. With Rajkumar early the next morning, he dashed down all the way to the bus stop on Cart Road to wait for vans bringing newspapers from the plains. The papers were full of the destruction of 7 Brigade and the Indian debacle at the Namka Chu. One paper likened the Chinese attack to an infantry Pearl Harbor three miles up in the Himalayan snows. *The Times of India* had asked Menon where he thought the Chinese might stop. His reply was frightening: 'The way the things are going, there is not any limit to where they will go.'

A third paper had noted that Rahul's idol – everybody's idol - Prime Minister Nehru, ever ready to talk to the press, had for once been unobtainable for comment. Rahul went through all the papers. Then he took the first bus going down south.

The first to see him was Terry. A mere glimpse of Rahul at that bend in the mountain road made him jump. He barked and bolted. Instinctively, the Kapoors knew. Shobana sprang to her feet.

'Rahul!'

It was ten. The Kapoors sat on the veranda in the morning sun. They sat in scorching silence. Shoki and Bimbi sprinted after Terry. There were hugs on the roadside. The two boys' eyes were red and swollen.

When they reached home, Kamla stood up and broke into sobs when she saw her son.

'Mummy!' Rahul flung himself at her and wiped her tears with his hands.

'Mummy!' Shobana also burst out crying.

'Stop it, Shobi. What is the matter with you?' Rahul shouted. 'Pithi is all right. Of course he is.'

'What can you say, son? Icy jungles, high high mountains and big Chinese guns. His brigade gone. All of it.' Kamla could not stop crying.

'Mummy, Pithi is a soldier. It's his duty to fight for the country. Wherever the battlefield.'

'I curse the day I let him join the military academy. I curse the day I let him sit the exam. I curse the day I let him go for the interview. Why did we let him, ji?'

Prakash didn't answer. Vacantly, he scanned the vast Solan Valley. A railcar was going across it, a white ant in a hurry.

'Mummy, that's what he always wanted to be - a soldier.'

Santram brought a glass of hot milk and a fried egg on a paratha. Rahul put his hand up - he had no appetite.

'Drink,' Kamla said, running her hand over his head. Then she caressed his cheeks. 'And eat.'

Rahul bent down to touch his father's feet. His father's face was ashen. The telephone rang. Rahul could tell a call was expected because it had been brought out to the veranda. Shobana got it.

'Daddy, Uncle Bishamber Sarin.'

Prakash hadn't said a word so far. He walked to the phone and everybody followed. Prakash had friends in high places in Delhi. He had spoken to them last night. A trunk call was expected from them this morning with inside information.

'Ah, Bishamber? Very kind of you. Very. So?'

'I have spoken to Chawla at the Ministry. Hello. Can you hear me?' Uncle Sarin said, and everybody heard every word because of his loud shrill voice.

'I can hear you.'

'The picture they are getting is very patchy. It was a surprise attack. Total surprise. The Gurkhas and the Rajputs bore the brunt of it. They fought back bitterly, but they had no chance. They were outnumbered twenty, perhaps fifty to one, and the enemy had superior firepower. Very superior. Their positions fell like nine pins. They fought the last assault with bayonets. By nine hundred hours, they were finished.'

'What about the Punjabis my boy is with?'

'I'm coming to that. The Punjabis and the Grenadiers on the right side of our positions were not attacked directly. You follow me?'

'I do. Go on, go on.'

'But the enemy engaged them by heavy firing from across the river. Their CO General Prasad ordered them to withdraw via a place called Hathung La. But the enemy had already got there.'

'So?'

'So they were caught. In a trap. Anybody's guess how many survived. The few who did must be making their way down to the Indian plains, avoiding that chakoochlau knife-wielding Chou.'

'How come we were so badly prepared?'

'Ask Menon. Ask Kaul. They're both useless, if you ask me. One is full of gas, the other of self-importance.'

'What are Pithi's and his men's chances, did Chawla say?'

'Good, if they don't get captured. More than that, he couldn't say. No one can. Nobody knows anything, not even that old windbag himself. Nor even the PM. Such is the scene. We all listen to the BBC World Service for the news, would you believe. My respects to bharjai Kamla and love to the kids.'

'When will the casualty list be published?'

'Much, much too early. I'll keep you posted.'

The Rana Saheb arrived. The Kapoors were glad just to see him, he knew they would be and that's why he had come. He made a trunk call to a minister he knew in Delhi. The minister knew nothing. He made a call to a more senior minister. Even he knew no better.

His Highness stayed to lunch but only ate a chappatti with a bit of dal.

'Kamla beti, Pithi is all right. He has the Kapoor luck,' he said, leaving. 'In the Palace, I'll be begging Krishna. You do the same here, my lotus flower.'

'We are, Pops.'

There were more trunk calls from Delhi during the day. An hour before dinner, the Rikheys walked over from the Moon House. They came on their own and carried an air of gloom.

'The army is puzzled by the speed and precision with which the Chinaman struck. He obviously knew where every single one of our units was,' the Colonel said, a glass of Scotch in his hand.

'And we knew nothing about his?' Prakash said.

'The Chinaman had been preparing for months.'

'Why weren't we?'

'That's Delhi for you, Kapoor sahib. Our politicians. They want to sell the world India as a paragon of peace.'

'Being prepared to defend your home is not being war-like exactly, Colonel, is it?'

'Tell that to Menon. The army has been trying for months, but he won't listen. I'm afraid it's ditto with our beloved PM. He has a problem. Vanity. It can immunise you against advice. This is the result.'

Prakash Kapoor usually had two pegs. Rarely three, but never more. Tonight he had four. And they were not ordinary pegs, they were Patiala pegs.

The Rikheys were asked to stay for dinner, but Mrs Rikhey shook her head. They had just come to convey their concern and 'heart-felt feelings'.

Usually, after a good drink, Prakash ate with a hearty appetite. Tonight, he hardly touched the food, all vegetarian - since last night, meat had been banished from the Sun House. Then he went and sat on the veranda, looking at the dreamscape of Solan lights, and ordered Santram to bring him yet another drink. Prakash sat upright. He sat still, smoking. The family watched him in painful silence from the drawing room. It was almost eleven when Kamla went out to him.

'Time to turn in, ji.'

A remarkable change came over Prakash Kapoor.

'OK, I had an extra peg. So what?'

'What did I say?'

'What did you say?' Prakash raised his voice. All his children came running out - their father never raised his voice at their mother. 'You gave me that dirty look. It was worse than anything you could have said with your tongue.'

'I only said it was time to turn in.'

'You turn in if you want to. GO. Let me be.'

'What's the matter, ji?'

'Pithi is alive, do you hear? Pithi is safe. He's a soldier. He has to fight. That's his profession. But he is alive. Do you hear? He is alive.'

'Of course he is.'

'That's what I am saying. Why shouldn't he be? I don't want to see a tear in your eye again. Understand? And go to bed, all of you.' It was an order. Everybody turned back. 'Rahul.'

'Yes, sir.'

'Son, you'd better get back to college in the morning. I don't want you to miss lectures. Understand? So take the early morning railcar.'

The Simla railcar was another Raj-time habit. Painted white, it was a single carriage propelled by its own diesel engine. The railcar began its journey at Kalka where the plains finished. This station marked the end of the normal broad gauge and the beginning of the 30inch narrow gauge. At the speed of 12-15 mph, the railcar raced up vertiginous heights that made you shudder. It roared through tens of tunnels and rolled over even more of lofty viaducts, leaving them breathless.

The railcar cost more than the first-class train fare. But then it took nearly half as long as the choo-choo toy trains to do the sixty odd mountain miles to the Queen of Hill Stations, a mere four hours. It was the Prince of Speed. It was heaven on wheels. It was the way to travel to Simla.

Very early in the morning Rahul telephoned station-master Gauri Shankar to ask if there was room on the 6 a.m. UP. Gauri Shankar checked with Kalka and phoned back to say yes there was. 'But only one seat, Rahul son, lucky lad. News of Captain Pithi? I hope good. God save him.'

The railcar arrived on the dot. It contained a loud-voiced Sikh Colonel, a very sleepy Mrs Colonel and their fast asleep two very young daughters. Then there were four English nuns of the Convent of Jesus and Mary in Simla. Behind them sat a semi-somnolent bania merchant and Madam Bania in tents of expensive pashmina shawls. On the last seat was a young woman. She wore a blue coat. Her head and face were shrouded in a matching chiffon dupatta like a bedouin's. She occupied most of the double seat. Tired, she looked out of the window at the other, more picturesque side of the valley.

'Excuse me,' Rahul said, after tucking his bag in the rack above. The veiled head turned to look and Rahul had a 440-volt shock - Meena Nath!

The question was, would she speak to him? Rahul wasn't worried if she chose not to - he had enough on his plate as it was. Nonetheless, he smiled - it was the gentlemanly to do.

'I don't believe it,' he said politely.

'I don't either. What on earth are you doing here?' Her brown eyes were piercing.

'I live here. And your good self?'

There was a whistle and a jolt and they were off. Miss Nath re-wrapped her face in her dupatta, crossed her arms on her bosom and fell promptly asleep, fast. Her answer. Fine, Rahul said to him-self, but felt kicked in his backside. To deal with his punctured pride, he put his chin up and looked in front of him. The Colonel was saying something important to one of the nuns, the only other wide awake person in the railcar.

'You see, Sister Inez, it is sixty miles long. It runs in continuous successions of reverse curves with a radius of 120 feet in and out along valleys, flanking mountains, rising to seven thousand feet, the steep gradient being three feet in a hundred. It has a hundred and seven tunnels, aggregating five miles in length, dozens of viaducts making up one and three quarters miles, would you believe?'

'Fascinating.'

'A great British engineering feat, this Kalka-Simla Line. This railcar should be called *The Flying Simla Man*. Or *The Simla Belle*.'

'Utterly fascinating. You know what, Colonel? I have been in Simla since `42 and have done this route umpteen times, but have never known these were reverse curves. How clever of you!'

Whenever the railcar negotiated a curve energetically, people got thrown from side to side. When it came to a steep bit, its wheels strutted. The engine then hiccuped, the railcar shook and Sister Inez said, 'Oh, dear.'

Rahul stole a sideways glance to see if Meena was really sleeping and heard the nun ask the soldier: 'Colonel, what's the latest on NEFA?'

'Total news blackout since Saturday.'

'What's it all about?'

'They want our land. Some fifty thousand square miles of it.'

'How dreadful of them. Are they serious?'

'Very.'

'Dangerous?'

'Very.'

Rahul sat up. 'My brother is serving there.'

'As what?'

'He's a captain, sir. In NEFA.'

'Oh, Thirty-third Corps?'

'That's right, sir. Fourth Division, Seventh Infantry Brigade in the high, high Namka Chu Valley.'

'That's Brigadier Dalvi's oufit. I served under him in Kashmir. He's an excellent commander. Conscientious and caring. Your brother'll be all right with him even if the Brigade's been in trouble.'

'Will there be full-scale war, Colonel sahib?' asked the man in pashmina, opening his eyes.

'No. The Chinaman has made his point.'

'The newspapers say there will be. The stock market is behaving as if there was one already.'

'Seth-ji, newspapers thrive on this sort of thing and our stock market loves acrobatics.'

Meena Nath opened her eyes. 'Any news of your brother?' she asked Rahul.

'No news.'

'No news is good news.'

'How kind of you to say that. I didn't know you knew I have a brother fighting in NEFA. Or cared.'

'All college knows. You told us yourself. I saw him when your family came. He was very handsome.'

'He is very handsome.'

'That's what I meant.' Meena had said the wrong thing. She was apologetic. Her eyes became soft.

'Where are you coming from, may I ask?' Rahul said.

'Delhi. Mummy and I had gone there to see Grandma. She had an eye operation - cataracts. Mummy is staying on with her for a few days. But I'm getting back so as not to miss college.'

'So you've been travelling since early last evening. Look, look, look!' Rahul cried. They rounded a bend and were cruising atop an almost vertical mountain with nothing below them for hundreds of feet, and grand vistas beyond with the sun balanced delicately above a distant peak. It was a staggering sight that had to be shared with another human being

Then, abruptly, they entered a tunnel. It was pitch dark here. Rahul stopped talking, but the Colonel went on. His voice rose above the roar of the tunnel.

'He hasn't stopped talking since we left Kalka.'

'Poor you.'

'And the poor nuns. One by one he killed off everybody except Sister Inez.' Meena laughed.

As they came out of the tunnel, the railcar shuddered and swayed. This time Rahul and his neighbour got pressed into each other - once, twice. Rahul looked out and loved what he saw.

'Reversing curves, those,' he whispered. 'We are rising three feet in every one hundred.'

They laughed.

'Strange, us meeting like this.'

'So?' Meena's eyes became piercing again.

'Do you believe in fate?'

'No.'

'Do you believe in chance?'

'No.'

'Do you believe in anything?'

'No.'

'What about God? You must believe in Krishna.'

'Humbug.'

'He did me a favour. He'll do you one too if . . .'

'What kind of a favour?'

'That, I am not at liberty to disclose.'

Tunnels were coming, tunnels were going, beautiful tunnels.

'Have you eaten anything since you left Delhi?'

'No.'

'There's a good restaurant at Kalka station.'

'A girl doesn't eat in restaurants by herself.'

'You must be hungry then.'

'Famished.' Meena smiled.

'What would you like to eat if you had the choice? What do you fancy?'

'Let me see. Cake. I fancy some cake.'

Rahul stood up and got his bag. He pulled out a home-made cake. It was still warm.

'But I can't eat. I haven't brushed my teeth.'

'Someone starving is hardly in a position to quibble in front of a hot cake.'

'Besides, I don't know you.'

'Distant neighbours we might be, but we are neighbours all right. Please try.' She took a bite. 'Any good?'

'Very good.'

'Tea?' Rahul dug out a Thermos flask and gave her a cup. He had had breakfast before leaving home, but he felt ravenous again. He ate the cake with her, and when she finished her tea, he drank from the same cup. It was an intimate gesture, which did not go unnoticed. By drinking from the same cup, Rahul felt he had touched her lips. He felt it foretold that their lips would touch before the journey was over. Her beautiful brown eyes confirmed what he felt - they spread an aura of inevitability around them.

Rahul thought that the railcar was going like a Formula One Ferrari. They heard the Colonel tell Sister Inez that they were coming to one of the longest tunnels on the line.

'For the first time in my life I feel grateful to the British for being such wonderful engineers.'

'Why?'

'Ask Krishna.'

'What has Krishna got to do with it? He was not English.'

'He has everything to do with it. And he is the greatest engineer of all time.'

A little silence followed - a loaded little silence.

'O Krishna-ji!' Rahul addressed the sky. Should he push his luck and . . . and what?

'Take matters into your own hands,' said the sky. 'Time's passing.'

Then came that long tunnel, the tunnel to heaven. It was long. It was black. It was beautiful.

Rahul put an arm around Meena. Meena neither pushed him away nor screamed, and the inevitable happened. They kissed and Rahul took matters into his own hands. The matters were firm, like those mangoes. The kiss lasted for as long as it was safe. They breathed out heavily in unison when the first light came. Meena was red in the face, Rahul on fire. They waited for the next tunnel. They kissed when it came. Hungrily, they looked forward to the next and the next and . . .

After the last one, Rahul died ten deaths as he opened his eyes. They were in broad daylight and Sister Inez's eyes were firmly on him. They were not accusing him. They were saying *naughty boy*.

Then Simla suddenly came into view, a large English town transplanted on the Himalayas. There soared Mount Jakhoo above tiers and tiers of tin-roofed, white painted villas, hotels and wooden structures ready to slip off the steep slopes, roll over and tumble down into a bottomless chasm.

The sudden appearance of Simla brought about an equally sudden change in Meena. She pushed Rahul's hands away and surreptitiously fixed her bra in her sweater. People in the rail-car began picking out the famous landmarks. There this, there that . . . and here in the railcar it was a different Meena Nath, silent, her face red but not with passion.

The railcar climbed on. It glided past Summer Hill, Simla second station, to slip into Simla proper in sultry silence.

'Is a servant meeting you?' Rahul asked.

'I had known from day one you were a rotter.'

'What have I done?'

'What have you done? What have you done?' She sounded like her father - beside herself with rage. Worse, she was on the verge of tears.

'Have I offended you? Are you angry with me?'

'Yes. Very angry. And with myself.'

'Why?'

'Ask yourself.'

'It was destined.'

'Humbug. Nothing is destined.'

'Some things are. Ask Krishna.'

'You ask Him.'

'When will we meet again?'

'Never. Don't ever even think of speaking to me.'

ELEVEN

It was billed as the Mother of all Union meetings. It took place in Principal Khurana's office. Two days' newspapers littered his desk. They wept tears of India's humiliation. Grief-stricken, those at the meeting stared at them helplessly. However little, Simla College had to be seen to be doing something. First, another urgent assembly in the college compound at the end of the day.

'Weather permitting or not permitting,' boy-faced Mr Khurana said. 'If our jawans can face Chinese cannons in snows high and mighty, we can put up with a bit of soaking if it rains.'

But it didn't rain; only honey poured on Simla.

The same people spoke again. They spoke with fire and heart. With Mr Khurana as Chairman, a National Defence Fund Committee was formed. Rajkumar Chuba Ao who alone hailed from NEFA, and Rahul, the only college inmate with a brother fighting there, were appointed Joint-Secretaries. The fiery Miss Moon Mehra was elected Treasurer with Miss Meena Nath as Joint-Treasurer. Moon spoke again, this time in her role as Treasurer.

'If you haven't got cash, give whatever of value you have. Give your ornaments. ORNAMENTS FOR ARMAMENTS.' That became the slogan for the day.

Mr Khurana took off his wristwatch and placed it in an empty box on the table before him. Rajkumar did the same. Rahul donated his gold cufflinks. Then Moon took off her gold earings and dropped them in the box. Meena dropped in hers. Moon took the box and the two girls went around the compound. Moon first went to the women - the teachers and the pupils. There was an avalanche of earrings. Jingling gold bangles, too, tumbled in the box. Now Moon and Meena went to the men. One look in their eyes and cash, gold rings and watches dropped in the box. When she approached Kumar and Mahendru, they both stood back. Rahul called out, 'Kumar! Mahendru!' Shamed, they had no choice. They added some change to the National Defence Fund.

In no time at all, the box was full. Mr Khurana gave Moon and Meena the key to his office. They returned with another empty box. That too got filled.

'Now we seek Simla,' Moon announced.

Headed by Principal Khurana and other professors in black gowns, Simla College began its march to the Mall. Lakkar Bazzar gave generously, shoppers and passersby, too. More people joined the march. On the Mall, the procession became 5,000 strong – Indians love being together. People embraced each other, singing pre-Partition songs of patriotism. Every shop gave. Every passer-by too. The Simla Mall was not a street of harsh commerce this evening, but one of tender embraces. Nobody had seen anything like it since August `47 when the last of the British, never regarded by Simla wallahs as 'enemy', walked here. Brahmins were seen embracing Untouchables. People said it was like 15 August 1947, when the tricolour of independent India was unfurled for the first time over the Ridge.

It was then that the first rock was thrown at a Chinese shop, Lin's father's, shatering its large glass front. Luckily, like all Chinese shoe shops, it was shut.

'Hold it,' shouted Principal Khurana who walked at the forefront, throwing an arm up in the air. The jaloos came to a standstill. 'Who threw the stone?'

'They are enemy shops, sir,' Kumar shouted.

'These people are not our enemy,' Rahul said.

'Whose side are you on, traitor?'

'His brother is fighting at the front,' Rishi roared.

'In fact, he is missing in action,' Kishi shouted.

'His brother may be fighting the Chinese. Or missing even. But this specimen from Solan is wining and dining them,' Mahendru barked.

'Lin is a friend of mine.'

'Only a traitor would call the enemy his friend.'

Nobody else thought anything of the smashed window. The march over, Rahul thought he would dip down from the Mall and pay Lin a flying visit to warn him to be careful. But that was not possible. The NDFC had to go back to the college. It had to count the cash and make an inventory of the rest.

Next Saturday, 27 October, was Diwali. Two invitations came. Rahul said no to both - he was desperate to go home for the weekend. But a letter from Solan on Friday changed everything. Shobana said Uncle Sarin's and Pops' friends in Delhi were hopeful; 4,000 Indian soldiers were missing in action, presumably cut off by the enemy. They could be making their way down to India through the jungles of Bhutan, avoiding the Chinese. The Kapoors were not celebrating Diwali. Naturally. Only praying. Daddy said Rahul should stay put, pray and concentrate on his studies. Love.

Rahul read the letter every half hour. Before going to the cricket net, he sent Bahadar Singh to cancel the 'no' with - *Sorry. But I'm coming tomorrow.*

On every Diwali night, every Indian rooftop and window sill is bedecked with little earthen lamps, candles or with strings of electric lights. Every street, every bazaar is a riot of light and noise shrouded in gunpowder smoke, courtesy of bangers, rockets, catherine wheels and the rest. Gifts are given and sweets eaten with disregard for the pocket or the tummy. Diwali celebrates the victory of the virtuous Rama over the evil Ravan, in which Hanuman, a flying visitor to Simla, played no mean a role. Indians love to go over the top when it comes to the business of celebrating. But what was there to celebrate this year?

It was a crisp, clear evening with the sky perforated by a countless number of pinpoints of light, grains of glowing sand flung apart. The Mall was a-buzz. It was a hushed buzz. With the season over, Simla folks no longer went out for walks in the evening. But in answer to a collective need for togetherness, they had turned up to promenade there this evening. There were no fireworks. The only sign to suggest it was Diwali evening was the presence of a solitary candle in every shop window except the boarded-up Chinese-owned. Last Diwali night, Simla had been a magic mountain of glittering diamonds. Tonight, it was a sullen hump of darkness.

The Malhotras had visitors. They sat in a large semicircle on the veranda, gentlemen on one side and the ladies and the children on the other. A candle burned next to the telephone on a table in their midst. When Rahul showed up, Bobby hastily set a match to a sparkler and waved it in his face. Then he lit a banger and threw it in the garden where it exploded deafeningly.

'Darling, stop that nonsense,' Mrs Malhotra cried.

'Only a cracker, Mummy.'

'We are not celebrating,' Mummy chided her son.

The Malhotra ladies hadn't tarted up for Diwali. They wore plain clothes. Sushma sat slumped in an armchair, her face wrapped up in her dupatta and her chin cupped in a hand. She seemed to be in mourning, as if she'd just been widowed. It annoyed Rahul.

'It would take more than a combined operation by the Chinese army, air force and navy to get my brother,' Rahul said to himself in his throat.

Rahul was introduced and handed a plate full of sweets.

'Eat. Eat shamelessly,' said Mrs Malhotra. 'Your uncle phoned Kapoor sahib. The news is of hope.'

Everyone held a plate like Rahul. But no one was eating. These people shared Sushma Malhotra's mood. This also annoyed Rahul.

The telephone rang. Bobby ran and grabbed it.

'Yes? Ah, of course. You certainly may. Mummy, it's Aunty Savitri. Wishing us Happy Diwali.'

The two women exchanged Diwali wishes. Then Mrs Malhotra passed the phone to Rahul.

'Happy Diwali, Aunt Savitri.'

'Same to you. Same to you. Are you coming?'

'Right away.'

'What for?'

'What for? To eat your sweets.' Rahul laughed.

'You don't deserve any.'

'I might as well not come then.'

'You might as well not, if that's all you are coming here for - sweets. Is that all you want to come here for?' Rahul had hurt Aunt Savitri. He hastened to make amends.

'Aunt Savitri! Of course not.'

'Then what for do you want to come here?'

'To tell you how much I love you.'

'And you are a top liar on top.'

Rahul heard Mr Malhotra say: 'Santoshi sahib, if I were Nehru, I'd boot Menon out tonight and take over Defence myself.'

Rahul said goodbye to Aunt Savitri and listened to the men.

'Menon is Nehru's chamcha and Kaul is the blue-eyed boy of both. You won't see the backside of either,' Mr Santoshi replied.

'American arms have started pouring in. Saw planes unload at Palam with my own eyes,' said Mr Pathania, just back from Delhi.

'Already? What happened to our non-aligned principles?' Mr Santoshi said.

'What bloody non-alignment? When someone is chopping off your balls, what do you do with your principles?' Mr Malhotra raised his voice.

'Still. Principles are principles.'

'What bloody principles? Enemy at the gate and...?' Ramakant was losing patience. It was time for the early evening news. The radio reported a continued lull on the NEFA front. This pleased everybody. But the last news item frightened them.

General Kaul is returning to NEFA to resume command of operations on Monday

'God save us now.'

'Meaning what, Malhotra sahib?' asked Mr Santoshi.

'Twelve days at the front. Leaves battlefield on the eighteenth, two days before the battle. Spends ten days in bed - at home, mind you, not hospital in Delhi conducting the war from his sickbed. And back to the front again. What is this, a game of Chinese cricket? How can Nehru let him play with the lives of our soldiers? Sickens me.'

More visitors arrived. Rahul got his chance.

'Tomorrow morning, Indu-ji?'

'We've guests staying.'

'Tomorrow evening?'

'No.'

'Day after?'

'Can't.'

'Day after day after?'

'No.'

'When then?'

'Next Saturday. Maybe.'

How could she live without seeing him for a whole week? Rahul couldn't understand. He simply could not. It was time to go.

Rahul stopped at the little Krishna temple. It being Diwali, Lord Rama's night, the shrine was empty and unlit. This suited Rahul. Leaving his shoes outside the door, he went in and struck a match. He spotted the familiar little earthen lamp at Krishna's feet. He lit the lamp and saw Krishna leap to life. Rahul sat down before Him cross-legged and shut his eyes, swaying his head in deep prayer.

'Sir, make him come back to us.'

The Mehras, too, had many guests, Meena Nath among them. They were dispersed on the veranda and the garden. The far side of the garden had a long line of earthen pots with holes in their sides and candles burning in them, giving the garden a fairytale look. On this veranda, too, only one candle burned, and the same question burned the guests' hearts - what now? The analysts and strategists only had cold sighs as answers. But the feeling was that the worst was over.

A little girl lit up a sparkler and Rahul saw Moon looking at him. It was a look Rahul hadn't seen for a very long time - sidelong, molten and full of Diwali candy. In that instant Rahul knew why he had come here. Moon didn't look at him again.

There were over twenty people here. Some more were coming and some were leaving. They were sipping tea and eating samosas and sweets and yapping. A little further on, Moon and Meena held hands and were going on and on about something, two birds chirping away. They sounded exceedingly happy. Rahul was baffled what the hell was there to be so ecstatic about? They were totally engrossed in each other and totally oblivious of him. It hurt Rahul. It puzzled Rahul.

Aunt Savitri was in her element, dishing out sweets. She gave orders operatically. She became angry when she was not obeyed instantly. Then she exploded. Then the veranda shook and the servants trembled and Moon cried: 'Mummy! Your blood pressure!'

Aunt Savitri thrust a plateful in Rahul's hands. 'Finish it. Eat. Eat shamelessly.' She was furious with him though. 'Why did you go to the Malhotras first? What are they to you? Nothing as yet.'

'Oh, Aunt Savitri!' Rahul tried to humour her.

'Why didn't you come here first? Explain.'

'So that I could spend the rest of the evening here with you.'

'True? It better be. Or . . .' Aunt Savitri said and moved on to other guests and Moon turned up.

'Monumental liar. You went there first for *her*, isn't it? Confess, admit and own up,' Moon whispered in his ear. She needn't have - the noise level there was equally high.

'What? Who? When? Where and why?'

'Shameless creep. Monumental lying hound. I am not talking to you. And if I am . . .'

'But you haven't talked to me all these days.'

'And if I am, it's only because it's Diwali.'

'If it wasn't, you wouldn't?'

'I wouldn't.'

'You mean you won't talk to me again till next Diwali?'

'Yup.'

'You mean nope.'

'Yup.'

A gust of breeze blew out the candles in the perforated pots spread out in the garden - magic hives of glow worms snuffed suddenly out. Moon took a box of matches from a table and ran to relight them. Rahul ran after her.

'Guess what?' he said in her ear near a high and dishevelled wall of sweet peas.

'What?'

'I have worked it all out. We are not related. We are not cousins. Definitely not.'

'So?'

'Just that. I wanted you to know.'

'What for?'

'So that we can do what we always want to do.'

'Namely what?'

'You know? Hold hands . . .' Rahul leaned into her ear, half brushing it with his lips.

'You are going to get two mince pies . . .'

Some children ran past them. 'Look, look,' they shouted, pointing upwards. Some idiot in a house nearby had let off a rocket. It was shooting into the steel-blue sky and then it exploded into a great orb of falling stars, casting a magic spell on the valley.

'Pardon?' Rahul said, his lips on her ear.

'I said you are going to get two black eyes.'

'I'll have a photo taken and frame it.'

Moon started rekindling the potted candles.

'You don't care for me at all.' Rahul lit up a cigarette.

'Shut up. My cheeks are burning.'

'It means you do.'

'Oh yaa? Just because my cheeks are burning?' Moon took the cigarette from his hand and had a puff, surprising him - Moon smoking! She blew out the smoke with a loud sigh.

Moon took another drag and handed the cigarette back. Rahul also took a drag before throwing the cigarette away because Aunt Savitri was coming.

'These sweet peas need fixing,' Aunt Savitri said irritably. 'The hedge needs fixing. Those beds need doing. And the mali has disappeared God knows where.'

'Aunt Savitri, I'll come and fix everything.'

'You never keep your word. You say this but you do that.'

'I'll come tomorrow and on Monday after college.'

'Promise, or I'll never talk to you again.'

Soon, people started to leave - it was dinner time. Only the closest friends remained, eight or nine of them, Meena

Nath, too. To stay overnight with her friend, Rahul presumed. At the dinner table, Moon's face shone. Meena's did not. Rahul was relieved that at least her face did not glow with anger like at the station the other morning. If anything, it carried a certain mystery. She had not looked at him once all evening. Rahul understood. Meena wanted to appear in command of herself.

They had just begun eating when the phone rang and a servant came to say it was for Meena bibi. Meena and Moon hurried to the hall. They were back within a minute.

'Meena's mummy is back from Delhi. They want her home.'

This posed a problem. Meena couldn't very well go out in the night on her own. Someone had to take her home. 'Eat dinner first, Meena beta. Then go,' Aunt Savitri said.

'Larka will take you,' Moon said.

'Why Larka? Rahul will. You both live there. Makes sense,' Aunt Savitri said.

It made sense all right. But it stole Rahul's appetite. Twenty minutes separated Balmoral and the Teak Hotel. Twenty minutes of largely dark and delicious jungle of haunted pines and ancient deodars where tigers once lurked and leopards stalked prey. And some of it was of anything-can-happen mountain darkness. Rahul had another of his premonitions - that whatever could happen in those twenty minutes, would happen. And this so soon after what had almost just happened!

'O Krishna-ji . . .'

For once, Rahul did not know what to say to Krishna. But the God of Understanding understood. He smiled, albeit enigmatically. Like the Mona Lisa.

Meena still didn't notice Rahul at the table. But Rahul thought that she looked less extinguished now. And Moon's eyes were on him all the time.

'Behave yourself, you hear?' Moon said just before they left.

'I hear.'

'What did you say about us not being cousins any more?'

'Just that.'

'What does it mean?'

'Just that.'

'Are you very sure?'

'Yup.'

'And another thing. Cut it out with Malhotra.'

'Sounds like an order.'

'It is.'

Rahul and Meena both breathed out loudly as they came out on the road. The first hundred yards were covered in silence. The second in deep sighs, getting deeper. Then Rahul took what was in desperately short supply courage - in both his hands and cleared his throat loudly.

'May I have your permission to speak?'

'Only if you have something pertinent to say.' Strangely, it was not the voice of a volcano.

'It is very pertinent. You know how we would be walking now if it was not India and was, say, England instead?'

'I don't, and I don't want to. I love India, my country.'

'I don't doubt your patriotism, Miss Nath.'

'What do you doubt then?'

'Your sincerity to yourself.'

'This is the most impertinent thing ever said to me.'

'You know what I mean.'

'I don't. I don't want to either.'

'I only wanted to apologise.'

'Having done that, walk in silence. Total silence.'

They walked in total silence. Dark patches became darker. Minutes passed faster. Not for the first time, Rahul's premonition had deceived him. He hung his head down.

'Not far to go now. What are you thinking?' he said as they began their climb to Christchurch on the Ridge.

'Nothing.'

'Me, I am thinking of railcar journeys.'

'Why?' Meena breathed out heavily. Somehow, from there on, their walk to the Teak Hotel became a railcar journey. Unpeopled patches became tunnels, long and short. The last bit, the steep rise from the public library, became the longest tunnel of all. Then it was all over. But the volcano did not erupt. Instead, it became the Sea of Tranquillity.

'Can we walk together sometime, Meena-ji?'

'My father would break every bone in my body with his stick.'

'Not if meet chori-chori, discreetly.'

'Where?'

'Leave it to me. I know just the place.'

'Maybe.'

'When? Next week?'

'Sunday. My parents are going to Summer Hill.'

Rahul kept his promise of fixing Aunt Savitri's garden. He skipped the cricket net. When he took a break, he lay on the grass in a bushy grove and lit a Gold Flake. Moon brought a cup of tea. She lay next to him and shared the cigarette.

TWELVE

A letter came every second day. The address on the envelopes was always in Daddy's hand. But their author was Shobana. First, she wrote what the newspapers said and Rahul knew. Then she spoke about life at home he longed to know:

Menon's gone. Nehru's taken over Defence and Declared Emergency. President Kennedy is 100% with us. England too. Pakistan is playing silly buggers, dropping hints of mischief. Commie Russia more on our side than Chou's. So things are looking up even though the Chinese keep pushing further down into India. Uncle Sarin is saying a big counter-attack is imminent. And a sure-shot victory soon. Pops comes every day. Stays to lunch but eats nothing, Daddy neither. But drinks every evening. 3-4 Patiala pegs (MAKE NO MENTION OF IT IN YOUR REPLY). Sits on the veranda for hours staring at the mountain. And at NEFA maps. Pops says he'll be all right once Pithi reaches India. Mummy and Daddy say look after yourself. Concentrate on your studies and eat properly.

The dakia postman and the newspaperman arrived one after the other at breakfast-time every morning. Rahul stood on the long Teak Hotel veranda, waiting for his letter. One cold Friday morning in mid-November, Rahul overslept and the dakia delivered for him a letter with a difference. It was not in the usual surface-mail 10P envelope. It was a 25P airmail.

Now airmail letters were no big deal. The 'Negro Sikh' Ranbir received them from Kenya, as did Rajkumar Chuba Ao from NEFA. No one took any notice of them. But something about this one raised eyebrows - the writing on it encased by those red and blue stripes! In a beautiful hand it said:

Rahul Kapoor Esq
Simla College Hostel
Simla
Himachal Pradesh

'Blow me arse and fuck me rigid if it not be a woman's hand which wrote it,' Atom howled, rolling his big royal-blue eyes. Interest multiplied tenfold. 'Without doubting a shadow,' Atom added as Rahul showed up, and waved the envelope in his face like a Tokyo fan. 'You can have it but on two conditions.'

'What conditions?'

'One, you tell us who it's from.'

'I don't know.'

'Two, you read it to us.'

More curious than anyone else was Rahul Kapoor Esq himself - an airmail letter for him? Solan was only twenty-five miles away and he knew no one at an airmail distance except Pithi. And Pithi never wrote to him.

Beside, Pithi was missing in action in Himalayan jungles. It was a joke. The bastards.

'Let me fucking see it at least.'

'Not unless . . .'

As the haggling continued, Rahul realised that the boys were not making an ass of him. It was a real letter. His curiosity rocketed. He made a deal.

'All right. But I want to read it first. By myself.'

That was allowed. Rahul took the letter. He went to a corner of the dining room and tore it open. It had a Bombay address on the top right corner.

Dear Rahul,
I know it will shock you to receive this out of the blue and I hope you'll forgive me. But I had been thinking of Simla and thought I'd drop you a line to say hello. I'm not sure of the address and hope this reaches you. So how are you?

The letter went on to describe the beauties of Bombay. There were mentions of magic names like Marine Drive, Juhu Beach, Church Gate, Gateway of India, the Taj Hotel . . . names radiating mouthwatering glamour which only London or Paris could match. The letter ended:

Write to me.
Love
Betty XXX

Before Rahul knew he'd been hit for six, the newspapers were delivered and a deafening roar went up. Every paper said what India had been longing to hear for so long - a big Indian push forward. Huge headlines screamed:

JAWANS SPRING INTO ATTACK

There were details of Indian military might. Stirring accounts followed of 'one of the world's most professional armies' achievements in the two World Wars. Iraq and the Somme were mentioned, as were El Alamein and Monte Casino. Victory was just around the corner.

Euphoria invaded the dining hall and Rahul's letter was forgotten. The boys went away to get ready for College. Back in his room, Rahul read the letter again. Bahadar Singh brought a bucket of hot water from the bathroom door on the balcony and Rahul gave him his army boots to polish. Rahul had been Bahadar Singh's demi-god since the wedding gift of forty one rupees and his speech. He would do anything for him.

Bahadar Singh sat cross-legged in the sun on the balcony to polish the boots. While he did so, Rahul had a bath. Then he got into his newly dry-cleaned NCC uniform. There was to be a big parade on the Ridge this morning - there was one every morning and all Simla came out to see. Later, there was to be a bayonet charge display in the college compound.

Putting the letter in his breast pocket, Rahul hurried down for breakfast. He ate and ran to the Ridge, hitting the mountain earth with the iron-lined heels of his boots. A war horse going to war.

The morning was bright, fresh and golden. The Ridge was sun-soaked but chilly. The news of the Indian counter-attack added colour to the parade. It took the chill out of the morning. There was another cheerful bit of news. It was local news. It said ice-skating was starting that evening at the Blessington Hotel. Ice-skating meant men and women 'whirling and swirling together'; even holding hands without a woman being called a brazen hussy, such being the nature of the sport bequeathed to Simla by its builders.

At the college, everybody knew about Rahul's mystery letter.

'Who's the letter from, oi?' everybody asked.

'Which letter?' Rahul replied, genuinely baffled.

'Rahul Kapoor Esquire?' Professor Nath accosted him.

'Yes, sir.'

'You'd better watch out, or I'll be reporting your activities to Mr Kapoor Esquire Senior in Solan. He asked me to.'

'Which activities, sir?'

'You just watch out.'

Indira's friend Manu passed, whispering, 'She wants to see you. Six p.m sharp.'

Well, well, well. What did it mean?

'Number One Eight.' Professor Lall saw them. 'No good will come out of that which is basically bad.'

'That's very philosophic, sir. But I don't get it.'

'You don't? That's your tragedy.'

'Sir? Why are you always after me?'

But Lall waved him away as if he was a bhangi.

'Simlaahh, you make me sigh,' Rahul hissed.

A bunch of girls passed. They didn't look at Rahul, but held their hands to their mouths and giggled. What the eff!

Rishi hadn't turned up for the parade, but he did for the bayonet charge. The boys lined the open side of the compound to watch. The girls sat on the covered verandas, knitting sweaters and socks for the jawans in NEFA. Pigmy, the seven-foot sergeant major, barked the order to charge. It was Rahul and Rishi's turn. Roaring like crazed lions, they leaped up and charged. They thrust the bayonets at the end of their rifles into the chests of straw-filled dummies with slanting eyes painted on yellow faces. Roaring again, they twisted the bayonets and pulled them out.

'What's this letter-shetter, Solan?' Rishi hissed.

The show over, they went to the loo and Rahul gave him the letter.

285

'Hummm.' Rishi grinned. 'Bucky Lugger. Women to the left of him, women to the right of him. Volley and thunder. What will you answer?'

'I won't.'

'Don't be a lidless bidet. Dash off a reply today.'

'Why?'

'Why? What a damnfool question! Why, to keep the fire raging. Maybe she'll come back next year and maybe you'll have her again.'

'I took advantage of her once, I shall not do so again.'

'What a damnfool of a mule you are!' Rishi was aghast. But his friend remained a damnfool of a mule. Nothing Rishi said would make him change his mind. Then Rishi clicked his fingers. 'I have a brilliant idea. What if *I* write to her?'

'You?' Now Rahul was aghast. 'Why you?'

'I'll reply in your place - as you, of course - and keep up the correspondence. Any objections?'

'Yes. It is being deceitful, it is unethical.'

'Don't give me your high-horse shit. There are no ethics in this sort of thing. She won't know. She'll be happy and you won't have a guilty conscience.' Rishi pocketed the letter. 'And I will have a nympho pen pal to fuck next summer,' he said to himself. 'Hopefully.'

The evening was mistless and clear. Rahul wished it was unclear and misty with zero visibility, which can make a mountain magical. Indira was all sparkle. But somehow it didn't seem real.

'How's the lover boy then?'

'Who, me? Feeling better than anyone else on this mountain. Or on any other.'

'Any particular reason?'

'Many.'

'But there is a special one. No?'

'In fact, two. One, victory's coming. Two, I'm not telling you.'

'Oh, please do.'

'I've been living in the clouds since the morning. Want to apply for permanent residency there.'

'Why?'

'Ever since Manu spoke to me. You must send me messages every day. Promise?'

Past Cart Road, they took their usual route, the hauntingly lonesome and dangerous road to Annandale. Rahul stopped by that rock where they always did for an 'English kiss' and a Customs Officer's search.

'Our silent rock. Our own private whispering jungle. And thou beside me in the wilderness. And the wilderness is - what did the chap say, that Omar Khayyam? It's just that.'

Indira had never allowed Rahul's hands in the forbidden city of her bra. This evening she did, wafting him beyond the stars and into the realm of madness total and utter - her bursting heavens through their magic casements. She even let his mouth wander, from her navel to her nipples to her mouth. Then she knocked him for six - straight over the top and into the pavilion. Rahul fell on the tin roof with a deafening thud.

'Who was the letter from?' She pushed him away.

Stopped dead in his tracks, Rahul was going to say 'which letter?' But he didn't.

'Indu-ji, I owe you an explanation.'

'You don't owe me anything.'

There was a noise.

'They are coming back, Bobby and Manu.'

287

But it was just a noise in the black foliage.

'Don't be mad at me. There's nothing to it.'

But Indira wasn't mad at him. She was only a heaving bosom. She fixed herself, looking dead calm. It alarmed Rahul.

'I want you to read the letter. Will that convince?'

'Where is it?'

'In my room. I'll give it to you in the college tomorrow.'

'It's Saturday tomorrow.'

'Monday, then?'

'OK. Let's catch up with Bobby and Manu.'

'But, Indu-ji?' Rahul pleaded. 'We've only been here a minute. I want more of the Krishna honey I have tasted.'

'You have had plenty of it and I am a damn fool.'

'Don't say that. You break my heart. Place your hand on it and feel what it says.'

She started walking quickly to catch up with Bobby and Manu. The moment they met them, she made everybody turn back to the goodbye gate.

What a, what a, what a walk! O Krishna-ji!

Rahul rushed back. He had two essays to hand in on Monday. If he didn't, God save him. Then surgeons Lall and Dyal would chop off his manhood and not with Major Doctor's imaginary knife - in public. He hadn't made a start on either yet. And the fool was playing cricket tomorrow and on Sunday. But as he came to Scandal Point, instead of going straight on, he found himself going to the Blessington Hotel down below on the left. Rahul wanted to see what he had never seen before - an ice-skating rink, this new wonder thing.

'Desist, Owl Rahul. You have so much to do.'

The Blessington was a middle-of-the road sort of hotel. Yet it was famous. Being directly below Scandal Point, it was minutes away from the heart of Simla. It had three tennis courts. In the summer, holidaying Indian super sportsmen – cricket and tennis stars - were often seen in action there, to Simla's delight. Come the winter, the courts were flooded with up to three inches of water. A chemical agent and the Himalayan weather did the rest, giving Simla the only ice-skating rink in India, blessing the hotel with stardom.

'Blow me arse!' Rahul cried when he came in sight of the floodlit sheet of ice. 'What the hell is going on?'

Light, colour, music and a hundred Simla stars. Men, women and children glided on a shining floor of white ice, going round and round in circles. Strings of coloured lights fringed the long covered veranda on the far side, the spectator stand. More people sat on it, sipping tea and watching the fun. A loudspeaker blared English and Hindi hit songs.

Rahul had been told that if he could roller-skate, ice-skating was a matter of ten minutes of trying. All he had to do was to be able to stand on his feet without falling. The rest was a piece of cake.

Resist, fool Rahul.

'A mere half hour only. Pukka promise.'

Rahul hired a pair of skates. Handing in his shoes, he went to the beginners' part of the rink. People here held on to the wooden railing and tried to skate. They fell and they laughed for having fallen. Two pretty things in blue jeans were trying hard. Suddenly they fell on their beautifully sculpted bottoms and giggled hysterically. Two more young beginners in fetching salwar kamiz and smart coats, giggled to see them giggle.

They, too, fell on their backsides. This proved hilarious for the four fallen angels. Rahul thought he should also fall on his bum - in sympathy. He got what he was positive were meaningful looks, as if he was different from other men, which he knew he was. Especially from one of the sculpted bottoms - she even beamed a slanting smile at him. It justified his having fallen. He felt pleased with himself.

Just then, someone shot through the galaxy of spinning stars and made a split-second halt in front of him.

Moon! She offered a hand and gave him a hypnotic look. Rahul struggled to stay upright.

'Stand on the blades of your skates,' Moon said, regally. Easier said than done. In the background, the music stopped for a second. Then a new record was put on, an English one – 'Living Doll' by Cliff Richard, Rahul's favourite.

'Your song, Jasmin,' said the second pretty thing with the sculpted bottom to the one who had smiled at Rahul, trying to stand up.

'Stand on the blades of your skates,' Jasmin said, imitating Moon.

'Anything you say, Miss Boss Sir,' her friend said and stood up, holding Jasmin's hands. As she did so, both of them fell again in fits of laughter.

Moon dragged Rahul away, muttering: 'Silly twits. Try to stand on the blades of your skates.'

'Anything you say, Miss Boss Sir.' Rahul tried, but fell in a heap.

'Get up.' Moon sounded angry.

'Not in a very cousin-like mood today, are we?'

'Cut your smartarse talk.' Moon was truly angry.

'What's the matter, my bulbul? What have I done?'

'What have you done? Two-timing bastard.'

Oh no. How could she possibly know where he was coming from - from extra-terrestrial orbits? Rahul should have listened to his inner voice like Mahatma Gandhi and gone straight on to SCH.

'Where is it?'

'Where is what?'

'That letter. Who is it from?'

Phew - relief! But Rahul was still in trouble.

'From a girl,' he replied with an honest face.

'Which girl?'

'You saw her with me once in Lakkar Bazaar.'

'Oh, that Anglo? What did she write?'

'It is perfectly innocent.'

'Then why can't I see the letter?'

'You can. It's in my room. Want to come with me to my room?'

'Ha, ha . . .'

'I'll give it to you after college on Monday. If you come with me for a walk.'

'Tomorrow. Bring it to the house tomorrow.'

'We are playing the YMCA tomorrow.'

'You and your stupid cricket. Sunday then.'

'We are playing Summer Hill on Sunday. It has to be Monday. I'll give it to you to read after college.'

'I shall never talk to you again if you don't. Understood?'

'Yes, Miss Boss Sir.'

Moon pirouetted on her toes and zoomed away.

'Phew.' Rahul wiped the sweat off his brow with his sleeve, thinking, Krishna! The games You play! Owl Rahul, all you need now is to run into Meena Nath tomorrow. Or the day after.

Neither tomorrow nor the day after, it happened only twenty minutes later. Unable to master the art of standing on the blades of his skates, Rahul postponed the learning of it. He got into his own shoes and set off for the hostel - he really had such a lot to do. He was waylaid near Mahatma Gandhi's statue on the steep road to Mount Jakhoo. Meena and Rover blocked his way. Was it chance that brought her there? The look on her face said it was not - she seemed to be waiting for him. The Sea of Tranquility had evaporated. Mount Vesuvius stood there in its place, fuming. How did she get the permission to be out and about on her own? Obviously she had - it was still early evening.

There was that horseplay between the dog and the man.

'Was just thinking of you, believe it or not,' said Rahul guiltily. 'Your name was on the tip of my tongue and a smell of roses in the air.'

There was a sulphurous smell about the evening – Mount Vesuvius about to make a Pompeii of Simla. While Indira was hurt and Moon imperious, Meena was simply about to explode. Amazingly, she didn't seem to care whether they were seen together - she did not leave his side when people passed them. It fell on Rahul to make sure they were not seen together. Else, word would reach home before her and then the Nath stick and her broken legs.

There were several benches in the little terraced park above the Mahatma's statue where people basked in the sun daily. A number of poor and scruffy hill folk huddled there in growing darkness shrouded in homemade blankets, watching the star-lit pedestrian traffic on the Ridge. The world never noticed these people, the scum of the earth. Normally, Rahul would not sit among them - it was out of the question. This evening it seemed just the thing to do – to sit among those poor people and become invisible to the world.

Meena wanted to talk. But talk would not come out of her. Even in that light, Rahul could see she was tomato red in the face. Rahul knew what she wanted to talk about. So he did all the talking. Meena heard him out. But she remained glum.

'You are a rotter. I knew from day one,' she said at last. 'I never want to see you again. NEVER.'

'Would you like to see the letter? Would that satisfy you?'

Meena did not answer.

'Monday. We both have a free period before lunch. We'll slip down the khud unseen . . . '

'Monday is a holiday.'

Of course. Monday was the College Founders' Day. Rahul had forgotten. Indira had forgotten. Moon had forgotten. It was strange that all three of them had, especially Cousin Moon whose memory was as sharp as her tongue.

'Early evening on Tuesday then. We'll go to our beauty spot and I'll give you the letter.'

'Swear on my head?'

'Why on your head? On my head.'

She stood up and they moved on. Meena stopped in a lonely bushy spot a hundred feet away. She turned, suddenly clasped Rahul in her arms and kissed him feverishly. The suddenness and passion of the kiss stunned him. Then she vanished. Only after she was gone did the reality of what he had done dawn upon him. The sweat of panic broke on his brow. He felt a cool breeze blow on it.

'Fool Rahul, what are you going to do?' Next morning, as he shaved to get ready for the parade on the Ridge, Rahul spoke to his reflection in the mirror: 'What are you going to do?'

He turned to God.

'O Krishna-ji, one last, final and ultimate favour. I'll never ask another. Get me out of this one. Inspire me with an idea.'

Instead of inspiration, Rahul received a lecture.

'You have made a jungle of a bungle, haven't you? You love being in a jam pot, don't you? Why did you agree to show the letter to all three of them? People sitting atop a heap of gunpowder should not play with matches. You know very well that I am usually very generous and full of understanding. But I don't care for too-smart fools. I let them sort out their own mess. *Dismiss.*'

Dismissed by his best god, Rahul had no one to turn to, not even his best friend. If there was anything Rahul was afraid of, it was being laughed at. Rishi, however, made himself available. Rishi guessed all was not rosy in his friend's garden, having a BA, MA and a Ph.D in mindreading.

'Out with it,' Rishi demanded as they marched in step on the Ridge to the beat of a military band.

'Have you got all day?'

'No. So be snappy.'

Rahul told him. Rishi did not laugh. 'Be grateful you have a friend who is a genius,' he said.

'Be grateful to whom?'

'To the friend.'

Rahul's best God had not inspired him with a brilliant idea, but He had inspired his best friend.

After the parade, Rishi took Rahul to a stationery shop and made him buy a pad of the flimsy blue airmail writing paper and two airmail envelopes.

294

Rahul had a feeling his friend hadn't eaten anything since last night, so he brought him to SCH and ordered tea with buns. Rishi first ate. Next, he sat down and made two copies of Betty's letter. He put them in two envelopes and wrote Rahul's address as Betty had done. Then, he accompanied Rahul all the way to the main Post Office and made him buy the airmail stamps. He licked them himself, stuck them on the envelopes and posted them.

'They'll get to your hostel first thing on Monday. Make sure you are down on the veranda to meet the postman. Get it?'

'Then what?'

'Then take this one to Balmoral after the game on Sunday.'

'But I said Monday to Cousin Moon.'

'Surprise. Best tactic in love and war. Just turn up and say you couldn't wait till Monday and see if she doesn't swallow it hook, line and rod. And . . .'

'Maharishi Mull, you sure are wasted on Simla.'

'. . . And somehow pass on the other to Miss Nath on Monday saying the same thing. Then deliver the third to Miss Number Two in a book on Tuesday morning at college. And . . .'

'And what?'

'And beat the shit out of this 3D guy.'

It was a tall order.

As things happened, the college had the shit beaten out of it instead by a vengeful Y. By the Summer Hill side, too. Yet Rahul was feeling on top of the world when he turned up at Balmoral. Surprise, surprise, no one was at home. Only . . . icing on the cake sweet cake.

'You look very pleased with yourself. Did you kill a century? Or a lady? Where's the letter?' Moon said behind the wall of sweet peas fixed by Rahul.

She read the letter twice.

'Why did she put these crosses under her name? It means kisses. Did you kiss her? Did you?'

'Heavenly Moon!'

'What are you going to write to her?'

'I am not going to write to her.'

'Swear on my head you are not.'

'I swear on my own.'

'Good,' Moon said, softening. Later, she did something which took his breath away. She permitted Rahul to do what she had never let him do before: she allowed him to behold and hold what the whole world was mad about.

'What do you think?'

'Can't think. I'm moonstruck.'

'What do you feel?'

'Over the moon.'

Moon smiled and Rahul buried his face in what he held and what he beheld – snow-white heaven.

'Paradise improved.'

THIRTEEN

Come Monday evening, a large crowd built up at the paan shop. Seeing it from afar, more men flocked to it. Nehru was to address the nation. So the people knew in their bones that it was something big. The mother-of-all-kicks in Chou's balls?

But unknown to any in the crowd, things had gone wrong for India, dreadfully wrong. The weekend had been soaked in Indian blood - rivers of it. All sure-shot predictions and calculations had gone up in smoke: the mighty British-trained Indian army had been completely destroyed in NEFA, as if a steam-roller had rolled over formations of toy soldiers. Assam of smiling tea gardens and the fertile green plain of Bengal now lay open to the Chinese without an Indian brave in uniform to stop them. India's only source of oil, the wells of Digboi in the east, and its greatest seaport, Calcutta, were theirs for the taking.

The killer question was - would the Chinese take them? The answer spelled virtual death. Nothing now stood between the enemy and the booty. They had started the war. They must have had an aim. And they had swallowed Tibet whole only thirteen years earlier without a world leader raising his little finger, including their own Mr Nehru. The Chinese could do the same to India with similar ease. At least to NEFA, Assam and Bengal in the north-east and Kashmir and Himachal in the north-west, including Simla! Simla was a mere 200 mountain miles from Tibet where the bulk of the Chinese army was based. Come to think of it, they could be in Simla in no time - Tibet was only forty or fifty miles as the crow flies. The Ridge was a first-class natural helipad.

In fact, it was like a giant aircraft carrier: several helicopters could land there at the same time, flooding Simla with little Chinamen.

Earlier in the day, there had been frenetic military activity in Simla. Soldiers had dug deep holes in the rough side of the Ridge for explosive charges to blow it up and render it useless, even though under the Ridge lay buried the city's main water reservoir. People had seen them dig trenches in the hillside above the Gandhi statue that offered a commanding view of the rest of Simla. At every main road junction, the soldiers had set up roadblocks with sand bags and machine guns.

The whole thing had looked surreal - war coming to Simla, the strawberry and cream city the English had built so lovingly! It was unimaginable. Insulting, too, to the memory of the English (whose shoes the Chinese used to make and polish), the same English whom Simla loved so much that it wouldn't mind at all if they came back. If truth be told, it would have welcomed them with open arms that Monday in particular, when it expected an 'any minute' Chinese landing.

Simla taken, it could be Chandigarh next - the new capital of the Punjab, a mere four-hour ride away. Then Delhi, and the rest of India perhaps. Would India once again become a colony - of shoe-makers this time?

A pin-drop hush fell when the announcer introduced the Prime Minister. Usually, when Nehru spoke, most Indians felt they were listening to their favourite god. Nehru never talked to his people. He lectured them. He harangued them. He became angry with them. But it was the lecture and the anger of a father who adored his children. And the children adored the father. Vulnerable and soft, Nehru's voice never failed to move. And he always knew what to say and how to say it, bringing tears to people's eyes.

Tonight, Nehru's voice was that of a worn-out old man with a broken heart. He had been stabbed in the back – he had trusted Chou. He had only sad tidings to give the nation - the destruction of an army, the loss of NEFA, the imminent occupation of Assam and . . .

Many a man in front of the paan shop had tears welling up in his eyes. Through Nehru's quivering voice, the loss of an army and unheard of, uninhabited and inhospitable mountain country nearly 2,000 miles away had become a personal loss. A faceless distant tragedy had become personal through the link of this voice people so loved. Nehru ended on a positive note, though:

'We shall not be content till the invader goes out of India or is pushed out.'

And the men listening to him in Lakkar Bazaar of Simla knew they were just words. Yet the tears came. One by one, the hostel boys embraced Rahul and Rajkumar. Then with arms around each other - it was a cold night - and chewing paan, they walked back to the hostel, talking in whispers.

'Bet there'll be a landing in Simla before the week is out.'
'Shut your face.'
'They can land military aircraft at Annandale.'
'Balls.'
'You think they'll really occupy Calcutta?'
'Tomorrow will tell.'
And tomorrow told the most extraordinary tale ever.

Rahul was booted out of sleep by loud banging on his window. Knowing it must be the Twins, he angrily kicked off his quilt and switched on his table lamp to tell them off. Then his jaw fell. For he beheld the face of a girl of fifteen and . . .

'Lin?'

'Very sorry for disturbing you,' Lin whispered. He had the air of a ghost.

'What?'

'Shut the light. They are after us.'

'Who?'

'Many goondas. Two hostel boys among them.'

'Where are they?'

'They've looted our shops and set fire to our houses. Come out and look.' Rahul looked. Far away on the right where he knew the Blessington Hotel to be - below Scandal Point and above Cart Road - there was a glowing wound in the belly of the mountain. Mighty flames a hundred feet high shot up, lighting up the valley and the sky!

'O Krishna!'

War had come to Mount Olympus! A dirty war.

'Save us, Rahul. You are my only friend.'

'Where are your parents?'

'The police took them. We hid. Hide us now, Rahul. They'll be here any minute. They have knives and swords and . . .'

'You stay here then. In my room.'

'No. Somewhere else. They'd kill you too if they found out.'

Rahul thought fast. He thought of locking them in his wardrobe. Lin didn't agree. A wardrobe would be the first place they would search.

'Somewhere else, Rahul. Hurry.'

'Come with me.' Rahul slipped into his shoes and together they ran up the hill to Bahadar Singh's hut. He knocked on the door.

'Sir, do you know what time it is?' The servant yawned, answering the door. 'Anything wrong?'

'Very badly wrong.'

'Must be, for you to come here at this hour.'

'My apologies to Mrs Bahadar, but I need your help.'

'Anything you say, sir sahib.'

'Bad men are after my friend Lin here and his sister. Will you hide them till the morning?'

'Done, sir.'

Rahul raced back to his room and got into his bed. Only minutes later, he heard noises outside below the balcony.

'The Chini has to be with him. This cunt is his only friend,' a voice bellowed.

Next instant, a torch-light was flashed in Rahul's room. Then there was a hammering at his window. Rahul leaped out his bed and switched the light on. Ten faces were pressed against his large window, those of mates Kumar and Mahendru among them. Their eyes were enflamed with hatred. They craved revenge. There were many more goondas behind the two. They were armed.

'Who are you?' Rahul screamed.

'Open up, pretty boy.'

'Wanker Kumar, what do you want?'

'We want that dining-wining Chini bosom pal of yours and his sister.'

'What on earth are you talking about?'

'Open up or we'll break the damn window.'

Rahul let the goondas in. They all wore brand new hand-made shoes. They looked in his bathroom. They looked under the bed. Kumar pulled out clothes from his wardrobe.

'Don't touch my clothes with your filthy hands.'

A giant goonda caught hold of Rahul's arm and twisted it. 'Where is he? Tell or I'll break it.'

'How should I know?'

Kumar advanced and gave a full-blooded lash at Rahul's face. Then another.

'I DON'T KNOW. I DON'T KNOW.'

'Tell.' Mahendru punched Rahul in the stomach. One, two, three.

'LET GO, YOU COWARDLY BASTARDS. I DON'T KNOW.'

Rahul's screams brought all SCH to his door.

'What the hell is going on here?' Atom said.

'Let go of his arm, man,' Balbir howled at the giant goonda, forcefully pulling his hand off Rahul.

A discussion followed.

'You are all mad,' Mr Universe spat, rolling up his sleeves over those biceps. 'What has Rahul to do with the Chinese? His own brother is fighting them in NEFA. Is any brother of yours fighting there? So get lost, cheapo Kumar, Mister. Take your lickspittle and other friends away, scum. As usual, you've made a bad mistake.'

'Maybe you have,' one of the goondas admitted.

'The Chini must have slipped down the tennis court to get to Sanjauli Road. There are a few Chini families in Sanjauli.'

The goondas ran and the hostel boys went back to their room to sleep. Rahul switched off his lights and lay down. The right side of his face throbbed with pain. There was a deep well of it in his stomach. An hour later he rose and ran up the hill to Bahadar Singh's hut.

'We heard the rolla-bolla, sahib. Thank you for letting me help.'

'Bahadar Singh, keep my guests here till early morning. Then I'll go and get help.'

'Your guests are my guests, sir.'

Dawn was breaking when Rahul left SCH. The morning was crisp and clear. Wishing it was neither, and that thick mist engulfed Simla, he hurried downhill. The morning was empty of humans. Only when he looked back from the middle of the Ridge did he see two figures under the Gandhi statue. They were too far away to tell who they might be.

Ten minutes later, he was outside the Mull house in the deserted Lower Bazaar. He was going to shout Rishi's name, but it was simply too early to call on anyone. Beside, the neighbours would wake up and, being neighbours, they would want to know what was going on. Within minutes, all Lower Bazaar would know, then all Simla, that he was hiding two enemies.

'You trying to call your friends?' A woman as old as Lin's grandmother and just as dignified appeared from nowhere and Rahul recognised her.

'Yes, Dadima.'

'You came here the other day when I was sick and angry, didn't you?'

'Yes, Dadima.'

'What brings you here at this unearthly hour? Must be something serious. You look as if you've seen the shaitan.'

'It is very serious.'

'Want to tell me?'

'It is also very strange.'

'I have seen a few strange things in my life.'

'But I don't know if you'll agree with me.'

'Try me.'

Rahul told her.

'Humm,' Dadima said, nodding. 'What made you think I wouldn't agree? Wait here.' Five minutes later, Rishi and Kishi were with Rahul.

'Take this,' Dadima said, coming after them and handing Rishi a twelve-bore double-barrelled shot gun. 'It is loaded and I'm coming too. We'll take your friends to the police station to be looked after, and we'll see who stops us.'

'Dadima!' cried Rishi. 'It's uphill all the way.'

'So what? I wasn't born in the mountains for nothing. I can climb them like any mountain goat.'

And she could, too. At the Mall, they took the steps going up to the Ridge.

'Look!' Rahul said. Fifty feet above them and holding the railing of the Ridge stood two familiar figures. As they climbed the steps, they came face to face with the goondas of last night - all of them. Rahul shuddered.

'Keep walking,' he said, despite his fear.

The sight of the gun had an effect - the goondas moved back but then followed them at a distance. At Christchurch, Rahul ran into Principal Khurana out for his morning constitutional, giving the man the shock of his life.

'Good morning, sir.' Rahul and the twins bowed to their Principal.

'Good morning, boys. Namaste, Mrs Mull. What a nice surprise. But where are you going with a gun, may I ask? Is it real? Is it loaded?'

'Namaste, Khurana sahib.' And Mrs Mull explained the whole thing.

'Oh, really? I had better come too then,' Mr Khurana said, taking the gun in his hands.

The hostel woke up within minutes. More than thirty boys escorted Lin and his sister. Just where their track joined the one coming from Lakkar Bazaar, they met a wall of the goondas whose numbers had now risen to more than fifty, but now Kumar and Mahendru were not among them. The goondas held aloft knives, swords and lathis. Hearts leaped to throats. Something awful was about to happen. Blood was about to wash the hillside.

Principal Khurana and Mrs Mull walked at the head of the procession, flanked by Rahul, Balbir, Atom and the twins. Lin and his sister walked behind them. The track was narrow and the slope leading down from it dangerous. Hearts fluttered.

'Keep calm, boys, and keep walking,' Dadima said, surprising everybody with her courage.

'Gentlemen, kindly move out of our way,' said Mr Khurana.

'Give us the Chinis and no harm will come to anyone,' barked the goonda leader, brandishing his naked sword.

'They are our guests. To us Indians, our guests are dearer than our life - surely you know. We are taking our guests to safety,' the old woman said.

'Give us the Chinis, old hag. Or there'll be blood.'

'We only want the Chinese skirt.'

Lin's sister let out a scream and clung to her brother. Something happened to Rahul at that moment. He snatched the gun from Mr Khurana and prodded the ruffian's chest with the nozzle.

'Get out of our way, or…!' Rahul also screamed.

'Or you'll shoot?'

'I swear I will. By God I will.'

'Shoot then.'

Rahul aimed the gun at the goonda's feet and fired a shot at the mountain earth. The effect was instantaneous. The ringleader was mesmerised. He moved aside. The others also parted and the hostel inmates walked through them in sizzling silence. Fifteen minutes later, they arrived at the police station on Cart Road. Six army trucks stood outside it. They were full of Chinese people - men, women and children, Lin's family among them.

'We are sending them to a camp in Rajasthan, for their own safety,' said the police inspector so well known to Rahul, with a bow to Mr Khurana.

Lin embraced his friend.

'See you next time,' he said, tears streaming down his cheeks.

On its way back, as the great hostel escort passed the bus stop on Cart Road, a van with THE TRIBUNE emblazoned on it came to a halt. It arrived daily with the newspapers printed in the plains.

The driver shot out of it, shouting hysterically: 'Read the NEWS. Read the NEWS.' The man showed off his paper. Disbelief filled the valley:

CHINA DECLARES UNILATERAL CEASEFIRE

Beginning from midnight tonight, the Chinese frontier guard will cease fire along the entire Sino-Indian border. From 1 December, they will withdraw to positions 20 km behind the actual line of control which existed before the fighting had broken out.

Every newspaper said the same. It left everybody speechless. Rahul and Rajkumar hugged each other. Everybody hugged them, then each other - the war over just like that. Just like that.

'What beats me is A, why the fuck the Chinis started it and B, why the fuck they have stopped?' Atom said out of earshot of Principl Khurana and Dadima, scratching his royal balls.

'You want them to go on, Mr MC Square?' Rishi said, thumping him hard enough to dislocate his delicate princely shoulder.

'Rahul,' Principal Khurana called out. 'Well done.'

Rahul looked up at the crystal clear sky and folded his hands on his chest.

EPILOGUE

If ever a man had cause to congratulate himself, Rahul did. Hook, line and rod had been swallowed by Balmoral and the Great Wall of China. One little hurdle remained. But Rahul knew his sweet and gentle Number Two-ji.

Indira didn't come to college on Tuesday. She came on Wednesday. She looked pale. She had not been well.

The class was filing into the Lilac Room for Professor Nath's lecture on *Much Ado About Nothing*. Rahul waited outside, book in hand.

Indira appeared. She was not expecting to be handed a book with not one, but two letters in it, the second from Rahul to her, a sonnet of which Shakespeare could have been proud - *Admit Me to the True Heaven of Thine Bosom Divine*. The 14-line poem spoke of *creation's best perfection* that caused *delirium fine*, and went on to dwell on the effect on the poet of his *lips' pilgrimage* from her navel to her nipples to her lips and of those *Albion kisses*, ending with a plea for *more, more, more* of what up till now had been *too little by too far.*

Taken aback, Indira fumbled with the book, the pages opened and the letters fell on the floor. Professor Nath, whom Rahul didn't see in the heat of the moment but who was right behind Indira, bent down and picked them up. He put them in his register and limped into the room.

Now Indira understood. Her face turned white - she was compromised, her reputation blown to bits! She walked in his wake, a mourner behind the hearse of a loved one, in this case, her own self.

Rahul, also white in the face - he was responsible for her disgrace - stayed outside. His heart was in his throat. His own destruction, for sure as hell he would be expelled from the college, paled before Indira's total ruin. He had to get the letters from the register before the end of the lecture, before Nath could read them, especially his ten-ton TNT sonnet. Even if it meant daylight robbery - dashing into the room and dashing out with the register. He needed Rishi. He waited for him in the corridor. But where was he? Five minutes into the lecture, then ten. Now panic swamped Rahul. Panic total and final. Time was running out. But what could he do?

Principal Khurana passed.

'Rahul, is this how you gain your education, by standing outside classrooms? Get in. Get in.'

'Professor Nath threw me out, sir.'

'He must be in a fiery mood then,' Mr Khurana said and walked on, and Rahul got an idea. He ran to the college office block, where office peon Labhu was sitting idly outside on the veranda. Labhu was in his mid-twenties, but he looked Rahul's age. Rahul pulled out a pink two-rupee note from his pocket and waved it at Labhu. This was mouth-watering. Labhu understood that a bribe was being offered. He shot to his feet. Two rupees! He'd do anything. He saluted Rahul smartly, army-style.

'Yes, Kapoor sahib? You wanting something?'

'Go ring the fire bell and this note is yours.'

The fire bell was a tuning-fork-shaped piece of railway line with the middle bit sawn off, found in all schools and colleges. When struck with an iron rod, it made a loud and unpleasant noise that could be heard deep down in the valley. It was 'rung' once a term for fire drill when classrooms emptied in a delightful pandemonium. Then it was put away in a locked cupboard, locked because it had been misused twice by some college jokers.

'The fire bell? It's been rung already this term, Kapoor sahib. Rung again, they'd think it was for real. Imagine the chaos.'

'That's the idea, Labhu.'

This coming from the Union President was bizarre. But the two-rupee note said it was none of Labhu's business.

'And I could lose my job.'

'Why should you? False alarms are not unknown.'

'No, sir.' Labhu shook his head.

'You could say you thought you saw smoke somewhere. You'd say worse than a false alarm is no alarm at all.' Rahul pulled out another two-rupee note.

'Well, sir . . .' Labhu looked to his left and right. No one was in sight. He snatched the notes from Rahul's hand and tucked them in a twist of his pyjama trousers at the waist. 'When do you want me to do it?'

'Now.'

'Give me five-six minutes, sir.'

Rahul went back to wait outside his classroom. His plan was simple. When the bell rang, the class would empty like a herd of wildebeests. Rahul would bump into Professor Nath. His register would fall. He'd pick it up and run away with it. Or he would snatch it from his hand. The consequences? He would see to the consequences - they couldn't be worse than those he would have to face otherwise.

Rahul waited and waited. But the fire bell didn't go, the fact of the matter being that Labhu couldn't find the key to the cupboard. Time ticked by with agonising speed, pulling the finale of the tragedy forward by powerful invisible threads. Rahul's end had come much worse, Indira's and her family's reputation. This made the whole thing unimaginably more horrendous. Minutes before the end of the lecture, someone thumped Rahul on the back.

'What the eff are you doing outside the class-room?'

Rahul had never been so glad to see another human being. He told Rishi the whole story.

The lecture over, the class spilled out. The two friends let everybody pass and waited. Professor Nath was the last to appear at the door, the register with the death sentence under his arm. As he stepped into the corridor, Rishi bumped into him from one side and Rahul from the other, taking care they didn't hurt the man. The register did not fall, but Professor Nath very nearly did and the fateful letters flew out of his register. Rishi grabbed them and put them in his pocket in a single movement.

'Rishi Mull, hand me those letters,' a very shocked Professor Nath thundered.

'Which letters, sir?'

Principal Khurana reappeared from nowhere.

'What's going on here, Mr Nath?'

'I have been physically assaulted, Mr Khurana. I have been ambushed and robbed of two highly sensitive letters compromising a certain young lady in my class. Ruining her reputation.'

'WHAT?' Principal Khurana howled. 'You had better come along to my office.' He marched everybody to his office. 'What have they done? Which letters? What were you saying, Mr Nath?'

'Letters dishonouring a young lady from a highly respectable family.'

The Principal ground his jaws in pain - letters dishonouring a girl from his college! His round boyish face became angular.

'Where are these letters?'

Professor Nath pointed his walking stick at Rishi. There was a commotion in the waiting room outside the Principal's office. But it was a very tense moment. He ignored it.

'Rishi Mull, give Mr Nath the letters.'

'Beg your pardon, sir?'

The commotion outside had become a loud noise. Among the number of faces out there, Rahul saw Bahadar Singh's. He was waving something at him.

Inside his office, the Principal roared, 'Where are the letters, Rishi Mull?'

'In my pocket, sir.'

'GIVE THEM TO MR NATH,' Principal Khurana glared at Rishi.

Rishi advanced, took the envelopes out of his pocket and handed them to Professor Nath.

'Open them, Mr Nath.'

Professor Nath opened them. They were empty.

'Sir, you love to make Much Ado About . . .'

'And what's this rolla-bolla outside? What's the meaning of it?' Principal Khurana shouted at the uproar outside his door.

'Sir, important wire for Kapoor sahib,' yelped Bahadar Singh like a frightened puppy. He didn`t wait to be given permission to come in. He rushed forward and handed the small telegram envelope to Rahul. Everybody understood what it was all about - the Chinese must have released the list of the Indian dead they had found. Rahul's brother was among them, shot or blown to pieces by a cannon.

Forgotten was the drama of the empty envelopes. A deathly hush fell all around.

'Telegrams don't always mean bad things, Rahul. Open it,' Mr Khurana said touchingly, hiding what was writ large on every other face - the boy's brother was not in this world any more.

Rahul tore open the telegram:

Wire from MOD says Pithi made it to Bhutan.
Safe and well. Come home.
Affectionately - Daddy

'Let me be the first to congratulate you,' Principal Khurana said, embracing Rahul.

'May I have your permission to go home to be with my family for a few days, sir?' Rahul said, and without waiting for an answer, ran. Out on the compound he ran right into an ambushcade.

Moon, Meena and Indira stood at the college gate like militants at a picket line, two of them holding up identical hostile banners, those airmail envelopes with blue and red markings. The Three Graces had taken to arms. It was clear what they wanted - blood - even sweet Indira Malhotra. But why did they also want to laugh, as it seemed? What was Rahul to make of female psychology now?

Rahul stopped in his tracks. How was he going to get out of this one? O, Krishna, please help. Now is Your real chance. Please.

Krishna smiled in answer, a true friend.

'My brother is alive,' Rahul shouted, waving the telegram.

'But not you,' the Graces shouted back. 'Not for long.'

Rahul did the only thing he could have done under the circumstances - he laughed and ran on. He didn't even go to his hostel to pick up his pyjamas or shaving kit. He ran all the way to the bus stop. No bus was going down south for another hour. But the man at Information said there was a railcar going from the railway station in fifteen minutes.

'You can catch it if you know how to fly, young man.'

The young man knew how to fly. The question was, how full would the railcar be?

'The railcar is full with one empty seat,' said the clerk at a window with iron bars.

'That will do nicely, thank you,' Rahul said, paying for his ticket.

A problem developed, though. For next to this empty seat sat a stunner, a curvaceous beauty. She moved her exquisitely-sculpted bottom to make room. Then she looked at him and beamed a slanting smile.

Rahul recognised both the bottom and the smile. Then he made an on-the-spot decision. He would never sit next to a woman in a railcar, train or a bus ever again. He would spend the entire journey standing by the door, looking at those reversing curves and admiring the British for having been such wonderful engineers.

But sit next to a girl in a bus, train or a railcar?
NEVER.

THE END

Acknowledgements

The author would like to thank Joan Deitch, James Bidwell, Rosemarie Hudson and Pierre Smith Khanna for their invaluable help.